CIR

Introduced to the world of broadcasting at the age of twelve when she began acting and performing in BBC children's programmes, Jill Arlon began her early adult career not only acting in radio drama but also researching and presenting current affairs.

She was working as a lecturer in English and drama when ATV launched its five nights a week flagship soap opera *Crossroads*. Jill Arlon enjoyed eight years playing the role of Josefina, one of the principal characters, appearing in over a thousand episodes.

During this period she married former fellow actor, singer Deke Arlon. They have two sons, James and Tim.

Following their marriage they co-founded D. and J. Arlon and together built an internationally successful music publishing company throughout the heady days of the seventies and eighties. They have managed and guided some of the world's leading actors, directors, songwriters and recording artists. They have produced theatre, movies for television and over fifty hours of entertainment for international television, receiving many awards both in the UK and the US.

This, Jill's first novel, is co-produced as a filmed drama series for television by YTV in association with Waterman and Arlon films.

CRITICAL OR DEATH?

CIRCLES *of* DECEIT

JILL ARLON

PAN BOOKS

First published 1995 by Pan Books

an imprint of Macmillan General Books
Cavaye Place London SW10 9PG
and Basingstoke

Associated companies throughout the world

ISBN 0 330 34181 2

1 3 5 7 9 8 6 4 2

A CIP catalogue record for this book is available from
the British Library

Phototypeset by Intype, London
Printed and bound in Great Britain by
Cox & Wyman Ltd,
Reading, Berkshire

For
Deke without whose love nothing is possible,
James and Tim,
My mother and father.

ACKNOWLEDGEMENTS

I would like to thank all those who helped me with the background material for this book, and I hope they will approve of the fictional use I have made of some of their facts. Especially I want to thank so many of the people of Ireland, no matter which foot they kick with . . . who down the years have opened their hearts to me and in particular, my dear friend, Ina.

My very special thanks to Dennis Waterman for being John Neil, for his faith and his friendship, and to Rula for her unflinching support.

Thanks too to Vernon Lawrence for his incredible insight and faith. Highest praise and thanks to all at YTV, David Reynolds, Andrew Benson and Geoff Saxe for their splendid and faithful portrayal of the original story, and to Simon Lewis for his integrity and care with the series. Finally I would like to express my appreciation to the fine company of writers, directors, casts and crews for their wonderful work in continuing the adventure.

Circles of Deceit is a Yorkshire Television production in association with Waterman and Arlon Films.

Executive Producers – David Reynolds, Andrew Benson. Producers – Andrew Benson, Simon Lewis.

The television series is based on the character of John

Neil from an original story 'Circles of Deceit' by Jill Arlon.

Additional material adapted from the television series writers – Wesley Burrowes, Ray Jenkins, John Brown.

CHAPTER ONE

The dirty sea mist, torn by the ship's passage, clung about him in tattered shreds. He leaned against the ship's rail and watched the oily water cream and curl back to the coast and he wondered, as he had so many times before, if he would live to see those shores again – only this time, he didn't care.

The black clouds rolling towards his new homeland he knew well, of course. He had touched them, in his former life, as he'd parachuted down, hidden in their billowing masses, his face blackened, to take up his position in some covert hide, one time in Tyrone, another in the bandit country of Armagh.

In his new life, as the dead man, he would walk boldly in the light.

The last few passengers who had braved the open deck now, at the first bucking of the open sea, fought their way back to the steamy warmth of the brightly lit bars and lounges, leaving the man alone.

Huddled in an old black duffle coat, his shoulders hunched against the cold, he cupped his hands and with the deft movement of a man familiar with such conditions, struck a match and lit a Marlboro, drawing deeply on the acrid smoke. He exhaled in a rush and straightened up, tensing his shoulders to parade-ground square, his body erect, at slightly above average height.

His tawny hair and short-cropped beard glistened

with spray and the recent frosting of a few premature white hairs.

Were it not for the length of his hair and the jeans that protruded below his coat he might have been mistaken for a member of the crew, so easily did his spread stance counterbalance the rolling of the ship as it hit the open sea.

He glanced round, his grey eyes sharp, with the instinctive awareness of his increased exposure as a target, then turned back and flicked the spent match into the gusting wind. The furious screech of a seagull, diving for the match, twanged his stretched nerves. He watched it swoop and snap, saw its long black tongue uncurl to spit out the splintered wood. With marksman's steady gaze, he fixed his sights and with deadly aim, targeted between the glaring yellow eyes.

Randall's eyes had been deadliest of all.

He'd contacted him as the man knew he would – called on the phone that never rang – where it lay forgotten in a corner of his isolated Highland croft, its covering of dust testimony to his self-inflicted isolation.

He took little with him, he had little to take. The rest, his books, tapes, guitar, his photographs – the precious frozen memories of his life – he locked away. They were safer in his head. He'd closed the door and headed south.

He knew why they'd chosen him. Had seen it in their calculating appraisal, as he walked to face the three of them across the bare boards of the empty classroom, in one of their many meeting places. Seen it in the cold shark eyes of Randall.

There were no niceties, no apologies, no condolences, no . . . 'How are you since your beloved wife, your little boy, your unborn child were blown to smithereens . . .'

He knew exactly why they'd chosen him – he'd been in the wilderness long enough.

John Neil – ex-husband, ex-father, ex-SAS – was alone and dispensable.

'Are you fit?' Randall had asked, his thin lips clamping in a line beneath the military moustache.

John Neil stared at the blond gelled hair, at the upright figure encased in the perfectly cut striped Guardsman's suit, at the tight waistcoat over the iron-flat stomach.

'Enough,' he'd answered sullenly and noted the gleam of arrogance in their eyes.

He'd had it himself once, along with all the other men in the Regiment, 22 SAS. The élite. The training was the toughest, the men were the fittest, but the sadistic endurance tests imposed in his youth, the endless marches up Pen-y-fan, were as nothing. How could he explain to these men who routinely broke the pain barrier that there was another hell beyond? Where the scream of his tested body, driven night and day, without rest, without sleep, was merely a diversion, a welcome relief from the torment of his loss, the anguish of his longing for yesterday.

'And the leg? The burns?'

'No problem at all.'

He'd been the last to leave the blazing circus tent. They'd dragged him out of the flames still screaming the names of his wife and child. He hadn't noticed his leg streaming with blood or felt the pain from the shards of glass embedded in his back. The enormous crystal ball had spun down from the roof of the big top, flashing its fiery reflection as it fell to smash and splinter beside him. He'd crawled on, searching through the blast-blackened timbers, ignoring the smoke tearing at his lungs, the scorching earth, the sickly smell of burning flesh. Somewhere in this carnage were his wife and child. He prayed they had survived. They had not.

'And your head?' The Etonian drawl of Havelock-

Davies, Randall's second in command, cut through the silence.

'You've read the report,' he said flatly.

They'd sent for him a year ago, summoned him from his Highland retreat, put him through tests with a psychologist, the usual thing. He'd been fine then, he was fine now.

The rage, the trauma, the pain, the unreasoning lust for bloody revenge – all had gone. The Regiment and the Gulf War had used him up. The murder of his family had tipped him over the edge. He'd received the ultimate sanction, Return to Unit. For Neil RTU meant self-imposed exile in the Highlands of Scotland. A year later, gaunt and empty, dried of all tears, he'd been ready to go back, needed to get back into action. The psychologists didn't agree. They'd left him out there, waited to be sure. He was a valuable man. The body was ready: the Regiment waited for the spirit to mend. In the shadowy world of Army Intelligence, a man can 'disappear'. They wanted John Neil forgotten.

Waiting to board the ferry, he'd checked the faces of his fellow passengers, compared them with those they'd instructed him to memorize. He recognized no one. He didn't have to, he knew that eyes were everywhere. 'Become one of them,' they'd warned him. 'Hearts and minds.'

After the last few weeks of intensive preparation incarcerated in a room, he longed to stay out on deck but the night was cold and he was too exposed. He felt that first rush of adrenalin. The dryness in the throat. His mission was beginning. His life was on red alert.

Neil pushed his way through the sliding doors, into the first bar. People turned at the unexpected blast of cold air, eyes raked him. Only a man whose senses were

so highly tuned would have noticed the almost imperceptible hush in the laughter of the two men at the bar, as
they monitored his voice when he ordered.

'Bushmills.' His voice had a Belfast growl.

'We have a job for you. Northern Ireland. Belfast, to be
precise,' Randall had said.

The words had exploded in John Neil's head. Three
pairs of eyes had scrutinized his face for a reaction. It
had remained impassive.

'Right,' was all he'd said.

'You realize, might come against one of the chappies,
planted the bomb, circus, Germany?' Havelock-Davies
had drawled in his affected shorthand. 'Cope with that?
Yes?'

'What's the job then, sir?' Neil had looked directly at
the Intelligence supremo. Havelock-Davies had coughed
nervously at the snub, a slight flush spreading across his
weak but handsome face.

'Gault will fill you in.' Randall had indicated the third
man. And he had.

Neil had expected to be installed back in Hereford,
headquarters of his regiment, 22 SAS. Instead he was
driven to a large country house hidden in the wooded
hills of Berkshire.

'No going back to the old "Sports And Social" for
this one,' Gault had informed him, skilfully manoeuvring
the Range Rover around the storm-torn debris littering
the rutted track leading to the isolated house. ' "Kremlin
boys" want you on your own for this!' And he nodded
back to where Randall and Havelock-Davies struggled
to keep up in their standard black Rover saloon. 'Still,
you always were a bit of a maverick, even for us.'

Automatically Neil's eyes tracked the terrain, registered landmarks, direction, sun, routes of escape. Except

5

this time he didn't want to get out. Only when he was alone in his room that night, restlessly anticipating his metamorphosis, did he allow himself to replay the precious memories of his life, before he wiped them from his head.

Julie in the snow, a smile of apology hovering on her lips, an anxious note in her voice as she hurried over to where his car had slewed across the road because of the snowball she had hurled at his windscreen, obliterating his view, forcing him to slither to a stop.

Cursing, he'd dropped the window. In the freezing snows of a misty December day in Germany was a face of summer – cornflower blue eyes, lips as soft as poppy petals, hair the colour of ripe corn in the sun. It was a face whose parts were clichés but whose whole was a masterpiece. At least so thought hard man paratrooper John Neil, as he crashed into love for the first and only time in his life.

Julie's face at the window, flushed with cold and embarrassment, her eyes sparkling with suppressed laughter; at that first sight of her, his breath had caught, his heart had raced and never stopped until she died – when it broke.

'I was throwing snowballs for the dog to catch. He missed!'

He'd stared, unable to speak, bewitched.

She'd stepped back, the huge blue anorak serving only to enhance the slightness of her figure.

He'd been stationed in Bavaria. She was the daughter of the CO – just home for Christmas. Her father, like all the fathers there with daughters, was only too aware of the dangers of army barracks buzzing with fit young men, sexually supercharged. He'd done his best to keep them apart – then given up. On a few days' leave they'd gone skiing together and returned never ever wanting to part. They had, of course. She'd gone back to teaching in England, he'd gone on with manoeuvres.

A few months later, in the cruel Antarctic conditions of South Georgia, as Neil and his men shored themselves together against the shrieking katabatic wind that threatened to tear them from the face of the treacherous Fortuna Glacier, their skin razored by the filings of powdered ice that froze their equipment, it was Julie's face that urged him on. Throughout the long night of that first abortive attempt, when their tent was whipped away by the knifing wind and they'd huddled together, bivvy bags their only shelter – it was thoughts of Julie that had warmed his soul. And as they'd struggled in the blinding snowstorm, to extricate themselves from the wrecked Wessex and prayed to be rescued from the freezing whiteout that had already dashed two helicopters to the ground, it was for Julie he was determined to survive.

'Take a good look at these men,' Randall had begun that first briefing as he pointed with his swagger stick at the screen, indicating with a staccato series of taps the enlarged, slightly blurred images of the faces in the crowd, gathered at a funeral.

'The McAuley family. Not all of them, of course. The eldest son was killed some time ago and the girl isn't in this shot.' He peered in at the picture, his shadow falling across the screen.

'But the others, Colum, Sean and Brendan are there, that's those three and this, this fellow here, this is the big man, Liam McAuley, the father, a dangerous man – and the main player.

'Big, wealthy Republican family, the McAuleys, all the way back to the Easter Rising. Joe McAuley, Liam's father, was close to De Valera, fought the Black and Tans

7

alongside Michael Collins. Liam joined the IRA when he was seventeen, a young idealist, under Terry Magan, fighting the Border wars at the end of the forties. All very chivalrous then, of course – non-sectarian too.' Randall sniffed dismissively. 'Family had land in the North then, sister still does, so Liam settled in Belfast. He was interned after the Brookeborough fiasco, an abortive attempt on army barracks, New Year 1957, and released in 1960. No one was particularly interested in IRA heroes at that time. He had a family by then, of course, and became a successful businessman but when the Troubles started again in '69, he was one of the first out there with Cahill raising money for weapons. And when the Provos broke away from the official IRA, there was McAuley side by side with MacStioffen and the men of violence.

'He still sees himself as one of the old idealists, but don't underestimate him, he's a powerful hardliner and just as cold-blooded a terrorist as the new breed of IRA thugs he pretends to despise. But he's a cunning and clever operator. For all the murders and atrocities he's planned, the blood is rarely on his own hands.

'Learn his face. You have to get close to him.'

Randall sat down suddenly and handed the stick to Havelock-Davies. But Neil noted the veiled loathing in the flick of his glance, the twitch of muscles in his cheek, the pugilistic thrust of Randall's jaw and he knew McAuley was no ordinary adversary – this was a vendetta to the death and he was the chosen weapon.

A new image flooded the screen. This time a thick-set man with short, crisp, curly hair and coarse handsome features looked round guardedly as he guided a reluctant young woman by the elbow.

'Gerry Hughes, one of McAuley's henchmen.'

Neil started. He leaned forward and stared at the girl.

That face. He'd seen it before. Where? His mind reeled back, fast tracking the years: places, events . . . nothing.

'The daughter, Eilish McAuley – family rebel. Joined the Women's Peace Movement 1976. Only about sixteen at the time but was very visible in all the marches speaking out against the violence, the killing of the Maguire children, etc. Great embarrassment to her father. Even more so when she married a Protestant. Real firebrand . . .'

Neil downed his drink and moved away from the bar. Oh yes, he'd remembered the girl. He hoped she didn't remember him.

The two men who had noted his arrival now watched him as he left. He strolled nonchalantly, checking the signs as he headed for the lounges and the duty-free shops. In the door's reflection, he saw them turn away reassured – no problem there.

This time of year, late September, the ferry was almost empty. There were a few backpackers, a coach party of returning pensioners, several small children ran around, mothers watched, fathers slept; lorry drivers on a regular run slumped bleary eyed. The usual hotchpotch, Neil decided, his trained eye taking it all in at a glance. A few eyes looked back but it was idle curiosity, nothing sinister.

'Which would be the best approach?' Havelock-Davies had pondered, studying the map of Ireland, at one of the last of their meetings. 'Maybe via Dublin? Give yourself time to acclimatize. Drive up across the border.'

Neil had shaken his head. Instinct had told him a man goes back the way he leaves, the way he knows. Besides, the man was a Celtic supporter. Of course he'd use

Stranraer. By that time John Neil was well into the man's skin. By that time he was beginning to think like him.

'Do what? Whose bloody brainwave is this?' had been his initial reaction at that first briefing. 'I'm a soldier, not a bloody kamikaze pilot! I've never even been to Belfast. Well – only briefly! I'd be sussed straight away. His brother would know, for a start! I'd be taken out before I'd even begun!'

'His brother hasn't seen him in years. Not since he was a boy.' Gault's worn face had puckered into a perplexed frown. This, the longest sentence John Neil had uttered in his presence, was not quite the reaction he'd expected. Over the top of his half glasses, his eyes darted anxiously first at Randall, who stared frostily at Neil, then at Havelock-Davies who gazed superciliously at the ceiling, his long frame stretched out on the wooden chair. Havelock-Davies raised an eyebrow and without looking at Neil spoke in the condescending voice of a headmaster to a recalcitrant child.

'Worked undercover before, I presume?'

'Not with another man's shoes on my feet,' Neil had snapped back.

'Been away too long perhaps? Grown soft, have you?'

Gault, equally antagonized by the taunt, looked on with sympathy at Neil, who, bristling with irritation, stared unseeing through the window. In his day Gault had been a top-rate fighting soldier, dedicated to the Regiment. He understood the frustration of being left in the wilderness. They'd done it to him. Told him he needed a break from operations, sent him off to do research. With John Neil, he noted, the yearning to get back into action was almost tangible. You didn't have to be a former trooper to recognize that that first laconic understatement hid a man who'd fought the devil to get back to his peak of fitness. You could see it in the spring of his step as he paced about the room, the set of his

10

shoulders, the width of his neck, the sheer physical electricity of his presence.

In all Gault's planning he had not quite anticipated Neil's resistance to his idea. He mentally measured Neil against the man, calculated height and build. Oh yes, John Neil was his man all right. Fitter, of course. Change the posture, that's all. He riffled through his file.

'Here. Take a look at these.' He thrust a batch of photographs at Neil. 'Now tell me you can't get away with it. You look just like him.'

'Oh, great – a fucking corpse! And that's exactly what I'll be if I go along with this.' Neil flung down the pictures taken in the morgue but his brain was working, Gault could tell.

Havelock-Davies, the master of mistiming, shifted in his seat, draped one elegant leg across the other, and said, 'Worked hard at this one, Neil. Do listen.' Neil and Gault shot him a look of pure malice.

'We've been monitoring our friend here for years.' Gault's stubby fingers drummed down on a heavy, well-used, black box-file. 'There is nothing we don't know about him and a lot he doesn't even know himself. We've recorded things he's forgotten, and things no one would remember. Incidents from his life, old friends, neighbours, teachers, family history; it's all filed away.'

And you knew without question that the filing and cross-filing and referencing and coding, the complicated networking of the man's history, would be indisputably correct in every detail.

'He left Ireland when he was just turned twelve, so it's those first few years you've really got to concern yourself with.'

'He must have gone back since?' Neil interrupted suspiciously.

'No. Never.'

'Not even to see his family?'

11

'No family left, close family, that is – only his brother.' Gault paused, aware of the flicker of interest in John Neil's otherwise impassive face.

'They were a small family. His mother suffered badly in childbirth. She nearly died having the brother. Six years and four miscarriages later, she conceived again; our friend here. He was the last. She was left very weak. Life was a struggle for her, but she did her best by the boys.'

Randall coughed impatiently.

'The family first came to our attention as regulars on the Stranraer ferry. Nothing sinister, the father was a Celtic fan. Always took the boys. We knew he was a bit connected, involved in a few skirmishes on the border, nothing much, but we kept an eye on him, especially as he was quite close to McAuley. They'd been interned together.'

'We don't need the whole history now, Gault. Neil can read that for himself,' Randall interrupted. 'The point is the mother died when he was twelve. The father was interned again at the time, so he' – Randall indicated the photographs of the corpse – 'came to live in Kilburn with his mother's sister.'

'What happened to the brother?' Neil asked Gault.

'He'd been accepted into a seminary to train for the Church. They were all very proud of him. It was also just as well because the aunt and uncle were getting on. Their family had left home long ago and it was all they could do to cope with the one.'

'And when the father came out he never went back?'

Gault shook his head. 'The father died of pneumonia in prison. The boy was deeply upset, started playing truant, caught shop-lifting, et cetera. The old aunt didn't know what to do. When she died the uncle finally threw him out. Our friend got into a lot of trouble at that time.

Small criminal stuff. No one to turn to, nowhere to live, he dossed down wherever he could.'

Neil was surprised to detect real concern in Gault's face. 'Didn't the brother try to help?'

'Oh yes. At first he used to write regularly but the boy never replied, not really, just the odd card. Then when he was thrown out, the brother lost track of him. He came to England at one point to try and find him but by then the boy was on a merchant ship working his way to Australia.'

'And that's where he's lived?'

'Not really. He stayed on as a merchant seaman, moved around a lot, the Far East, Hong Kong, India. He liked the Tropics. Never really settled anywhere. Never any family or close friends, just his shipmates and any girl in any port. No one to identify him, you see. Ideal as a cover.'

'So . . .' Havelock-Davies drawled. 'Not such a forbidding prospect now, eh?'

Neil didn't bother to reply. He prowled about the room, then turned sharply.

'What made you pick up his trail again?'

Havelock-Davies pursed his full lips in a self-satisfied smile. 'One of those happy coincidences that make our lives such a pleasure. We were investigating the movement of arms in the Far East, especially around Hong Kong. Been tipped off the IRA had become "new best buddies" with . . . er . . . a couple of our Triad friends over there and were looking for deals. Not to miss out on anything, followed every lead we could. The Hong Kong police – particularly helpful. Gave us names of every seaman listed in their waters over the last bloody century by the length of it. Millions of the buggers. Including the name of our friend.'

Gault picked up the story but Neil sensed in all three

13

the excitement generated by the painstaking sifting of facts.

'We'd been watching the brother. He'd spent most of his priesthood doing missionary work in Africa. Then a few years ago, he suddenly appeared back in Belfast to take over at St Augustine's. Nothing extraordinary in that except—' Gault's sense of drama again took over. 'Who should be his most devout parishioners? The McAuleys! And not only that but suddenly he's visiting on a regular basis. Now, we've seen no evidence at all of his involvement with the IRA, the 'Rah', in fact he is quite vociferous in speaking out against the violence. Nevertheless he is a frequent visitor to their house, seems very close to the family and, don't forget, has known them from way back through his father.'

'We know a big arms deal is going through.' Randall held up his hand, there was a new urgency to his voice. 'We know there are plans for an escalation of the violence, destined not only for Ulster and the mainland but possibly our troops in Europe too. And we know the man behind it all is McAuley. But what we don't know and must know is where and when. Somehow we have to get someone on the inside.'

'We'd thought of trying to turn the priest,' Gault added.

'But the priest is not for turning.' Havelock-Davies smoothed back his hair. 'Besides, didn't know his colours. Too dangerous. But the long-lost brother eh? Gault made the connection.'

'It was a long shot.' Gault continued to build the case. 'After all it was a very common name, but our friend here had been in a dock-side brawl only twenty-six months previously so the Hong Kong boys were able to fill in a few more details. Not much, really, apart from country of origin and age, but it all matched so it was worth pursuing.'

14

There was romance in the ex-trooper yet, Neil thought, watching him. The old lust for adventure. Like all SAS Gault still believed in the *Boys' Own* story.

'I tracked him down to a bar in Taipei – very down on his luck, trying to get a job, waiting for a ship. We got on well, became drinking buddies. Told me his life story.' Gault patted the black box-file. 'I promised I'd help him. Pay his airfare. Get him a job back in London. He was very grateful.'

'I take it there was no Rah-IRA connection? I mean he had nothing to do with the gun-running?' Neil interrupted.

'Not a thing. No, quite the opposite. Called them a lot of bloody fools. Wanted nothing to do with them and their petty politics. Swore they should see how some people lived, they didn't know how lucky they were, etc. No, no, in fact he seemed to blame his father's death on them – said he'd never have died in prison if he hadn't got involved. He seemed our ideal cover.'

'And he was willing to go along with it?' Neil queried.

'Oh God, no. He knew nothing about it. No, no. The plan was to get him back here. This operation is too big to risk putting in the wrong man. But I was convinced he could do it. I just needed time.'

'Time, however – not on our side,' Havelock-Davies said. 'Time he and Gault had returned, things had moved on.'

Neil noted Randall's face had frozen to a blank mask and Havelock-Davies' usually effete features had hardened.

'No one knew he was coming,' Havelock-Davies continued. 'No one knows he's gone. Bad luck about the accident. 'Course,' he leaned back nonchalantly, 'hit and run. No witnesses. No record. Should anyone check Heathrow arrivals, he flew in from Taiwan two days ago, booked into a small hotel off the Cromwell Road, dropped off his luggage and told them he'd be back in a week. Which he will be.' And he looked at Neil.

There was a defeated droop to Gault's shoulders, his large flat hand rested lightly on the pile of photographs while unconsciously his huge thumb gently stroked the image of the dead man. He had looked up and by the pain in his eyes Neil realized that what Gault had suspected was now confirmed. The man's death had been deliberate.

'Then we'd better make the sacrifice worthwhile,' Neil declared. 'But I don't even know the poor bugger's name.'

'Jackie,' Gault said, 'Jackie O'Connell.'

CHAPTER TWO

He'd been Jackie from then on, he was Jackie now. Gault was right, he knew everything about the man. Far more than John Neil remembered about his own life.

Studying the photographs it was obvious, even in death, that the man was fleshier than Neil, the skin slack with years of alcohol abuse and dissolute living, but there was a passing resemblance in the shape of the face, the set of the eyes, the general colouring, certainly enough similarity of features to persuade the hotel receptionist he was Jackie O'Connell when Neil went back a few days later. By that time, of course, Neil had trimmed the beard he'd cultivated in the isolation of his Highland retreat and cut his long hair to match the shorter curling style of the Irishman. He'd picked up the baggage and with it the threads of the man's life.

Over the next few weeks he'd absorbed a million facts, anecdotes and memories. Gault had fed him the minutiae of the man's life, from the perfume his mother wore, Evening in Paris, to his favourite gift for Christmas. Neil could only marvel and wonder at the hours spent and the drinks drunk for Gault to have extracted all that knowledge. Did Jackie O'Connell ever realize, over those few friendly jars in a bar in Taiwan, that his life's history was being pirated?

Havelock-Davies had walked him down every street in the Belfast of his birth, introduced him to the occupant of every house on the model street in the model city spread across the table. Reminded him of the location of every exploit, every incident, every person that had crossed his path or marked his life, the when, the how and the where of those first crucial years.

Randall had taken him to Kilburn and pointed out the scenes of his juvenile crimes, his school, who were his friends and enemies in those wild days. Had shown him his old haunts, the house he'd shared with his aunt and uncle, and reminded him of the shadowy figures who'd visited under cover of darkness, to flee before dawn. Figures whose names were only ever whispered, who'd hold subversive meetings, sing rebellious songs around the piano. Figures he was about to meet again, who would remember him.

He'd spent hours listening to tapes, adopting the guttural vowels of a long forgotten Belfast accent, layered with teenage cockney overtones, softened with the mellowing of years spent abroad. And as the days passed Neil left himself behind.

It was Randall who fed him the plot; introduced him to the cast of characters he would meet. The major, the minor, the lead players; rehearsing, planning, preparing – for what performance? Which dangerous roles? What murderous acts? What treacherous action? And where? And when?

Then suddenly it was over. Havelock-Davies, pale blue eyes glittering with excitement, had burst into the room with the news that the operation was on. There was no more time.

A funeral was to take place. The McAuley clan would be there. Jackie's brother, Father Fergal O'Connell, was officiating. It was the opportunity they needed.

'Whose funeral is it?' Neil asked.

'Who knows? There are so many,' Havelock-Davies answered. But Neil knew he knew and guessed the death was planned.

18

Randall supplied the details later. Sean McAuley, one of the sons, had been shot. Another sectarian revenge killing. All rather vague. But nothing with Randall was vague, thought Neil.

It was time for Jackie O'Connell to go home.

On board the ferry, John Neil checked his watch. Another forty minutes to go. He smiled at the woman on the till in the duty-free. 'The Marlboros for me. The Bushmills for my brother. If I can stop myself from drinking it that long.'

Her plump round face creased in a broad smile. 'Home to see your family, are you?'

'My brother. Hope he remembers me, I've been away a long time.' Neil threw the line casually over his shoulder as he moved away. But the two men behind him who had watched him in the bar heard it, just as he'd intended they would.

'They'll be tracking you from the moment you get on that ferry,' Randall had warned him on that last day, as they'd walked in the wooded grounds of the old house. 'And not just the IRA, the Rah, or any of the other self-styled paramilitaries – our boys too.'

Neil sneaked a glance at the older man, at the thick brows bristling above the frosty eyes, the chin that jutted forward and the mouth, clamped tight. It was the face of a man determined to do his duty whatever the cost either to himself or to others.

'I can't give you any back-up on this one, John,' Randall said. 'This is strictly a one-man op. The fewer who know about it the better and that includes all the bloody Intelligence bodies and all the other covert teams.

They know the minimum they need to know – a man's going in and will want to come out fast. I'll brief them where and when. No ID, no tongues can wag. I don't need any slip-ups with this one. You'll report to me and only me. Understand?'

'Right, Boss.'

Alone with Randall, Neil had slipped back into the casual relationship of former years when Randall was his commanding officer in the SAS before he lost his soul and joined Military Intelligence.

'Don't underestimate this man McAuley for a second, John. Your life may depend on it. He'll take you in, he'll charm you, even maybe sway you that his Cause is just . . .'

Neil shot him a look of contempt. An alarm rang in Randall's head. Was this man ready to go back in the field? Was the thirst for revenge too fresh? When the heat was on, would the mask of control be in place?

'And I'll believe him. Sure your man's right, 'tis the Armalite not the ballot box that'll win the war,' Neil said. Randall allowed himself a tight smile.

'He's very well connected.' Randall steered back on course. 'Powerful friends in high places, especially in the South. Influential Republican families, rich, heavy hitters – discreet. He's a frequent "weekender" across the border. The surprise guest to entertain the rich and famous; the dangerous swashbuckling rebel; the legend – given his life to the Cause, etc., etc. Good fund-raiser. He'll be looking for funds now.'

'The Hong Kong connection? The arms deal. That him?'

'Not directly. Triad weren't too interested. It's a big shopping list for the IRA – not a big enough deal for them. But something's turned them. Not the Irish boys, they went home. Someone else has done a deal with the

20

Triad and on their behalf. Some big arms dealer, we suspect, no doubt a sympathizer, who's put their order under another umbrella. We've lost the track. Triad interests are so far-spread these days. No idea where it's coming from. We only know it's soon. Up to you to find out when and where it's going to land. It's a big cache this time. That we do know.

'There's a glut in the arms market. With the end of the Cold War everyone's selling off everything, even state-of-the-art arms. If the IRA start getting hold of some of those, God knows what we're in for.'

Both men fell silent.

'There's something else, John. I've been after McAuley a long time and I know him well. Whatever one thinks of the man, he was always meticulous in aiming at military targets. Oh, a few bystanders might get caught in the cross-fire but he regarded that as acceptable – one of the hazards of war.' Randall's eyes narrowed. 'But recently he's changed tactics, gone for bigger and bigger targets especially on the mainland – indiscriminate civilian targets, crippling and killing: not just people, the economy. I think he feels time's running out. He's been a powerful figure for a long time, now there's a new breed eager to muscle in. McAuley won't give in easily. This next operation is going to be his show of power – I know it.'

Randall punched his right fist into his leather-clad palm. 'McAuley.' He dragged the word slowly from the depths of his throat. 'He's taken too many of my men! Too many friends!'

Then he coughed, afraid he'd revealed too much. 'Too much blood on his hands, John, too much blood. He's got away with it too long.

'You have to forget all that. Get close to him. Make him trust you. It won't be easy. He's cunning, suspicious and conceited and a fanatical Republican but he has one soft spot and that's his daughter.'

And there she was, in John Neil's mind, her image as fresh and vivid as when he'd seen her all those years ago, marching from Hyde Park, her arms linked with the other Peace marchers that cold November day. On that day of hope when Joan Baez sang, when Jane Ewart-Biggs, whose husband had been murdered by the IRA, had joined hands with Betty Williams and Mairead Corrigan, co-founders of the Ulster Peace Movement, when all the world seemed to have gathered in Trafalgar Square to pray for peace, despite the counter-demonstrators' cries of 'Troops Out!' Her young face had symbolized the conviction that peace was truly possible.

Neil had fought his way to the front of the rally just to be touched by the power of faith that radiated from that slim teenage girl. She'd seen him and she'd smiled. They'd linked hands, stranger with stranger, joined in the belief that they could overcome.

He'd been young himself then; even so, the first frost of cynicism had already blighted his life and the blood of war was fresh on his hands. The faces of the Arab rebels he'd fought in close combat had been masked by their head-cloths but their eyes haunted him and the shrill cries of battle woke him at night.

Outstanding boy soldier, John Neil, first class paratrooper, John Neil, youngest selected SAS trooper, John Neil, was well noted for his courageous spirit when he was approached by a senior officer at that time seconded to the Sultan of Oman's army. The officer, recognizing Neil's exceptional qualities, had persuaded him to join his special force of selected men, fighting the rebels in Oman. A speedy course in Arabic was ordered. Neil arrived just as the final bloody onslaught was beginning, pushing the rebels back to the Yemeni border. It was a military victory but a tough baptism.

When young John Neil linked hands with the girl that day, the war had been over but a few weeks. She'd smiled at a tanned young man in civvies but he knew that despite the call for peace he was the enemy and that the cries of 'Troops out!' referred to him. He'd broken away, aware that one day, they might meet on hostile ground.

Neil glanced at the senior officer who'd fought alongside him in Oman all those years ago.

'There's a division between the girl and her father,' Randall was saying. 'He never forgave her for marrying a Protestant, but, since the husband died, he's never stopped trying to win her back. Adores the grandson, of course. Another McAuley to carry on the tradition. The girl must hate that! She could be very useful. Good way to get to him.'

'Was the husband murdered?'

'Heart attack. Five years ago. One of the few to die in his bed.'

They'd walked for a while in silence.

'Confident, are you?' Randall asked. 'Don't want to lose you. One of my best men.' With a huge effort he'd muttered, 'And – er – sorry about your family. You didn't deserve that.'

There was a sudden change in the pulse of the ship's engine. Passengers stirred, peered through the dark glass windows, fancied they saw lights and began to gather up their belongings. John Neil got ready with the rest.

He'd decided to hire a car rather than hitch a lift. He needed to concentrate and he did not want to answer questions. It was an easy drive, despite the control points which were still a shock in a country one regarded as part of home. After a few questions, the soldier waved him on, but the moment was fraught with the fear of recognition, even though he told himself the chances were remote. He entered the city limits down the Antrim Road, passing the high sandstone banks of the Zoological Gardens to where the floodlit outline of Belfast Castle rose up on his right. Across the black expanse of Belfast Lough he could see the distant lights of the docks, the navigational lights of ships reflected on the vast waters and the warning lights of the distant Harbour Airport. Ahead the glow of Belfast filled the sky, its people, streets and houses penned in for the night by the slumbering hills.

Jackie eased down to a moderate speed, allowing himself time to assimilate passing street names, signposts, buildings, locations, correlating the reality with the model city of his briefings. A sudden flurry of bed-and-breakfast placards and bright hotel signs warned him he was drawing closer to the centre. Surrounding the larger, more notable ones, broken glass or coils of barbed wire topped high walls and security gates loomed up, the legacies of former bomb attacks.

He turned the car around and headed back out of town to where he'd noticed a discreet sign advertising 'Vacancies' in a small hotel situated in a side street. He drove past slowly. A full-bosomed, sandstone Victorian house offered 'Warm, comfortable rooms. All mod cons. CH. Own phone and TV.' It looked clean and friendly, if a little shabby. A large arrow indicated 'Off street parking' at the front and side.

By the light of a street lamp, Jackie checked his map. The road had several others leading off it. All led back to the main Antrim Road. No way could he be trapped.

Security seemed minimal. At his ring a disembodied voice instructed him to 'Push'.

The tall figure of a woman, outlined by the wall light at her back, stood to greet him from behind a large curved mahogany desk that carved out the reception area from the shadows of what appeared to be a cavernous marble-floored entrance hall. For a moment she said nothing, her face in darkness, but Jackie could feel her eyes scrutinizing him and his luggage. Obviously satisfied, she switched on a desk lamp. Jackie assessed her: stern face, ramrod back, old school, followed her man, tamed the natives, colonized the world. Hair, white. Age? Sixties? Fine bold features. Aristocratic – down on her luck.

She stood, crisp in a man's white shirt, her hands resting on the desk top, staring directly at him over heavy framed glasses that had slipped down the aquiline nose, and waited for him to speak.

It was like being back at school and this was a test. He offered his most winning smile, slightly crooked, schoolboyish, charming. It had worked before.

'I need a room for a couple of nights, if you have it? Maybe more. I saw your sign. Nice place.' He nodded appreciatively in the general direction of the main house.

'You've had a look round then, have you?' was her short response.

'Well, no. Not yet.' Jackie stumbled.

'Then how d'you know?'

'Intuition?' Jackie shrugged and pointedly checked for eavesdroppers. 'No, the truth is, I'm a close friend of the Dalai Lama and I happen to be an exponent of the third eye.'

'That'll do.' She nodded at him, her face lit from within by a secret smile that did not quite reach her mouth. She sat down decisively, picked up a heavy, cut-glass tumbler of whiskey and drank appreciatively.

'If I have to have strangers in my house, at least let them not be dull and boring! Now, no cheques – they bounce; no credit cards – too often stolen; no address – usually false. So cash only – two nights up front and a name? I don't want to have to keep calling, "Hey You!" '

'Jackie O'Co—'

'Jackie. Ah, that'll do. I can't be doing with all that red tape. Now, you can take the big blue room at the back. It's quiet there.'

She handed Jackie a key, her tapering fingers stained with ink, nails cut short and mannish. She had been writing something – but not bookkeeping, that was clear.

'Do you have many staying?' Jackie asked as he caught the sound of voices from a room somewhere.

'Just visitors. No guests. Two came. I turned them away. Travelling salesmen!' And she wrinkled her nose. 'Dead as dodos! And old beyond their years. Withered on the bough. You could smell the hopelessness on them. I won't have that!' And she flashed him a smile.

'Right now I must get back to my friends. I'm sure you could do with a drink. The bar's open.' She pointed vaguely in the direction of the hall. 'You just help yourself now. Make a note of what you drink and we'll settle up when you go. I'll get my girl to put up some sandwiches for you, too late for anything else this time of night. You'll find everything you want in your room. Sleep well.' With that she pushed open the door behind her and was gone.

Was this the right setting for Jackie O'Connell? For a split second John Neil slipped his role and felt a twinge of panic. Then it stopped. He'd found the place as Jackie would, driving along the road. The price was right, no questions asked. And it was near his brother. St Augustine's was but a mile away. Jackie O'Connell would have wanted his return to pass unnoticed, his homecoming to be – not secretive, but low key. He would be uncertain of his reception, Neil was sure. He'd been away a long time. Like a vulnerable animal, he would want to sniff the air, test the ground before he made his presence known.

John Neil slipped back into Jackie's skin.

'Belfast is a village – remember. Beneath the charm lies suspicion. Never drop your guard!' Randall had emphasized that.

Jackie locked the room behind him as he left, the exact state and position of his possessions already imprinted in his memory. He checked the corridor for signs of life. Nothing, apart from the light beneath his door – all was silence and shadows. At the foot of the stairs he paused. A faint murmur of voices filtered through the closed door behind reception. He stepped closer but could distinguish nothing, only hear what seemed to be the soft rhythmic cadences of a chant or a prayer, something ritualistic.

He found the bar off the hall, in a room which also served as the dining room. Several small tables were set for breakfast, each laid with a place-setting for one.

He poured himself a whiskey. On top of the bar a sheet of paper was waiting with the name 'Jackie' scrawled across the top, ready with a pencil for him to list his drinks, a plate of sandwiches beside it. Tension and tiredness had made him hungry and he ate quickly.

Clearly no bureaucracy, no red tape, meant only one thing – no evidence. The solitary travellers who rested here could not be traced and did not want to be traced. Had Jackie O'Connell flown into the hornet's nest? Was this a refuge? A safe house for people on the run? It would explain a lot. And if so, what had made the woman trust him? This was a Republican house, no doubt. He hadn't mentioned his surname, anything – how had she known which foot he kicked with? Subconsciously he checked his image in the mirror behind the bar and saw the light flash on the gold chain at his neck. Jackie's crucifix, of course, he'd forgotten.

And the bag, he realized. She'd assessed that too. The beaten-up sports bag that served him as a suitcase, the one he'd retrieved from the hotel on the Cromwell Road, that held all Jackie O'Connell's few possessions. A man on the run would travel light, just as he did. She would be used to that.

John Neil was cast back. He was high in the Lake District, fifteen years old, leading a group of four youths across Scafell, as part of their training for the Duke of Edinburgh Award. A heavy mist had fallen. They were cold, frightened, they'd got separated from their leaders and they were lost.

One of the boys shrieked out, stumbled and slithered away on the loose scree. A rough shrub stopped his fall and somehow they managed to pull him back to the track but his leg was broken, they could tell, and he was shivering with shock.

Following the trail of a small stream John Neil led them down. The injured boy was from Belfast, so was his mate. They'd come over together on a Boys' Club exchange. It was August 1969. They took it in turns to carry the boy, holding him, spread-eagled across their backs. His mate insisted on doing more than his share. When they rested, which they were forced to do, he cuddled the boy to keep him warm, wiped his tears when he whimpered in pain, gave him his emergency rations, encouraged him to hold on.

The boy safely in hospital, his mate visited him daily, cheering his spirits with gossip of the day's achievements.

On 12 August 1969, news of the riots flaring in Northern Ireland glared from every newsstand and television screen. There had been marches and protests already that year, but the violence of these clashes, the bloody confrontation of Protestant versus Catholic, was unexpected, something few boys on the D. of E. course understood. The 'Irish Troubles' were history, not happening today. They turned to their Irish friend for reassurance but his face was hostile and his answer shocked them. He talked angrily of discrimination, injustice, unemployment, the bastard Paisley and fighting on the barricades. He railed against the division of his country, the Free State, the Six Counties, in terms the boys barely understood – war-like terms: 'The Republican Army', the British 'occupation' and ousting the troops. The invective of generations suddenly was released. They had listened in amazement. They were all British. Denomination? They never even questioned it. He was Protestant, Catholic, Irish, British, who cared? He did. He stood his ground. He was an Irish Catholic, a Republican. He wanted a United Ireland, ruled by an Irish government. A country free of British rule. It was time to fight.

But it was his last statement that really shocked them, when he announced he was going back and without his friend, the injured boy, his fellow Irishman. Their friendship was impossible, he'd said. The boy was a Protestant and if it came to it, to a fight on the streets of Belfast, he'd kill him, along with every other 'Orange Proddy Bastard'.

Neil didn't understand it then. He didn't understand it now. Intellectually, historically, politically, of course he did. He'd seen enough war and hatred to comprehend the manipulation of the masses by big business and power-hungry leaders. But that indoctrinated hatred in the name of religion could shatter a friendship, and turn

29

two caring people into the bitterest enemies, emotionally to him, it was an anathema.

Jackie O'Connell had to believe it.

Senses tingling, he checked his room. Nothing had been touched. He went to bed and tried to sleep. Tomorrow was the funeral. Tomorrow Jackie must come face to face with his brother Fergal. And the others. McAuley, Brendan, Eilish. Tomorrow he must outwit them all.

There was the sound of voices. The 'friends' were leaving. He went to the window and looked out but could see nothing, only the flash of headlights reflected on trees. Engines revved in the car park. Two of the three cars he'd noted on his arrival drove off. The third obviously belonged to the woman. He heard her brisk footfall on the stairs to the floor above. Then silence.

Back in bed, sleep evaded him. He lay there, eyes wide, alive with 'pre-battle' nerves. Over and over he rehearsed his lines, his approach to Fergal. The funeral was timed for eleven a.m. He knew the cemetery, he knew who would be there, he knew Father Fergal would be conducting the service. Now he had to forget it. He would seek out Fergal at the church, timing his visit for about 11.10 a.m. Someone would be about, someone would direct him to the funeral party. He'd watch and wait, catch Fergal at the end when his attention would be focused on other things, his wits perhaps not quite as sharp, so that any slip-ups Jackie might make, any nervous hesitancy, would go unnoticed. Convince Father Fergal he was his long-lost brother and the others would be hard pressed not to accept him.

Out of nowhere Julie's face was there, her sweet pervading presence, her perfume . . . he could smell her perfume. He sat up suddenly. She was there, she had to be there. He looked round wildly, then sank back, his body, mind and soul consumed with longing just to see her, hold her, touch her, be with her.

The last morning when he'd kissed her goodbye, she'd been wearing that perfume, he'd given it to her that day, Tommy's birthday. It was her favourite, the one she always wore, a sensuous summer blend of musk, vanilla and blossom. She'd laughed, her arms twined around him, drawing him in to nuzzle her neck, whispering loving promises. He'd teased back, called her 'temptress', 'wanton hussy'. Tommy had overheard.

'Mummy want an horsey? What horsey, Mummy?' He'd spoken with his thumb plugged in his mouth, trailing his teddy by one arm, sleepy again after the excitement of his birthday morning.

They'd both laughed. 'The circus horse!' Julie had said.

John had swung his little son high in the air. 'Just you wait, birthday boy – there'll be lions and tigers and elephants and clowns. Everything at the circus!'

Tommy had giggled delightedly. Julie had been just as excited. 'I wish we could all go together!' she'd said. 'Couldn't the army do without you for once?'

'I'll be there as soon as I can, I promise. You don't want to miss the beginning – I might be held up. It's the parade. Tommy must see the parade. And he'll love going on the minibus with the others from the base. The boys have laid on all sorts of surprises for the kids.'

'But I want you to be there for all of it,' she'd said. 'It's his first circus!'

'Believe me, I'll be there – soon as I can.'

The parade music was ending as he parked his car. He could hear the drums, horns and hurdy-gurdy organ, the trumpeting elephants, the calls of the animals, the high-pitched cheers of young voices, the uproar of approval from the audience, all blaring out across the

31

grounds, the sound caught and amplified by the loudspeakers.

Then the bomb exploded.

John Neil buried his head in the pillow, tortured again by the scene that would haunt him for the rest of his life. Then he was calm. An icy detachment permeated his being, his nerves stilled. Tomorrow could come. He was ready.

CHAPTER THREE

Someone directed him, as he thought they would, to the burial ground. An old man, withered as a leaf, was leaving confession. He looked too fragile to have the strength to sin, Neil could only imagine his memory was good or his mind agile. His bones had long since given up the task of supporting his body. He drooped like a dying plant, supported from toppling by a stick on which he leaned heavily. But his eyes were bright as a bird's.

'Father Fergal? Father Fergal is it you're wanting? Ah no, no . . .' He shook his head sadly, then brightened up. 'Now, would you not like Father Michael? He's a lovely fella. Does a lovely confession.'

'No, it's Father Fergal I have to see, but if you don't know . . .?'

'Oh I do, I do. But he's at the interment.' He paused and for a moment his thoughts drifted away.

'Terrible thing,' he muttered, 'terrible thing. That poor soul. Shot down, shot down. Orange bastards, Orange bastards.' His thin voice trembled with anger and a long projectile of sputum was suddenly ejected with astonishing violence from his gumless mouth.

His awareness heightened by danger, Neil moved out of the shadow of the church and approached the scene in the cemetery. A magnified landscape of brilliant white gravestones, vivid green grass, and black crowd against a bright blue sky confronted him, stark and unreal in the autumn sun. It seemed he watched himself from a great

33

height and saw Jackie O'Connell in slow motion move among the gravestones, keeping a respectful distance between himself and the mourners. He watched himself, as others did, hesitate, retreat, turn back and listen, his head bowed as he crossed himself in response to the prayers for the dead that echoed on the still air from the Tannoy speakers.

Now, as a more strident voice demanded attention, he moved forward. At the same time, two figures broke away from the crowd. A slender woman, head bent, arms protectively around the shoulders of a young boy, strode off defiantly, ignoring the heads that turned to shame her. The boy tried to look back. She pushed him on. Even at this distance and after all these years, Neil recognized Eilish McAuley. The boy twisted round in her grasp. She pulled at him impatiently, distancing herself from the ceremony until she disappeared among the gravestones.

The voice of the speaker thrilled dramatically, the mourners murmured and swayed, their attention gripped by the fervour of the oration.

'And if killing every damn British soldier or Loyalist is the only way, then we'll do it! And if shedding every drop of Irish blood is the answer, then so be it. I'll join all those who have gone before. Like my father did before me. We're past talking peace. Leave that to the politicians. Let them wave the ballot boxes – believe me, the Armalite will win the day!

'Remember the words of Terence McSwinney before he died: "It's not those who can inflict the most but those that will suffer the most who will conquer." So today we suffer – we lose our sons and our grandsons, our young heroes. But I promise you their sacrifice will not be in vain. We will be avenged! Ireland will be united. Our suffering we give gladly to the glory of Ireland.'

The mourners sighed and stirred, revealing for an

instant the white eagle head of Liam McAuley at the microphone, his eyes closed, his head thrown back, his fist held high in defiance of the attendant military helicopter flying above.

Black-hooded gunmen leapt to attention. A salvo of gunfire saluted the air, flags of white cordite smoke hovered then faded above the covered heads of the mourners who now moved as one, camouflaging the tracks of the masked gunmen as they melted into the sympathetic crowd.

People began to drift away, leaving only the main funeral party still at the graveside. Neil, rooted in character, watched, his hands jammed in his pockets, itching for the cold, comforting steel of a trigger beneath his finger.

The black-and-white photographs he'd studied sprang to life in colour and dimension; Father Fergal looked shorter, McAuley far taller.

Eyes were on him now. McAuley's henchmen inched closer to their man. Gerry Hughes whispered something in McAuley's ear. Unabashed, Neil looked back, his gaze slightly averted – trained on Fergal.

The violence of the death had been reflected in the speeches. In contrast, Neil saw there was a gentleness about the priest who moved among the mourners. He more than anyone seemed to bear the sadness of the occasion. Even the daughter, Eilish, returned, but still stood apart, clutching anxiously at the thin, young shoulders of her son, seeming impatient to be done with the ritual. Father Fergal noticed her irritation and caught her arm. She listened to him but didn't hear – poised like a bird for flight. John saw her nod, smile briefly at him, then speak curtly to her father and walk off, her slim legs flashing from beneath the enveloping black coat. McAuley watched her go, issuing instructions for Hughes to follow. Without turning, McAuley, his head for the first time bowed low, reached out behind him. Father Fergal moved into his grasp, offering a shoulder for the man to lean on.

Was it the instinct of the man of God that made Fergal anticipate McAuley's need for comfort or some other more earthly understanding? Did Fergal condone – share, even – the same political ambitions and convictions?

'The Church is reluctant to condemn,' Randall had warned him. 'We do not know Fergal's involvement. We only know he is a regular visitor to the house. Do not trust anyone.'

Neil paced the grass and waited. McAuley leaned to whisper in the priest's ear. Neil sensed Fergal glance in his direction and saw the priest reassuringly pat McAuley's arm before he headed straight for him.

'Convince the priest and you'll win the others!' Randall's voice rang out in his head.

Jackie O'Connell took a deep breath and prepared to meet his brother.

Ignoring the path, Father Fergal came striding across the grass. He walked confidently, a man used to respect, his feet kicking out briskly beneath the black robe, his lithe body upright, its slimness owing more to a hard physical life than the vanity of the gym. His short hair had looked blond from a distance, bleached blond by the African sun, but as he drew closer, Neil realized it was the strands of white that gave this illusion. There was a querying half-smile on his lips, a questioning, troubled look in the blue eyes that had not lost the habit of narrowing against a blazing sun. John Neil stood his ground.

Close to, Fergal's skin was leathered and lined, more than his years deserved. But if he tried, Neil could see a resemblance, justify a likeness between the two of them.

'Fergal,' Jackie said with a teasing smile, 'do you not know me, Fergal?'

The priest stepped back, surprised, and frowned. 'Should I? I don't . . .?'

'Oh, but you do.'

Father Fergal scratched his head.

'Oh Jesus, Fergal, I've never forgotten that.' Jackie caught the priest's hand and stared at the little finger with its missing top digit. 'Or the beating Daddy gave us when I slammed your finger in the door.'

Father Fergal snatched back his hand as if it had been scalded, crossing himself in panic. He stared, his face white, his mouth gaping in shock.

'I'm not a ghost. It's me – Jackie.' And he grinned. The older man still stared, his eyes wide and confused.

Jackie reached out and squeezed his arm reassuringly. 'Jesus, I didn't mean to shock you like that. I should have written – warned you I was coming.'

Fergal released his pent-up breath on a great rush and a prayer. 'Holy Mary Mother of God. I don't believe it. I just don't believe it. After all this time. Jackie . . . Jackie! My God, Jackie!'

He shook his head in disbelief. His eyes scoured every feature of Jackie's face, desperately seeking to identify, to recognize in this stranger something of his long-lost younger brother. He stared into eyes that looked back fearlessly, grey eyes like his father's, with the hint of a warm smile, like those of his mother – and the mouth, the crooked grin that had charmed his teachers and got Jackie out of so much trouble, yes – that was there. The more Fergal searched, the more he could see; the hair – that strange tawny colour, a few grey hairs now, lighter than his own but still the same. And the same square jaw, similar physique, but more than that; there was something in the presence of the man, the easy familiarity of someone who knew him well. The man before

37

him didn't shy away from the intensity of the scrutiny, nor was he brazen; quite the opposite – Fergal detected a diffidence in his bearing although the gaze returning his never faltered.

Visualizing the young Jackie, it wasn't hard to imagine that in adulthood he might look like this. Taller, certainly, than Fergal remembered and beneath the bulky duffle coat, with a great physique, but then, that last time, just after their father had died, Jackie had been a scrawny kid caught up in the turmoil of a particularly difficult adolescence.

To all appearances Neil stood easily before the older man but inside he burned with the deception. Transparent as glass, Fergal's face mirrored every emotion. Doubt and suspicion, Neil had expected; it was the love and the hope he regretted betraying. Physically, Fergal had recognized similarities, Neil had seen that; now he waited for the questioning to start.

'How many years is it, Jackie?' Fergal began.

'Oh God – when was it?' Neil stroked his beard. 'Let's see now, Daddy died February '68. I saw you not long after that. March? April? March, it must have been.'

'Don't be too glib in remembering. Memories are never that good. Hesitate, make mistakes, correct yourself,' had been one of Gault's instructions.

'I've always regretted it, you know, Fergal, never going to Daddy's funeral. I was so mixed up at the time. So angry with him for dying, for leaving me, for not coming back like he'd promised. He'd sworn on Mammy's grave, remember? Promised faithfully that if I was a good boy and did everything Auntie Maire said he'd fetch me home. I was so bloody good at first, it hurt! Then when he died, still in prison, I felt he'd let me down. I wanted to hurt him back. Pathetic, eh?'

'Not really. You were very young. So was I . . .'

In his mind's eye, Fergal saw the tear-streaked furious

38

face of his young brother. He'd gone to England, indignant and angry with Jackie for refusing to come to their father's funeral. Jackie had flung himself into his big brother's arms, begging him to take him home. Fergal, the trainee priest, pompous with new authority as head of the family, had pushed him away, and instead of listening and understanding the twisted logic of the confused adolescent, had castigated him severely in the name of their father and of God. He'd regretted it ever since.

Steeling himself against nostalgia, Fergal concentrated on testing the man purporting to be his brother.

'Where now did you say you hid when Aunt Maire and Uncle Patrick were leaving for the funeral?'

'Oh God in heaven, do you remember that? I could hear them yelling at me all over the place, cursing and shouting as to how if I didn't show up, they'd miss the plane or go without me – and me, all the time, crouched in the back of the cupboard under the stairs. Then just as I heard the car drive away, this bloody great spider started crawling up my leg. Ah Jesus, I nearly went berserk. I thought it was God paying me back for my wickedness. I went screaming after them. Too late, they'd gone. God, I cried.'

'You always were terrified of spiders.'

'Still am.' Neil, alert to every nuance, detected an almost imperceptible pause.

'Do you remember the song Mammy always sang to us at night to keep us safe?' Fergal's voice was deceptively light.

'Oh God, Fergal, she sang so many . . .'

'Not at night!'

The words, loaded with suspicion, hung on the still air. The priest held his breath. Neil sensed McAuley watching from a distance. He'd noted him dispatch the funeral party on ahead, while he and his men waited for the priest to be done. Abruptly, his tolerance exhausted,

McAuley signalled his followers and started his approach. Far away, a dog barked. An aeroplane droned overhead.

The priest exhaled. A long slow expiration of air that hissed between his teeth. 'Jackie would have known,' he said bitterly, and turned his back.

'*Oh my dear old Nellie Gray, they have taken her away* . . .' Softly, Jackie began. '*And I'll never see my darling any more* . . .'

The priest froze.

'*I'm sitting by the window, weeping all the day* . . .' Jackie's voice rose.

'*Now she's gone from our old Kentucky shore*,' Fergal joined in.

'*Poor Nellie Gray*.' John Neil added the stamp of authenticity. ' "Mammy, Mammy, where've they taken her?" I used to cry. Remember?'

Fergal flung his arms around his brother, tears streaming down his cheeks.

Caught in the emotion of the moment, Jackie hugged him back. And opened his eyes to stare directly into the piercing black eyes of McAuley.

Father Fergal broke away. 'Liam,' he said to the powerful figure now standing by his side. 'You know who this is? Look, look carefully. It's more than twenty years since I last saw his face, but I know it now like I know my own. It's Jackie. It's my wee brother Jackie! Remember?'

'I remember you, Mr McAuley,' Jackie said easily, holding out his hand.

A huge liver-spotted fist clasped his, but the granite face was as impassive as a carving on Mount Vernon.

'Jackie O'Connell! Well now, isn't that something after all these years.'

'I'd have recognized him anywhere,' Fergal said proudly.

'Sure I remember.' McAuley nodded. 'A bad wee

article, always racing round.' And the thin lips cracked across the lantern jaw in semblance of a faint smile.

'Bring him along, Father. To the house.'

Jackie drew back, his hand held up in protest. 'Sure you're very kind, but there's no way I'll intrude on your sorrow. My sympathies on your loss, Mr McAuley.'

'Thanks, son. It's a sad day. You join us now. Come with Fergal. You're welcome.'

Fergal nodded eagerly and indicated his car.

'I'll follow on. I've my car with me,' Jackie acknowledged.

'Do that and don't get lost, now. Still, Belfast is a small place, we'll always find you.' McAuley's words held an underlying threat.

The three henchmen who had kept vigil nearby now fanned protectively around the big man as he walked the short distance to his waiting car.

Neil had recognized them immediately. Brendan McAuley, tall, arrogant and handsome, was unmistakably his father's son. He'd looked at Neil suspiciously with the same deep-set eyes but he lacked the intelligence of McAuley, making him even more dangerous. Throughout the meeting, his hand had restlessly stroked the lapel of his jacket, itching for one false move, one excuse to draw the gun John Neil knew was hidden there.

The other two, both obvious bodyguards, bulky in shape, hefty in build, dressed uncomfortably in ill-fitting suits, Neil identified as Micky Maguire and Joseph O'Shea, both in their thirties, both long-time members of the IRA, suspected but never convicted of a number of bombings and killings.

Maguire, with long fair curls, huge baby face, broken nose, bore the cauliflower ear and huge ham fists of the street fighter. Unquestioning in his loyalty, he acted for McAuley as a human shield against the many enemies who threatened his life.

O'Shea, his weasel face and small bullet head weaving threateningly on the over-developed body, was a killer of cunning. He was the tactician. He plotted routes and times and safe houses, outmanoeuvring would-be assassins. He planted evidence on others, lied and cheated against friends and enemies alike and kept his master safe. What McAuley hardly dared to suggest, O'Shea did and bore the brunt of the big man's rebukes, knowing in his heart of hearts that what he'd done was what McAuley wanted.

Following behind Fergal, John Neil mentally sifted through the filed information on the three men. McAuley was something else. Physically, he was even bigger and more powerful than Neil had expected. A magnetic field of energy emanated from him, a charisma, a charm, but underneath there was something sinister, a violence in his very stillness, like the threatening silence before a volcano erupts. He'd welcomed Jackie too easily. Neil knew, even now, as they were driving to McAuley's son's funeral breakfast, the inquisition would soon be under way.

'Oh Christ, Gault, don't be so bloody pernickety,' he'd cried, tired and irritated during those last long hours of intense briefing when Gault had striven, day and night, to drive into his head those fine details which could save his life.

'I can't remember my own mother's favourite colour – why would he?'

Now he thanked God for Gault's meticulousness. He hoped they would not be as thorough.

Stopped at traffic lights, Neil caught Fergal watching him in his mirror. He grinned back. With his right fist clenched he gave him the thumbs-up, then bent the top digit at right angles to signify 'Not bad!' in a silly sign Fergal and Jackie had shared as kids.

Fergal laughed.

As Jackie parked his car, O'Shea was there to lead him and Fergal into the house, one of several similar, substantial houses, sheltered behind high walls.

'I'll take youse in,' he muttered, through the side of a mouth tight with secrets, while all the time the bald, domed head swivelled round, surveilling the area.

'Cheers,' said Jackie, all open and friendly.

It was the girl, Eilish, he was dreading confronting. Would she remember?

Every room in the high-ceilinged house was crowded, yet as Jackie pushed through, a lull descended. Eyes narrowed, voices faded, there was a stranger in their midst. Then they spotted the priest at his side and the word went round; Father Fergal's brother, wee Jackie O'Connell, was back.

McAuley found them immediately.

'Well now, this is something. Jackie O'Connell, bad wee article! You'd no idea about his coming then, Fergal?' he quizzed, but it was Jackie's face he studied.

'Biggest surprise of my life, but I'd have known him anywhere.'

'Been living across, all this time?'

Jackie shook his head. 'I'd have been back before now, if I had. No, the Far East. All over. I was a merchant seaman. Few other odd jobs. Anything to make a bit of money.'

'So what made you want to come back now?'

'Don't know, really. Got talking to some fella in a bar. Started reminiscing, the way you do. Suddenly made me want to see the old country again. Maybe settle down. Just had enough of wandering, I suppose.'

43

John Neil struggled to concentrate. The girl was coming towards them, pushing through the crowd. He saw her pause, as someone caught her attention, noted the way she listened, her head tilted to one side. McAuley noticed and called her to him.

'Eilish. Meet Jackie O'Connell. Father Fergal's brother.'

'You're welcome, Jackie. Can I get you something?'

'A Guinness?'

'I'm sure we can manage that.' A fleeting smile and she was gone; no sign of recognition. John Neil breathed more easily.

Brendan McAuley muscled forward, followed by his younger brother Colum, smaller boned, finer featured, with a sensitive intelligent face, like his sister. McAuley introduced them. They nodded curtly at Jackie, sizing up their man, before reporting back to Gerry Hughes, who kept his distance across the room.

'Are you staying a while, Jackie?' McAuley asked.

'I think I might. Get to know my brother again.'

'We'll see you, then.'

There was a waft of perfume, vanilla, spices – Eilish was back, holding out his drink. She was wearing the same perfume as his wife! Taken aback, Neil stared at her. Eilish's glance held his until she broke away, embarrassed, to attend to her son, who called to her. Looking at the boy, John Neil saw Tommy.

He had to get out. He fought his way to the door.

'Ready to go then, Jackie?' Fergal had followed. 'Let's be off. I've done my duty.' He lowered his voice confidentially. 'They'll be here till the wee hours, singing the songs, praising the Cause. Time was – I might have joined them.'

From the window, Eilish watched them leave. He was attractive, Father Fergal's brother. There was some-

44

thing . . . something about him. It was a long time since she'd even noticed another man.

Fergal insisted Jackie move in with him. John Neil was deliberately vague as to the whereabouts of his hotel. It was a sanctuary he might need. He wanted it kept secret. There were no questions asked when he paid his bill.

That night he and Fergal shared the Bushmills he'd bought on the ferry and talked way into the night, catching up on each other's lives.

It was amazing how much more Jackie remembered than his brother. So much so, Fergal commented on the power of his memory.

'Being so far away, I probably thought about home a lot more than you did,' was his excuse, but it made Neil more cautious thereafter.

'Eilish seems a nice girl,' he commented casually.

'Best of the bunch,' Fergal replied with feeling. 'Quite a girl too. Real firebrand. Won't let herself be pushed around. Not even by her father. Lot of bad blood between them.'

'She's not involved, then?'

'Quite the opposite. Firm Republican, mind, every bit as much as her father. But against the violence. Always has been. Joined the Peace Movement when she was just a slip of a thing. Old Liam McAuley, apparently, ranted and raved as to how she was making him look a fool. He was a powerful man in the organization, even then. The IRA hated the Peace People. Considered them pro-British, traitors to the Cause, hypocrites for speaking out against the violence of the Rah, and supporting the Security Forces. The Peace People wanted the law upheld by the proper authorities, not the paramilitaries. Eilish, with the rest of them, urged ordinary Catholics to report IRA activity. But nobody likes informing. Lost

45

them a lot of support, that. The Provos retaliated, stoned the marchers, daubed their houses with threats, did everything to destroy the movement. Oh yes, she made things very difficult for the McAuleys.

'Don't suppose you heard much over there. Visiting priests, in Africa, used to bring us all the news. It was a sad time, so much hope turned into so much hate.'

'What happened with Eilish?' Neil probed.

'Eilish!' Fergal said fondly. 'I suppose she must have been at the university by then. Bright girl, not like that young hood, Brendan.' Fergal frowned. 'Anyway, she defied her father, joined in organizing mixed-religion camps, marches, that sort of thing. She became one of the lead campaigners speaking out against the rough justice meted out by the Provos against their own. That's how she met her husband, Chris. God in heaven, did that upset her father! Chris was a Protestant, you see. Took her off to live in a mixed area. Her father would have nothing to do with her after that. It was only after Chris died – a heart attack – they started speaking again. Must be four, five years ago now.'

'Shame. Not remarried then?'

Father Fergal shook his head.

'There was a fella at the house.' Neil swirled the whiskey in his glass. 'Curly brown hair, not bad looking . . . Seemed to be with her?'

'Gerry Hughes? No, he'd like to be, I'm sure. He's one of McAuley's boys. A bad lot. You steer clear of him. All of them!'

'You never got involved then, Fergal?'

'Never. I've seen too much. They've enough heroes.'

Most of the mourners had gone. A few hard-core drinkers, Sean McAuley's fellow volunteers, still caroused down below, bellowing out their Rebel songs, planning their revenge on his killers.

Eilish closed the bedroom door, shutting out the noise.

In the darkness, she pressed her forehead against the cool wood. She wanted to be home, back in her own house, maybe back in the peace of the Mournes. She looked across to the bed where Michael, her son, was lying fast asleep on his back, arms flung out against the pillow, his face at peace, like an alabaster cherub. The thought made her shiver. Everything was a reminder of death.

Her entire being ached. She felt drained, angry at the futility of Sean's death and frustrated at the mockery of his funeral. The military ritual. Sean, her brother, was dead; all day she'd choked back the tears. It had been a hard day and an even longer night. The Troubles had claimed another victim, another brother, and to what end?

She moved towards the window. On the dressing table, she caught the reflected gleam of a silver-framed photograph. It was the one her mother had been polishing that day, so many years ago it seemed, not long after James, Eilish's eldest brother, had been buried.

Her mother hadn't known she was there. Eilish had watched her from the half-open door. She was standing by the window, gazing unseeing, rocking gently on her feet, cradling the photograph of her dead son, crooning a lullaby. It was the first betrayal of sorrow her mother had shown since James's death. Eilish had reached out to comfort her. Her mother had pushed her away. She was polishing the picture, she'd insisted, nothing more. Tears didn't help anyone, she'd said, and she should know. She'd already lost her father and two brothers to the Cause. 'Don't you go making up things to your

47

Daddy now, telling him I was weepin',' she'd warned. 'Your brother died a hero. We all should be proud.'

Eilish could see her mother now, rigidly upright, tight-lipped and withdrawn.

'And where's Daddy now?' Eilish had asked.

'Away. He has a job to do.'

'A job?' Eilish had stormed. 'You mean planning more deaths? Jesus Christ, has he not done enough? His whole life has been for the Cause. Could he not stop now?'

White-faced, her mother had put her hands over her ears.

Eilish had raged on. 'Oh, Mammy, I hope you believe all this bloodshed is worth it! How do you bear it? Your first son dead, Daddy half the time in jail or on the run, from one safe house to another. Never knowing where he is, what he's doing. When or if he's coming back. When or if one of your other sons will be killed.'

'Enough!' her mother had shouted. 'Enough! I don't want to hear. I don't want to know. I just want youse all coming back to me. No more funerals – I don't want to know! I just want to live quietly. Losing James was almost more than I could bear . . .'

'But you never even cried!' Eilish was stunned. 'When they told you he was dead, you said nothing.'

'No, no . . .!' The haunted look on her mother's face was something Eilish would never forget, nor the bleakness of her answer.

'I sometimes think I'm dead myself,' she'd said. 'All cried out, you know? I've seen too much – lost too many. Lived with the Troubles too long. We all have. Look at us. We see people maimed, killed – people we know. We see it on the news, in the papers. "Isn't it dreadful!" we say. "Desperate. That poor man." A week later, we don't even remember the fella's name! We're all guilty of it. And at the end of the day, who really cares? Just the family, left to pick up the pieces.'

Her mother had died a year later. Eilish was thankful she had been spared Sean's death.

In the darkness, Eilish could hear the soft breathing of her son. She leaned over and kissed Michael gently, longing to squeeze him to her. He stirred, half woke and wrapped his arms around her neck. In sleepy innocence, he forgot he was growing up and whispered his baby name for her, 'Mamma.'

The ferocity of her love was overpowering. 'I won't let them get you, Michael, I promise.'

Her father and brothers were clearing the empty glasses and brimming ashtrays when she walked into the kitchen. Automatically, she pulled on rubber gloves and began to wash the last few things. The men said nothing but the air was heavy with accusations. She could see them behind her, reflected in the window, glancing at her and at each other, waiting for her to finish.

They remained silent until she reached the door. Brendan blocked her exit, glowering drunkenly. Colum, flushed and nervous, scraped a chair along the stone floor as he pulled it out from under the table and her father commanded her to sit.

'I'm tired, Daddy!' she tried to say, but Brendan cut across her roughly. 'Do as your father says!'

Wearily she dropped into the chair, head down, her hands twisting anxiously in her lap.

'There's things that have to be said and you're going to sit there until I've said them,' McAuley began.

Eilish lifted her sagging shoulders. 'I'm exhausted, Daddy. Let me be.'

'Today you turned your back on your family and disgraced the memory of your dead brother.' The voice, though slurred, was censorious.

49

'I loved Sean as much as any of you. I prayed at his graveside . . . !'

'You walked away from your own brother's funeral!'

'From the celebration, not the funeral. You – with your flags and your guns. I'll have no part of it. I'll mourn Sean my own way, not at that circus!'

McAuley's hand flew up in anger. Eilish did not flinch. Slowly he lowered it. He leaned heavily on the back of a chair. 'Time was you'd have stood with the rest of us. I was proud to call you my daughter, then you turned away from us. Turned your back on everything this family has fought for. That was your choice and I respected that. Now, your husband is dead. It's time for you to come back. To come home!'

'I have my home.'

'That's no place for my grandson!'

'It's my choice. I have the right!'

'And doesn't my grandson have rights? Doesn't my grandson deserve to live amongst his own people? To learn about the glory of his heritage? To take up the role for which he was born?'

'No . . .' The scream issued spontaneously from her lips. She leapt to her feet. 'Never! Not my son.' Terrified, she glared at them. 'Tomorrow, Michael and I are going home.'

CHAPTER FOUR

Like any man returning home after a long absence, John Neil trawled the streets of Belfast, rediscovering his roots. Sometimes Fergal drove with him, reminding him of places, people and things past; more often it was to point out the harsh reality of the present.

'I remember Auntie Maire and Uncle Pat going on about the Peace Wall . . . way back. I never thought it'd still be here,' Jackie O'Connell commented, that first day with Fergal. 'Graffiti's improved, mind!' he added, twisting his head round to view yet another enormous mural, covering the side of a building. This one glorified the INLA.

'Sure, those were always there.' Fergal frowned. 'No, you're right. Not like today. INLA, IRA, UDF, UVA, they're all at it, proclaiming their Cause from every bit of spare wall there is! God in heaven, I'm so used to it, I don't even notice.'

John Neil did. As did the nervous young British soldiers, whose thankless task it was to keep those same warring factions apart. A surreal game was being played out on the streets of Belfast. Amid the seeming normality of city life, figures in battle fatigues crouched in doorways and edged along streets, eyes darting everywhere, in fear of their lives. And nobody noticed. Nobody even looked. Nobody cared. Anger spurted deep inside fellow-soldier, John Neil. Jackie O'Connell stifled it.

'I can't get used to this.' Neil indicated the huge grey bulk of a Saracen rumbling towards them.

'You will. The occupying forces have been with us a long time.'

Again Neil noted the jarring use of words: 'The occupying forces', the derisory term of the paramilitaries.

'Now this you will remember.' And they'd turned into the terraced street of his boyhood.

'OK, let's go over Rosemary Street again,' Gault had insisted.

'Not again. Give me a break, Gault, for Christ's sake.'

'Sorry mate, no time. Gotta keep going. Someone's bound to ask.'

'Right now. Let's see how good your memory is. Who lived across the street from us, then?' Fergal teased.

'Glorie Maguire. My first love! I remember saving up my pocket money to buy her sweets from McAteers, at the corner. Is that still there?'

From the first day he'd noticed a white car tailing them. He'd said nothing to Fergal. He'd seen it in the side mirror, turning as they'd turned, stopping where they did. It was so obvious, it had amused him. The next morning, there was a youth almost hidden in the shrubbery by the gateway, opposite the presbytery. It was the cigarette stubs that gave him away. A thick scattering of them where he'd waited all night for his quarry to appear. Neil was trailed by a motorbike, that day. The more exposed excursions had them puzzled. Cave Hill, he'd had two of them puffing behind him, until he'd turned round and stared at them, and they'd scurried off and fidgeted at a distance, waiting for him to return to his car. At Shaws Bridge, they'd driven on past his parked car, then returned, back and forth across the bridge, watching his progress from above the river. As he disappeared along the towpath they panicked, parked and rushed after him and he'd met them face to face, coming back. He'd said nothing, just smiled. They were mortified and he'd deliberately lost them driving back. It was a game he played while he marked out his space, kept a low profile and waited for McAuley to check him out.

'Today, I'm taking you somewhere special,' Fergal had announced as they were rounding up the memories. It was the Boys' Club that had been a home from home for both of them, where all the restless energy of their city-bound youth had been directed, by an inspired leader, into sport and club activities, instead of being misspent on the streets.

'Ah, the smell of it!' Neil breathed deeply, blissfully inhaling the heavy masculine odours of fresh sweat, hot bodies, chalk, resin, oil, his ears filled with the grunts, thumps and groans of bodies being tested.

'Where's old Paddy? He has to be here.' He searched eagerly, peering through the shafts of dust-laden sunlight barely filtering through the cathedral gloom of the Victorian hall.

'Old Paddy died years ago. He must have been over sixty when we were here.'

Neil shook his head ruefully, but it was his own youth he was remembering.

'I help out whenever I can but there's another fella here, been running it for years now. Terry!' Father Fergal called out. 'Come over here. There's someone I want you to meet.'

An athletic figure detached himself from a group of would-be gymnasts, his body half turned as he shouted instructions over his shoulder. On his way, he stopped, distracted by the wavering arms of a boy attempting to lift too heavy a weight. It was then John Neil saw his face.

He was the last person on earth he'd expected to see. Fergal caught the sharp intake of his breath. To disguise his shock, Neil swung round to the punch bag beside him and, dancing on toes that had 'Ali-shuffled' many rings, he feinted and air-boxed his leather foe, delivering a vicious left blow to the kidneys.

Fergal laughed. 'Still a southpaw, I see. You look pretty nifty there, Jackie! What do you think, Terry? Could you do something with him?'

'Not bad, not bad at all. Good to meet you, Jackie.' The voice was deeper, older, but there was no mistake. Neil grasped the hand held out to him and looked into the face of the injured Irish boy they'd carried down Scafell, all those years ago.

A quick frown of recognition creased the man's brow. Head on one side, he peered at Jackie. 'Do I know youse from somewhere? You look awful familiar.'

Fergal answered, amused, proud, 'Not unless you were over in the Far East these last twenty odd years. This is my young brother, Jackie. He's just come over.'

'My God! 'Course! That's what it is. You're so like your brother it's uncanny. I'd have known you for brothers anywhere!'

'Yeh?' Jackie laughed faintly.

Fergal pulled a wry face. 'I'm the better-looking one, remember!'

'You look pretty handy with your fists, Jackie. Maybe you could help out, teach the boys a thing or two?' Terry radiated the encouraging air of the youth leader, used to enthusing reluctant volunteers.

'He could do that all right, I was on the receiving end of those fists when he was just a wee lad and it hurt then!' Fergal eyed his brother. 'By the look of you, Jackie, you've put in some practice while you've been away.'

'Some of the places I've been, I've needed to, believe me.' The answer slipped out easily, but for a moment there, in the crossing of lives, John Neil and Jackie O'Connell had become confused.

It was John Neil, London Boys' Club and boy soldier, ABA champion, who had pounded the punch bag. It was by happy coincidence he'd led with his right. It was Fergal who'd informed him his brother did both. Gault had never mentioned O'Connell did either. It was the club setting, and meeting the Irish 'boy' that had thrown him.

Surreptitiously, the man was studying him and the perplexed look was still there. Terry shook his head. 'I keep thinking we've met before.'

'Here maybe? But a long time ago,' Neil bluffed.

'No, no. Not here. I belonged to a club on the other side. East Belfast. This is a mixed club now!'

'I don't know, we all seemed to mix a lot more then,' Neil countered.

'Isn't that the truth. OK boys, I'll be over,' Terry called out and lightly patted Neil on the shoulder. 'Come down any time, Jackie. Always glad of help.'

Undercover agent, John Neil, was suddenly very vulnerable. He'd slipped up, dangerously. He should have remembered the two boys. Gault could have checked them out. He was also severely jolted by his reaction. He'd done the unforgivable and for a moment there lost his concentration. It must never happen again.

Fergal, his hands relaxed on the steering wheel, displayed not a hint of suspicion.

'So, are there quite a few mixed clubs about now, Fergal?' Neil tested.

'Not as many as we'd like, but we're trying. We have to get to the young ones if we're ever to get peace. But it's hard. Too often the hatred's indoctrinated from the cradle – on all sides.' Father Fergal's whole body sagged wearily at the enormity of the task. Resolutely, he straightened up.

'But there's a lot of good people out there, working hard to make it happen and we will . . .'

'People like Terry?' Neil probed lightly.

'Exactly. He's a good man.'

'For a Proddy?'

Fergal's head jerked round at the provocative gibe. 'Not at all. He's just a good man. He wants peace, like we all do, and if a United Ireland gives us that, then that's what we must have. He believes that. It's not just the Catholics want that, Jackie. There's many Protestants too who believe we should be one country, one people, with no discrimination whatsoever. You've been away a long time, Jackie. There's a lot you have to understand.'

Jackie was thoroughly rebuked, but Fergal was coming through very clearly and John Neil was relieved.

They turned off the main Falls Road into a maze of narrow streets and terraced houses.

'Clonard Street,' Neil picked out. 'I know this. Isn't there a bar round here Daddy used to drink in? Not far from the church?'

'That's right.' Fergal cheered. 'Just round the corner. I'll introduce you. There might be one or two you'll remember. Then, if you don't mind waiting, I've a couple of visits to do in the area, won't take long.'

'Note this bar.' Havelock-Davies had prepared him, on one of their many journeys around the plaster model of Belfast. 'Could be useful. Heartland of the Rah. Regular watering hole for several of the players. Good contact point. O'Connell's father might have drunk there. Check with Gault.'

The bar was small and busy. The Republican tricolour was prominently displayed; above the framed verses of 'The Provo Cat' proclaiming its Rah allegiance. Father Fergal, obviously a regular, was hailed as he pushed through to where a tot of Bushmills was already poured and waiting for him. A wary silence followed Neil. Eyes dropped as he passed, heads turned away, yet he knew that his every feature was being studied. He, in turn, prepared to smile at a familiar face and primed himself for the one he dreaded, Terry's opposite number, his one-time friend.

'Joseph.' Fergal's voice rang out. He picked up his glass and tapped the tankard the barman was lifting to his lips and paused, his sense of drama heightened by his years in the pulpit, aware of the straining of curious ears.

'I want you to welcome a fella dear to my heart, Jackie O'Connell, my wee brother. Come home!'

The whole bar breathed out as one, their heads turning, their lips buzzing with the news of wee Jackie's return. It was his father some of the older men remembered, as they peered at him with rheumy eyes, scratched their ears and shook their heads. But not him, not him at all! Even so, they bought him a drink for old times' sake. The women, two of them, recalled him as a 'beautiful boy', but mostly they remembered his 'poor wee mother' and thrilled to be the sole purveyors of their little scraps of knowledge, they held court for anyone who'd listen.

Neil nodded, encouraging their reminiscences. Acceptance by the locals was crucial.

The younger people, most of whom did not recall

'wee Jackie', shrugged and got on with their lives. But there were others, seated away in a room at the back, for whom the news was not new and who shifted uncomfortably and glared suspiciously, and questioned Fergal's sense in bringing the 'stranger' to this particular bar.

'Have we heard anything yet?' one of them asked.

'Not yet. But Sinead's been sent across to see what she can find.'

'He seems right enough. All he does is sightseeing. We've been following him the last few days.'

'Well, I don't trust him. He's turned up too easy. I tell youse, the man's not what he seems.' Gerry Hughes scowled. 'One youse go listen. See who he talks to. What he has to say.'

A hand clamped Neil's shoulder. He swung round, prepared for the worst. A grinning bulbous face, heavy with beer and five o'clock shadow, ducked behind fists that wove teasingly, in mock defence. Neil hesitated as if struggling to recall a once familiar face then quick as lightning his fist shot out and contacted the soft belly, catching the man by surprise.

'Desi Gill! You old rogue. Thought you'd get me, eh! Not a chance!'

'You've been bloody practising since you've been gone, that's why.' The man laughed.

'Well, you bloody haven't! What's all this? Sure you were thin as a pick last time I saw you. And who's this? Not Doyler? Not wee Doyler? I don't believe it. You were at least a foot shorter than me!' Neil shook his head. 'I might have known. The first bar I go into, and you two's drinking it dry!'

'T'was you set us on the road, remember?' Doyler, aged too soon, with an old man's stoop, shyly stroked the few remaining hairs plastered to his balding pate.

'Not in front of my big brother, please.' Neil shifted

his position, the better to observe the swarthy youth ferreting a path towards him, and felt him ease in behind his back. The eavesdropper was in place.

Fergal signalled his leaving, and headed for the door. Doyler and Desi, thrown back into boyhood, rounded up the drinks and excitedly steered Jackie to a table. The eavesdropper glanced after them anxiously, his acned skin moist and purple with the importance of his mission. Neil shifted his chair and created a space. The youth slipped into it, his face ostentatiously turned away from the group, his ear angled to it. The old friends recalled old adventures. Some Jackie remembered, some they'd forgotten. He threw in names Gault had taught him, pronouncing them clearly for the youth to hear. He recalled music they'd shared and loved, Billy Boyle, the Freshmen, Dickie Rock, the Witnesses. He reminded them of Sundays watching the showbands playing five-a-side football and how the three of them had crept out at night and inveigled their way in, to see Dave Glover and Muriel Day at Romano's. And all the time the youth listened, his face contorted with concentration, his lips moving in repetition of their conversation as he struggled to retain the information it was his duty to repeat.

Jackie was beginning the story of his life in the Far East when Fergal returned and waved from the door, indicating it was time for them to leave.

'I'll see youse,' Jackie announced loudly to Desi and Doyler. 'I'm not going anywhere. I'm home for good.'

Before Neil had even left, he noted the youth elbowing his way to a room at the back of the bar, bursting to make his report, before he forgot it.

'Amazing, seeing those two again.' Neil slammed the car door. 'Funny, you'd think with all the Troubles they'd have changed. They're still exactly the same. They're involved, I suppose?'

'I doubt it. Not those two. Like most, they'll help out from time to time, hide the odd weapon, that sort of thing, but not much else.'

'When you're living over, or away, you tend to think everyone's in there, fighting. You ever tempted to get involved, Fergal?'

There was a beat before the priest answered. 'I came back from Africa, thinking I could help. I should help,' he corrected himself. 'Not to take part in the violence, you understand. But to join the fight for peace. I believed it was God's will that I stood up to be counted; that the years away had been but a preparation for the part I had to play, had given me a special insight.' He drew in a deep breath, and shook his head as if bemused at his own audacity before he continued, 'Like so many of us who live far away, I made the mistake of thinking distance clarifies your vision of the situation. It doesn't. It merely simplifies it. I came back believing I had a voice to be heard – that I understood. I was wrong . . .'

Neil waited for him to go on but the priest was lost in his own thoughts, digesting the paradox. He drove automatically, following the route home, but Neil sensed the struggle of a man still trying to come to terms with what he had discovered. When finally Fergal did speak it was as if he was voicing his inner thoughts to himself, unaware of Neil's presence.

'Holy Mary, Mother of God, forgive this presumptuous fool. I saw only what I had been conditioned to see, what history had taught me to see. How could I have forgotten one man's war is another man's gain? How could I have ignored the devious manoeuvring of the devil?'

Suddenly aware of his brother, he cleared his throat and shifted to attention, peering keenly ahead.

'What you said, Jackie, to young Terry there, was right. When we lived here, all those years ago, we mixed more. I can remember crossing town, walking from the Shankill to the Falls late at night with no worry at all. There were areas of West Belfast back then where Catholics and Protestants lived happily side by side. 'Course we joked about who was a Proddy and who was a Taig but the jokes didn't have the vicious sting they have now.' He shook his head and stared out at the bleak prospect. 'We had a . . . a sense of freedom then, we moved about the city as we liked. Not any more. We've had ethnic cleansing since then. Nobody calls it that but that's what it is!

'The paramilitaries and the powerful Catholic and Protestant Godfathers have herded the people into their marked-out territories and carved up the cities into ghettos. They've made them believe it's for their own protection that they'll keep them safe from the enemy without, the Catholic safe from the Protestant, the Orangeman from the Fenian. But it's protection from the enemy within they need more. Protection from the powerful leaders and the self-styled paramilitaries who have grown fat on the fear of those they pretend to defend and who use that power to persecute their own. They promise the poor believers they, not the law, will take care of the welfare of their own, they will keep order and they do – with breezeblocking and knee-capping, young offenders, kids! God in heaven. It's shameful, that's what it is. A terrible thing when a man, for fear of being shot, is forced to watch his family, his children, go without, rather than risk working for the military or an employer of a different denomination. When hard-pressed businesses are forced to pay protection money or risk being bombed or burned out. Protection! Extortion is what it is. Criminal is what it is. And there's many have grown rich on it.' Fergal's colour was high; he shook with

61

indignation, his voice trembling with the vehemence of his delivery.

'I tell you, Jackie, it took me a while to recognize it wasn't just politics and religion keeping us apart, most of it was money. God forgive them, the Movement has become a great front for the criminal mind. Oh, there's a few old believers in the Cause . . .'

'Like McAuley?'

'McAuley?' He snorted. 'Maybe. Once. Not now. Too much money tied up in it. It was principles or power and power is an awful strong persuader, especially when there's a younger breed itching to take over. The McAuleys have always been top players and this one has no intention of moving over. And that's the trouble, you see. They're hard men at the top, on both sides. They're making a lot of money out of this war. They don't want peace. There's no profit in it!'

'You make it sound like the Mafia.'

'That's exactly it. It is the Mafia. Be careful, Jackie, don't get involved. It's too dangerous.'

'Me? God in heaven, I've come back to enjoy life, not to get myself killed. Besides, I know nothing about it.' Neil shrugged guilelessly.

'That's never stopped them. You've talents they could be after. You know about engines, electrics, communications . . .'

'I learned a bit on the ships, yes – but I'm no expert.'

'Few of them are. They take what they can get.'

An uneasy silence fell between the two men but Neil was conscious of a new tension gripping the priest. Fergal crashed the gears as he moved away from a red light.

'It's a bad time! A bad time for you to have come back.' The words exploded from Fergal's mouth.

'Oh? In what way?' But Fergal was already regretting his outburst. He stared grimly ahead, his lips pursed tight.

'Why should now be such a bad time, Fergal?' Neil persisted.

'Never mind. The less you know the better. There's rumours, that's all.'

'What sort of rumours?' But Fergal would not be drawn. He pulled into the drive of the presbytery and stopped the car with a jolt.

'Listen to me, Jackie. You're new here but there's one thing you have to learn – don't ask too many questions. Information can be a very dangerous thing to possess. People kill for it.' He jumped out of the car, then peered back in. 'Don't get involved, Jackie, I beg you, for God's sake.'

When Neil followed him into the house a few minutes later, Fergal was already at his desk in the study. Neil watched him through the half-open door, riffling through a sheaf of messages. One in particular seemed to disturb him. He reread it several times, then slumped down into his chair and stared out abstractedly. At Neil's cough he started and tucked the offending note at the bottom of the pile.

'I don't want to be a problem for you, Fergal,' Neil began. 'Would you rather I went away, lived across, maybe?'

Impatiently Fergal slammed down his hand on the desk. 'God in heaven, what's put that idea into your head? Can you not tell how much I enjoy having you here? You're no problem to me whatsoever!'

'That's great. Because I've been thinking about setting up a little business here and I've seen a very good van for sale.'

It was part of the plan agreed between him and Randall, just before he left. The cover for their first contact. The timing was up to Neil. Whenever he felt confident he

63

had been accepted and was ready to start moving in on the players.

A small electrical business had been Randall's choice. 'Perfect foil for everything you might need for surveillance. Perfect cover for getting into houses, checking under floorboards, et cetera. Never know what you'll find. Whatever it is – say nothing. Earn their trust. They'll test you. Hearts and Minds, remember! Whenever you're ready, make the phone call asking to see the van for sale. I'll tell you where and when.'

Neil already knew the van, had gone over it carefully with Gault, checking the covert equipment, the electronic wizardry necessary to feed back the vital information.

Fergal insisted on driving him to see it. Neil, who had surreptitiously prompted the offer, at first resisted, then gave in. Having the priest with him would reassure anyone who might be watching of the authenticity of the negotiation between him and the van owner.

They'd arranged to meet in one of the big impersonal bars on the outskirts of the town.

'What'll you have, Fergal? I'll buy you a drink while we wait.' Jackie led the way to the bar.

The bored young barmaid flicked a cloth in desultory manner across the counter. She stood up smartly at the sight of the priest and smiled gratefully in response to Jackie's flirtatious wink.

'There was a fella hanging around,' she told them, anxious to please. 'He had a cheese roll and a Guinness. But then he left. Had to get back on the road, so he said. Then the old fella from the insurance came in. Always has the same. Meat pie and a tomato juice. Oh, there was another, not so long ago. A Bushmills. That's right – a Bushmills.' She nodded sagely. 'But he didn't hang around waiting for anyone. Just said he'd be back later. Ah, God in heaven, speak of the devil!'

The man looking around with shifty eyes took off his pebble glasses and wiped his brow with the oily sleeve of his overall, leaving yet another streak across his heavily stubbled face. Then, spotting the two men, he clumped towards them, his feet spread wide to avoid tripping on the shoelaces that trailed from his open boots. He was sweating profusely, probably from the padding he was wearing plus the additional layers of shirts and sweaters that served to add to his bulk. He stood near them, his face turned away, slung his black donkey jacket across the counter and called for a pint. Only when he'd drained the glass and called for another did he attempt to make contact. He looked straight ahead, his expression surly, flexed his shoulders, then squinted at them sideways, his eyes darting suspiciously behind his glasses before he decided to speak.

'You the fella wants the van?' Even the voice didn't sound like Randall. Neil was impressed.

Fergal, acting the responsible older brother, hovered over the engine while Neil kicked tyres and looked for rust. The vehicle road-tested, the deal done and papers exchanged, satisfied his brother was not being ripped off, Father Fergal left Jackie to drive back in his van, instructing him to give the man a lift back to work.

Randall indicated the direction. Swiftly Neil reported his progress, Randall listened intently. Only when Neil recounted the meeting at the gym with his boyhood colleague did the intelligence man react.

'Stupid. Bad mistake. Can't afford those. I'll look into it. Let you know what we have on the other one, his friend "Hogan" – that right? Meanwhile avoid Terry. Don't want his memory jolted further. Anything else?'

'One thing. Fergal seems very disturbed by something, some rumour flying about. He got very upset recently, insisted this was a bad time for me to come back. Then shut up like a clam. He seemed scared, as if he fears things are going to get worse. Is there anything going on I should know about?'

Randall's face was bland, he shook his head and changed tack. 'When are you seeing the McAuleys again?'

'Don't know. I don't want to push it. Fergal was summoned there this week. He didn't tell me. I went through his messages. Again he seemed quite distracted, as if he's being called in against his will. Maybe they're questioning him about me?'

'They've certainly been checking up on you but you're in the clear so far. Every alibi's held up. I don't think it can be that. You've got to start getting closer. Use the girl.'

They were in the Belfast docks area. Randall barked at Neil to stop and clambered out, then ducking his head back inside, he threw a white envelope on to the seat. 'Ticket there for the next Celtic match. Take the usual ferry,' he said and shambled off.

CHAPTER FIVE

He was crouched in the back of his van when he heard the car come round again. Like a photo-shot the image came back to him clear and sharp. An Allegro, blue, three faces looking out, searching. They hadn't seen him. He didn't want to be seen and he had a feeling neither did they. There was something furtive in the way they looked. There were any number of spaces for them to park. They ignored them. They drove slowly, covering each aisle, seemingly checking each car. Now they were circling the outside edge of the multistorey car park again, approaching Neil. He pressed up tight behind the seats. It was impossible for them to see him from the outside. A special shelf fitment built into the van was hinged on a frame behind the seats which, when lifted, acted as a work surface. Its main purpose was for times like these when he needed a hide. A simple instrument, a magic eye like a periscope, gave him a 360-degree view of the world outside.

He had chosen to park on this particular floor because most of the spaces were let to city centre businesses whose workers parked at regular hours and random visitors were few. John Neil wanted to work unobserved. For most of the day he'd crossed the city seeking different suppliers for the requirements on his list, the tools and appliances, the electrical gear necessary for his new career. To have bought from only one would have created interest, spawned too many questions. He wanted to spread his net wide, to have as many contacts and sources as possible. Besides, there were certain items Jackie O'Connell, Father Fergal's brother, would never need but John Neil, undercover agent, did. He was checking through his purchases confirming he had everything and disassembling the suspicious into innocent parts, when he'd heard the car grinding up the ramp. It had stopped when it reached the level and waited, its engine idling. It was this that had alerted him. The ramp was on the east side of the building, his van was on the north, facing the main thoroughfare but he'd angled his side mirror so that he could see the car facing away from him. At that distance he could make out three occupants, nothing more. The car began to move, anti-clockwise, south. He waited for it to park and when it didn't, he swept away the spread of evidence from the work surface, and crouched down. He watched it cruise the floor then start again, stopping at the odd enclosed vehicle, like his van, where a short man would get out and illumine the dark interior with a torch. Now they did the same to him. The beam played across the neat racks of tools fitted to the sides, the coils of wire, the various boxes and cartons of his trade. He froze as the man whistled appreciatively, he heard him rattle the door handle and a voice shout out a warning: 'Don't touch – the sign – fucking alarm!' There was a disappointed 'Shit.' The man moved away but not before Neil had heard the harsh whisper, 'OK. That's it. That's a good place – there!'

They pulled into a space at four cars' distance. Neil's view was somewhat obscured. He could see three men, the short one, one who was very slight and another of average build with dark hair, but he couldn't see their features clearly. Their manner was furtive, their heads swivelled in constant surveillance. He'd initially suspected they were car thieves, now he feared something more sinister. The dark-haired one appeared to be the figure in command. He issued an instruction and the slight one ducked out of sight. Neil could only guess he was retrieving something from beneath the car. He guessed it would be a gun, a high-velocity rifle, the kind used by a sniper, something like the L42A1, the reliable bolt-action sniper rifle he'd used himself in the Falklands and he blanched remembering its devastating effect. He heard the sound of metal hitting concrete and the scrape as it was dragged along the ground. Probably it had been hidden in some piping, undetectable in the cursory security search at the car park entrance. The short man kept watch while the other bent down to assist the third. When the leader stood up, Neil was in no doubt, there was a rifle cradled in his arms. There was an increased excitement in their movements; they checked their watches, conferred, then split, moving swiftly apart in long low lopes to different sides of the building. Two of them flitted in and out of his sight among the cars, the one with the gun he lost, but it was obvious the others were keeping watch, signalling the progress of what he knew must be a military patrol.

John Neil, ex-trooper, could almost hear their boots ringing on the highway below, knew they would be looking round, looking up, covering every angle and direction, their hearts thumping, alert to the danger of snipers. He wanted to shout out, to warn them. He did nothing and he ached with the impotence of his position. Every nerve in his body was steeled for the shot. Then he heard it – the whoosh and ting of elevator doors opening, women chattering.

A voice yelled out, 'Get the fuck out of here!' and something smashed against his van, to emphasize the point. It was a rifle butt. The sniper was there at his back.

The women gasped, too scared to scream, and fell back in the lift. Whether the door closed or not Neil had no idea. The shot seemed to explode in his ear, rapidly followed by another. The man cursed. He was panicking now, Neil could tell, he called out to the others to run. Frozen in his hide, Neil heard a car start, the engine scream, stutter and roar to life. He heard the harsh grate of gears smash into reverse and the screech of tyres. The car ripped out of its space, thrashing its way heedlessly as it hurtled towards the ramp. Shouts and heavy footsteps rang out from every approach. The car spun on a turn and plunged down the ramp. Gunfire rattled out, the car tore on, its engine and tyres screaming in its mad descent. Rapid staccato gunfire drilled the air. There was a gut-wrenching crash that reverberated on and on. Then silence.

Neil listened intently, his eye pressed tightly to the spy-hole, scanning the area. He had no idea who else besides the sniper had been in the car. He hoped all of them. Troopers were searching the aisles, wheeling slowly as they walked, their weapons held at the ready. Every so often they ducked down, surveilling the area at ground level for signs of further fugitives, their covert reportage terse, low-key in the face of danger. They found the empty shells some two cars' distance from Neil's van. Listening intently, Neil tried to gauge the exact position. He guessed the sniper, disturbed by the women, must have fired on the run. The search fanned out from the epicentre. There was the scrape of boots circling the surrounding vehicles, the snap of locks being tested. Neil tucked back in his hide and prepared for discovery. Torchlight flooded the van, the doors were tried, the trooper moved on, Neil heard him report 'All clear'. For their sakes, he prayed he was right.

This was a routine John Neil knew well, perfected in the hours he'd spent dug down in a foxhole, behind enemy lines, observing, waiting, and though he eased his position and closed his eyes, his vigilance was unceasing.

From a decline in the level of activity on the floor below, he guessed the operation was concluded. He heard a final search being conducted. Office hours were already over and the public would be anxiously waiting to retrieve their vehicles. He monitored the last manoeuvres as the troops withdrew until there were only two men left, covering either side of his floor. One had now reached the stairs, the other was almost level with his van, when the call came over, 'All clear'.

He heard the trooper at the stairs call out and his footsteps disappear but it was the response of his partner that made Neil stiffen. It was a voice he knew. He peered at the man's retreating back and saw a figure with a bearing he recognized. They'd shared hell together in the Falklands. He pulled back just as a shadow passed his windscreen, momentarily blocking the light. There was a soft, brushing sound. Someone was sidling along the side of the van. Neil was in no doubt it was one of the snipers and the target was his mate. Instinct propelled him. Timing told him when. In one fluid silent movement, he shot the bolt and slammed the back van door into the face of the sniper. The rifle flew from his hand, the man staggered back, his nose streaming blood. The trooper fired. The sniper's body folded, then dropped in a disorganized heap. From the splay of his limbs and the twist of his neck, Neil knew he was dead.

John Neil came out slowly, his hands high, his cover blown. He saw it at once in the slow grin of recognition on his friend's face, the soft swearing of affection when the man spoke, in the outstretched arms of welcome. The grenade came out of nowhere, it blew his friend apart. There was no warning, it didn't even land, just exploded at chest height in the trooper's face. He didn't stand a chance. Neil, at a distance, protected by the van door, felt the heat of impact. He fell flat to the ground. The soldier's gun, remarkably still intact, clattered and skittered across the floor. Neil slithered after it. When the second grenade clunked nearby, he threw himself as far as possible, rolling over and over away from the explosion. Car debris flew, fires exploded, but the gun was still in Neil's hand. As he lifted his head he spotted the man, the slight, shadowy figure darting for the stairs. He fired. The body rose gracefully at the impact and in that split second as it hovered there, John Neil saw the astonished face of a young boy, surprised by death. Shocked, Neil hurled away the gun. He leapt for his van and locked the door, and buried himself in his hide.

Pale and shaking he joined the queue of departing cars. The boy could have been no more than fourteen and a young fourteen at that. How could he not have realized? When he saw the slight figure, how could he not have known? How could they have used a boy that age? Bile soured his stomach, bitterness wrenched his guts, black anger consumed him.

When he arrived at the exit, to complete the formalities, Jackie O'Connell, brother of the priest, was most helpful. It was his van, they could certainly search it; yes, everything was new, he was starting in business – an electrician. He'd left it locked. He had been alone and had heard and seen nothing. Any further questions, any help he could give in this tragic affair, please call, care of the rectory, Father Fergal.

In the privacy of home he was violently sick.

He wanted to be culpable. They hadn't even looked. The case was cut and dried. The trooper, surprised by the unsuspected snipers, had fired back, killing both terrorists, before the second explosion blew him apart.

CHAPTER SIX

Belfast was shocked, outraged and jittery. In the wake of the shooting incident and the much publicized death of the fourteen-year-old boy, there had been another random killing. A bomb had been planted in a Protestant area fish and chip shop, supposedly owned by a former British soldier. When it blew, the shop was comparatively empty, just two teenagers, a young child and her grandmother, all Protestants, all dead. The owner, a man in his late sixties, was not there but the young woman who was helping out received severe burns, was critically injured and not expected to live. The Irish National Liberation Army claimed the credit. Another sectarian murder to add to the list.

Liam McAuley raged. Random senseless atrocities by the extremist murderous INLA were constantly discrediting the paramilitary front presented by the IRA. It was this semblance of being an organized army of freedom fighters, with a well-elaborated code of 'operational ethics', killing only 'political' or 'military' targets, that earned them emotional dollars from the millions of Irish Nationalist supporters around the world. Killings like this, of innocent victims, dried up funds. Funds McAuley and the Army Council were desperately trying to raise for the plans they had in hand.

It also endangered his family. Revenge murders would be inevitable and Eilish and her son away from the protection of the family would be particularly vulnerable.

McAuley slammed down the phone.

'Damned girl, damned stupid fool! She's the devil's own, that one. God in heaven, I'll drag her home by the hair of her head if I have to . . .' His huge ham fist slammed into the wall.

'Daddy, Daddy, calm yourself. I'll go get her. The bitch. After all you've been through, and Sean not yet cold in his grave!' Brendan savagely delighted in stirring his father's anger.

Colum sensed it and snapped back, 'You keep out of it. You'll only make things worse.'

'Quiet, the pair of youse.' McAuley, silent and impenetrable as granite, rocked gently on his feet. When he spoke, his voice was silky with cunning. 'Get me Father Fergal. Tell him I want him here. Now!'

Colum jumped up nervously.

'No. Wait,' McAuley glowered. 'What's the news on the brother, Jackie? Have we heard any more?'

Colum shrugged. 'Got a job. Seems right enough!'

'Fool! I don't mean that. Has his story checked out? Is he for real? You two are useless. Get me Gerry Hughes. He'll know if there's anything going on.' A crafty smile twisted the grim line of his mouth. 'I think we'll try the fella out. We'll soon know if he's some "four square laundry job" or not!'

Security forces were everywhere. Patiently John Neil waited at road blocks, answered questions and chatted nonchalantly to the hyped-up young troopers who searched his van.

Father Fergal had proved to be an excellent promotion man and John Neil, electrician, was already in demand. He was returning from his final house call when he saw Eilish, restlessly pacing the sidelines of an open football pitch, where teams of young boys were playing a match with enthusiasm if not much skill.

A fine drizzle was drifting down from a louring sky. Eilish, a lone figure wrapped in a long, pale-coloured mackintosh, her hands plunged deep in her pockets, shifted from foot to foot or ran to keep up with play, stopping every so often to lean forward eagerly, encouraging the boys with a cheer.

From his van Neil watched her. There were a few other figures dotted about the sidelines, but Eilish kept her distance and spoke to no one. He parked his van away from the entrance and strolled back.

She started violently when he greeted her and backed away.

'Hey!' He lifted his hands in mock surrender. 'I come in peace! Father Fergal's brother, Jackie. Remember? We met at your brother's funeral?'

He reached out to shake her hand. She barely clasped his in return.

'Oh yes,' she said, unsmiling, and looked away quickly but not before Neil had noticed the hostility in her eyes.

'Is that your son playing?'

'They've sent you, haven't they?'

It was Neil's turn to be startled. Acid hit his stomach. 'They?' he asked nonchalantly.

'My father and brothers. They've sent you. To watch over me?'

'No.' Relief flooded through him. 'Why on earth would you think that?'

'Why else would you follow me?'

Bemused, Neil stared at her. 'Well now,' he teased, 'I was on a job across the road when I noticed the kids playing. It wasn't until I was up close I recognized it was you.'

'Oh!' She swallowed and blushed, focusing her attention on the game just as it finished.

'Did your son's team win?'

'A draw.' She moved away rapidly, calling out to her son, 'Hurry Michael, get your things. We have to get home.'

'Can I give you a lift? The sky's about to open by the look of it.'

She turned slowly to look at him, her eyes narrowed in accusation, her mouth curled contemptuously. 'They have sent you. I knew it! Well, you tell them, I don't need any looking after and I certainly don't want you following me about. Besides, I have my own car. Just leave me be!'

There was no use protesting his innocence. She was not there to listen but already striding out across the field to meet her son. Something had happened to change her opinion of him, of that Neil was certain.

Neil slid down low in the seat of his parked van and in his mirror watched the knots of young footballers dawdle home. It was some time before Eilish emerged. She looked cautiously up and down the almost empty road before she called to her son and his friend. The heavy rain that had threatened to fall now deluged down. Eilish, driving with limited vision, was too busy concentrating on the road ahead to notice Neil's van. He waited for her car to turn the corner, then followed at a distance. It was a short journey to another soulless estate of similarly built respectable houses. What surprised John Neil was the number of houses displaying flags or banners boldly proclaiming Loyalist sympathies. Eilish drew up before one of the few which did not.

He watched her struggle with the lock and usher the boys inside the house before he drove slowly past.

Fergal was out when he arrived home but a note in the housekeeper's writing informed him of a message from

Desi Gill asking him to meet up that evening for a drink in the Clonard bar. He hadn't heard from either Desi or Doyler since that first occasion and something about the formality of the request alerted him.

He knew his instinct was right as soon as he entered the bar. The two men were sitting stiffly at a table, both facing the door, obviously waiting for him to appear. When he did they started nervously and looked away before greeting him over-effusively in a bravura display of camaraderie, tumbling over one another to buy him a drink in their attempts to escape the inevitable confrontation. Desi won. Doyler, forced to face Neil, struggled to find something to say. Neil was deliberately silent. Agitated, Doyler resorted to stroking the long strands of thinning hair over the polished dome of his head.

'It's still there,' Neil said, wickedly amused.

'What? Wha . . . what?' Doyler was even more confused.

'Your hair.'

Doyler snatched away his hand and flushed. 'Habit,' he muttered and looked beseechingly across to where Desi was still waiting to order.

Neil smiled encouragingly.

Doyler coughed and cleared his throat before mumbling something.

'What was that?' Neil enquired.

Doyler cleared his throat again. 'Terrible weather. Wet!'

Neil agreed. 'What with that and the road blocks, it was devilish hard getting round the city today.'

'Terrible,' said Doyler and collapsed in miserable silence.

'I was pleased to get your message. I needed a drink. Was there something special?'

Doyler's startled rabbit's eyes stared glassily. His mouth opened but nothing came out.

77

'Here's Desi!' He sighed with relief as the big man clumsily banged the glasses down in front of them, spilling the frothing liquid which streamed across the table.

'A cloth!' Nimbly for a graceless man, Doyler leapt to his feet and was gone.

Desi, his face flushed and perspiring with embarrassment, sat down heavily, rocked the table again and sent another flood oozing across the surface.

'Fuck!' He pulled out a filthy, dirty handkerchief and began mopping up.

'Shit!' Guinness oozed between his fingers from the sodden rag. He looked around helplessly, then for want of somewhere to dispose of it, with a grimace shoved it back in his pocket.

'Friggin' hell!' Doyler dropped the cloth in the middle of the brown puddle, caught a glass and almost toppled it. A stream of liquid flooded into Desi's lap. Resigned, he dammed it with his forearm.

'You two should be in pantomime,' Neil said.

The two men giggled but both darted anxious glances at the door to the side of the bar.

'So, lads, what have you twos been up to, then?'

'Nothing, nothing,' Desi answered, too quickly. Doyler buried his face in his drink.

Neil put down his glass. 'OK. Enough of the Laurel and Hardy routine. There's something up so you might as well tell it.'

'There's a fella in the back wants to see you,' both blurted out in unison, then slumped exhausted, their message delivered.

Neil nodded thoughtfully. 'Fine,' he said brightly. 'Now my round. Same again? Full ones this time, eh lads?' He stood up.

Desi caught his arm. 'Now, they said. Don't keep them waitin', Jackie.'

Neil eased away the sweating hand, still clutching at his sleeve. 'Drinks first, lads.'

Before they could protest he was gone. He delivered his order in a loud voice. In the bar mirror he watched a head appear at the door to peer at him and saw a hooked arm jerk impatiently in the direction of the two men. Immediately Desi was by his side, whispering nervously.

'Please, Jackie. Go in now. Please.'

Feeling sorry for the old friend, Neil sauntered to the back-room door and leaned casually against the frame, observing the gathering before they observed him.

Gerry Hughes, one foot up on the rail of an empty chair, lounged back self-importantly, tilting back his own chair at a dangerous angle. Opposite him, with his back to the door, Brendan McAuley, dressed in black, posed languorously, his legs extended, his feet in black cowboy boots up on a chair. A slim girl, her titian-red hair cut boyishly short, sat next to him, her body pressed tight against his, her arm draped possessively round him. Colum McAuley hunched over his drink. A fourth man, thirtyish, small and ferret-faced, was riffling a deck of cards. It was the youth, the eavesdropper from Neil's first visit, who suddenly noticed he was there.

They all started and looked up, except for Brendan. He did not move. The girl glanced quickly at Neil then turned in profile but not before Neil had noted that even bare of makeup her face was extraordinarily beautiful.

Gerry Hughes dropped his chair upright and with his foot kicked away the other chair, indicating that Neil should sit down.

Neil ignored it but stood directly behind Brendan, forcing Hughes to look up at him.

'You wanted to see me?' he said nonchalantly.

Hughes nodded, skimmed a sheet of paper across the table and sat back.

Neil made no move to retrieve it. Irritated, Colum snatched at the paper and held it out.

'For me?' Neil raised a mocking eyebrow. He read it slowly, feeling their eyes watching. It was everything needed to make a very sophisticated timing device for a bomb.

'Well?' Hughes barked.

'Good. Only one mistake – electrical's spelt with a C not a K.'

'Can you get it?' Hughes snarled.

'Sure.'

'How fast?'

'When do you want it?'

'Yesterday.'

'Give me two days.' Neil folded the paper precisely and tucked it into his inside pocket, aware of the flash of the girl's unusual green eyes watching him.

It was the test he'd been expecting. He had to get in touch with Randall. A device like this meant certain death for someone, maybe many. He'd had enough of that. He needed assurance that his instinct to sabotage the materials was right.

The lights of the car he'd noticed slip out from a side street to tail his van were following at an even distance. He guessed they had a scanner tuned in to his business cellphone. He'd detected the change in the quality of reception when he'd used it before when they'd followed. To have scrambled the frequency would only have aroused suspicion. His experienced ear had noted too that from the time he'd moved into the presbytery, the phones had been tapped.

The covert equipment in the van was for the big event, not for now. He pulled into the presbytery drive and jumped out of the van, taking his time securing it, checking the back doors. His trained ear heard the tail car stop, its engine idle. He heard the door close softly and feet rustle the dry autumn leaves nestling close under the rectory hedge. The watcher was in place.

In the house, he changed into jogging gear and called out to Fergal, who was working in his study, that he was off for his run. It was a routine he'd established, a way of keeping fit and a means of getting out without raising questions. He'd deliberately left the front door slightly ajar, now he slammed it noisily, crept back along the hall and slipped out into the garden via the kitchen. It was a route he'd negotiated on several occasions, running through the presbytery grounds, over the dividing fence into the garden beyond and out onto the next street. There were a series of public phone boxes he'd already marked for his use. He headed for one of them.

Randall's response was brusque and immediate. 'Get it.'

'But it could kill.'

'What they have planned could kill hundreds. Do nothing to jeopardize your position. Do exactly what they ask. You have to convince them. Time is running out.'

'Any trace on the other matter? Terry's friend – Hogan?'

'Nothing as yet, we're still trying.'

Angry and frustrated at what he was being forced to do, Neil sprinted back.

He entered the way he'd left. He had just locked the kitchen door behind him when he heard Fergal approaching. Quickly he picked up a glass and as Fergal entered, pretended to drink, his head tilted back as if draining the last drop.

'That was a hard run!' he said, refilling the glass from the tap.

'Mmm . . .'

Neil glanced round. 'What's up? Something wrong, Fergal?'

'Ah, another call. Another kneecapping. God in heaven, they get younger. I swear it. The boy's all right. Doctor's strapped him up. It's his mother. Distressed out of her mind. I best get there. No father, you see. It's tough. I can say the words but do they listen . . .' His voice faded wearily. Neil had never seen him look so despondent.

'I'll drive you there, Fergal. Give me a minute to change.'

John Neil drove quickly through the dark streets, the older man slumped down beside him. A few desultory comments passed between them but for the most part the priest stared out, preoccupied.

They turned off the Falls Road into a street of recently built neat little council houses.

'This is new,' Neil said.

'Rehousing. Mostly from the Divis. They've pulled down some of the old blocks of flats. Not all of them, of course. Some of the old folk still miss it, the community feel, you know.'

The lights from two of the houses spilled out into the blackness. Neil parked in front of them and noticed a curtain tweaked back as someone peered out.

'Here we go.' Fergal clambered out wearily. Neil was about to follow when Fergal stopped him.

'Do you mind waiting? Might be better if I go in on my own.'

'Sure. Just let me know if there's anything I can do.'

There was a sudden commotion, a door was flung open and a voice, harsh with anxiety, called out. It was the neighbour, a stout woman.. She came waddling across the small front garden, her hand making the sign of the cross over her huge pendulous breasts that heaved with the exertion. She was gabbling away, the words tumbling over each other in feverish excitement and fear.

She grabbed frantically at the priest's sleeve and without stopping the vociferous flow began pulling him back to the house.

'Oh God in heaven, Father, you gave us a fright, coming in that there van, we thought they were back! She's in here, Father, with us. Oh God, the state she's in! You should see what they've done. The poor ducksey. And the wee ones, crying and screaming, frightened to death. Jesus, Mary and Joseph! Wait till I get my hands on that there wee hood . . .'

'Wait. Mrs O . . . Mrs O'Hara, will you please hush your talking.' Fergal dug in his heels. 'Now, where's the boy?'

'They've kept him in. This is the second time that young hood's done this to his poor wee mother . . .' She stopped suddenly, her mouth gaping as she noticed Neil watching from the van.

'Who's that?' She gasped in astonishment at seeing a stranger with the priest.

'My brother. He's given me a lift. Now what hosp—'

But she was gone. The drama forgotten, her curiosity aroused, she peered in at John Neil, her face alight. 'Oh God, he's a good-looking fella. Will you not come in? Don't leave a lovely man like that in the car, Father. Come on, come on in. Let's get a look at you!' Eagerly she pulled open the door and hauled Neil to his feet.

Fergal knew better than to argue; he strode ahead into the house followed by the woman, her arm firmly linked in Neil's.

The tiny living room was dominated by an enormous television screen, vibrant with the lurid images of some video horror film, the soundtrack blasted out at full volume. Three young children dressed in pyjamas clustered around it, totally absorbed in the violent action, seemingly unaware of their distraught mother collapsed on the sofa behind them, sobbing bitterly.

The noise level was unbearable but Mrs O'Hara sailed into the room and presented Jackie with all the panache of a top hostess introducing the prize guest of honour. The children ignored her, the mother took one look and wailed even louder. Immune to the noise, Mrs O'Hara smiled benignly, the trauma of the evening forgotten.

The mother, Maggie Devenney, her head cushioned in her arms, her painfully thin body racked with sobs, her brown frock twisted around her white scrawny legs, looked like a mangled sparrow mauled by the cat. She lifted her head and although Neil realized she must be relatively young, her face was that of an old woman, the eyes dead from too much suffering. Words spewed out of her, a confusion of curses and pleading and vindictiveness. Against the noise of the television, it was impossible to hear. She screamed at the children to turn it off, to turn it down. They looked round in mild irritation at being interrupted, then ignored her.

Fergal took her arm and lifted her gently to her feet. 'Don't disturb the children,' he said. 'We don't want to upset them further.' He grimaced wryly at Neil and indicated the door. She came reluctantly, protesting she did not want to go back, did not want to see what they'd done to her beautiful home.

Mrs O'Hara, sensing her impending abandonment, seized Neil's arm. 'I'll show them, Maggie. I'll tell them. Don't you worry.'

'We need you here, Mrs O'Hara, to look after the little ones.'

'But—'

'Please, Mrs O'Hara.' Neil smiled his crooked smile, patted her hand and she submitted, grumbling.

The Devenney house was in chaos, furniture upturned, clothes, comics, toys and papers scattered, the

84

remains of a fish and chip supper splattered everywhere. What at first appeared to be blood was tomato sauce. The blood was outside in the yard. They'd spread-eagled him, she said, face down on the concrete – to make it hurt more. Then they'd shot him, four times, in the legs.

'I thought they'd just breezeblock him again, like last time, that was bad enough. But they didn't, they shot him!' she sobbed.

John Neil was appalled, sick to his stomach. He did not trust himself to speak. Fergal despairingly cradled the broken mother against him, murmuring what consolation he could. Neil righted the furniture. He pushed forward a chair and the woman collapsed into it, her crying exhausted.

'I'll make a cup of tea,' Neil said gruffly. The kitchen, obviously shambolic at the best of times, bore more evidence of the violence of the struggle as the men had dragged the boy outside. Chairs and tables lay upturned, a fridge was pulled away from the wall, a shelf tilted at a precarious angle, its contents of crockery smashed in drifts across the floor. Neil cleared as much as he could then set about swabbing down the yard, washing it clean of bloodstains.

When he returned with the tea, the mother was calmed. Fergal sat opposite her, his hands folded comfortingly around hers, attempting to still the twitching fingers that plucked nervously at a handkerchief crumpled tightly in her palms. Her nose glowed raw red in the tired grey face, the thin membrane barely covering the jutting bones. Without looking up, she accepted the tea with shaking hand.

In between sips and sobs she talked.

It was a familiar story of the hardships of unemployment. Her husband, unable to find work within the Catholic community, for the sake of his family had gone outside. He'd taken a job on a building site, for a Proddy.

The 'punishment squad' had made him pay. He'd been 'breezeblocked'. They'd come for him, held him down while another stood on a wall high above his prone body and smashed down breezeblocks on his legs. Then just to make sure he never carried a builder's hod again, they shot him in both elbows. To make ends meet, when he could walk, he turned to crime, minor offences – but he'd been caught and locked away in the Maze.

She spoke simply, without rancour, accepting the inevitability of the situation without question. Listening, the two men could only guess at the pain.

'Why did they come after the boy?' Neil asked.

'He hates them. For what they did to his dad,' she said bleakly.

'But he must have done something, Maggie, for the Rah to come round?' Fergal prompted gently.

'Oh, the usual,' she answered resignedly. 'Drinking too much, joy-riding. That was the first time. This time he'd been shoutin' his mouth off. He got himself a little job, delivering. Seems he was in the back one night the men came round for the money – the usual "donation" – you know what I mean? He heard his boss begging to be let off. Things were bad, you know? Anyway, they started threatening him. Started pushing him around, breaking things, the usual. Kevin heard it all going on, went in and had a go at them. Hot-headed young eejit! Just like his daddy.'

'And they kneecapped him for that?' Fergal said, astounded.

'No, no, not just that. The Rah put the fear of God into the man, said if he could afford to pay Kevin, he could afford to pay them. It wasn't his fault. They forced him to sack Kevin!' Her face contorted with bitterness. 'You know how hard it is to get a job?' she cried out in anguish. 'Kevin was so proud he could help out and those bastards . . .! Anyway, they warned Kevin, next time they caught him acting up he'd be for it.

'Young hood was caught joy-riding again, wasn't he! Holy Mary, Mother of God, I've done my best by him. I've tried to keep him straight so I have, but there's the devil in him, I swear. He knows what the Rah will do if he goes against them. He knows it and he doesn't care! He proudmouths about them, swears they can do what they like to him, that they'll never break him like they did his daddy. Swears he's going to get even. My God, if he only realized, you can't get even. And next time they'll . . .!'

Terrified, she broke down, her weak frame racked by tormented sobs. There was so little the men could say. Both felt the woman's sense of hopelessness well over them.

'Calm yourself now, Maggie,' Fergal said gently but firmly. 'We have to decide what to do. When does your husband get out?'

She blew her nose noisily and wiped her eyes with the edge of her dress before answering in a dull voice, 'Eighteen months . . . I don't know.'

'And what's happening with Kevin now? He's in the Vic, I take it.'

'Home tomorrow.'

'Then I'll be round to see him. Talk some sense into him,' Fergal promised. 'Jackie, would you mind getting the little ones? I'd like a moment for Maggie and I to pray together.'

'What will happen next time?' Neil asked when the two men were alone.

Fergal rubbed his eyes with the back of his hand. 'A boy like that. He's too much trouble. They'll make him leave.'

'Home?'

'Ireland.'

'And if he doesn't?'

'They'll shoot him. In the head this time.'

It had come to him in the middle of Mass, a sudden sense of *déjà vu* and the answer to his prayers. Father Fergal dismissed his flock somewhat perfunctorily and strode off. Today he did not notice the dank leaves massing in the churchyard nor did his keen eye spot the plume of smoke rising from the guilty cigarette of the errant caretaker lazing behind a gravestone. Fergal was intent on getting home.

All night long he'd been haunted by the image of Kevin's young body sprawled in death, in some forlorn place, two shots through his head. A sight he'd witnessed before. He'd searched for some inspired approach, rehearsed the line he would take, dug deep to find something new to say that would dispel the boy's entrenched hostility, avoid the inevitable end. A whirlpool of platitudes had spun in his head, he'd tried them all before. In the middle of Communion it had come to him, the parallel – Jackie's turbulent teenage years and Kevin's.

'Jackie!' At the urgent call, John Neil dropped the paper he was reading over the breakfast table and jumped up.

'Oh, thank God you're here. I was worried I might have missed you.' Fergal grasped both his brother's arms. 'Now I know why you're here.'

Neil froze.

'God has sent you.' He shook his head emotionally. 'For this very time. You must talk to Kevin!'

Surprised, Neil waited for Fergal to elaborate but the priest just nodded at him enthusiastically.

Neil scratched his beard.

'Great, Fergal – sure. Happy to, any time! But why? I don't even know the boy. Why would he listen to me?'

'Because you've been there. You know what he's going through!'

'I do?'

'Remember the things you told me when we first met?'

'Don't test me, Fergal, it's too early.'

'How angry you were when Daddy died? How mixed up you were? How much you blamed him for being in prison, Mammy dying. How isolated and frustrated you felt? How you hated the Rah? Well, that's just how young Kevin feels. It suddenly came to me, that could have been you. If you hadn't been across, you'd have been here – proudmouthing it just like him, in trouble just like him. Maybe facing death just like him! You have to realize, Jackie, they mean it. This is his last chance. Someone has to get through to him. God knows I've tried.'

Fergal had already phoned ahead and warned the hospital that his brother would be collecting Kevin and taking him home. Neil, deep in thought, thrust open the door to the ward just as Eilish pulled from the other side. The force of his entrance threw her back and she landed across an empty bed.

She was not amused or placated by his apologies. Neil squirmed beneath her wrath as she stormed out. But it broke the ice with Kevin. Along with the others in the ward he waited until Eilish was out of earshot, then burst out laughing.

Neil had been expecting a hard case, a tough kid more brawn than brains. Kevin Devenney, looking younger than his seventeen years, was slight in build like his mother, and bright. He was waiting in a wheelchair, a black windjammer tucked around him, his jeans torn back to accommodate his bandaged legs. Neil noted the desperation in the short-lived laughter, the stubborn lines about his mouth.

Neil started on common ground and from curiosity, asking about Eilish. She was from the Centre, was the brief response. She was there to talk to them, him and the other boy. The Rah had done them both. He answered Neil's questions politely but economically, glancing at him sideways with a puzzled frown, anticipating there was more involved than just the casual offer of a lift . . .

'Which Centre?' Neil asked as he helped the boy out of the wheelchair and lifted him into the van seat.

'The Falls,' the boy said, surprised he didn't know.

'I've been away a long time. Could have done with that m'self, when I was a boy. Trouble I was in!' And he left the boy wondering while he collapsed the chair and stored it in the back of the van.

'Did you have to get out?' the boy asked, intrigued.

'I was out already, living across.'

The light died from the boy's eyes. John Neil fought to get it back. He recalled everything he'd learned about O'Connell's early life, recounted anything to which he thought the boy might relate. Kevin listened. Sometimes a secret, knowing smile played upon his face; more often he stared stonily ahead. So many times Neil caught himself about to embark on episodes from his own life, little incidents that perhaps might give the boy some hope, persuade him that he could be master of his own destiny, that the choice could be his. Always he stopped himself, dug deeper into Jackie and tried to find another way to allay the boy's deep sense of injustice, his determination for revenge.

They drew up before Kevin's house. A group of youths were kicking a can around the road, others watched, indolently smoking. Cans of beer or Coke passed from hand to hand. They stopped at the arrival of the van and waited for something to happen.

'See them,' the boy said suddenly. 'Not one of them's had a job since they left school. Their dads, their brothers, uncles – most of them have never worked either. It's not that they're lazy. There's no work. There's no point looking, even, now or later. That's their life, forever. What you see now . . . just hanging around.

'Well, my daddy fought against that. He wanted me to fight against that. He got a job, the only one he could get, and look what the Rah did to him. I got a job and look what they did to me. Do you think I can let that go?'

John Neil understood. 'I'll call in. See you again.'

It would make no difference, Neil could tell, but he had to try. It might also be a way to get closer to Eilish and though the chance was slim, it was the only one he had. With a heavy heart he helped Kevin back into his wheelchair.

CHAPTER SEVEN

Gerry Hughes sauntered into the big man's study and perched himself on the edge of the desk. McAuley was talking on the phone, facing the window, his back to the room. He did not acknowledge Hughes' unbidden entrance but the venom in his gimlet eyes when he eventually turned round made even the cocksure Hughes uncomfortable. He got up slowly and threw himself down in a chair where he sprawled insolently, like a wayward child.

'Has he delivered?' McAuley demanded.

'He said two days. That's tonight.'

'Good. I want to make sure of the man. I think he could be useful.'

'Useful? I think he's dangerous. I don't trust him. His eyes are too busy.'

'His brain's busy, I know that. He's already set himself up in business. We could do with a few bright fellas like him. We might be doing better than we are.'

This was a deliberate provocation. McAuley sensed a rival in Hughes and a devious and dangerous one at that. As a young volunteer Hughes had been all passion for the Cause and McAuley had become his mentor. He'd proved particularly adept at raising funds, and even though McAuley knew it was by devious means, through extortion, protection and fraud, he'd turned a blind eye believing anything was justifiable if it enhanced the greater Cause. Now, the old rebel realized it was hunger for money and power that motivated Hughes. He was using the Rah as a front for criminal activities which McAuley suspected were now benefiting Hughes himself rather than the Provos.

Gerry Hughes was pretending hurt innocence. McAuley knew the arrow had hit home. He decided to let him sweat.

'I'm away a couple of days. A special meeting,' he said meaningfully.

Gerry Hughes played on. 'We've been pushing for donations real hard but times are bad.'

'Then try a little harder. We haven't much time. I need to see the power of your money. It's a big job, this one.'

'Do we have a date?'

'Maybe. When I get back. And watch out for Eilish. There'll be reprisals for that last bombing, make no doubt. I don't want it to be her or the boy. You take care of them both.'

Hughes nodded. There was nothing he'd like more. A match with Eilish would serve him well in his bid for power. 'I waited to pick her up from the Centre. She'll have none of it. Insists she drives herself. Other than kidnapping there's not much you can do,' Hughes said plaintively.

'That's a damn fool place to try. The reason the bloody Centre's there is to save kids from the likes of you. There's no way she'd want to be seen with a fella from the punishment squad. Use your brain – check her car, follow her. Keep her safe. Oh yes, and keep me informed on O'Connell.'

'Right,' he said sulkily. 'We've already leaned on a couple of his old mates. They'll not let anything past, don't worry. And . . .' he paused triumphantly, 'there's Sinead's brother.'

'Sinead's brother? I haven't heard of that one in a long

time. Not since he escaped and went over. A wild one, that one, a bad lot – one of the devil's own. He still involved?'

'Sure.' Hughes smiled knowingly. 'He's in the Far East right now. We've been trying to reach him. If there's anything to find out, he's your man. We'll know soon enough.'

John Neil had enjoyed the match. He'd enjoyed, so soon, being back on British soil. He'd left the ferry and made his way to Glasgow with the throng of exuberant Celtic supporters. At the ground he'd cheered every goal and when they'd won he'd bought rounds of drinks along with the rest, except he hadn't really drunk and they had. But no one had contacted him. No one he'd expected. Desi and Doyler had. They'd turned up on the ferry out of nowhere and hadn't left his side. At one point he'd deliberately lost them, then watched their frantic search when they realized he had disappeared. He'd already guessed they'd been got at from that last evening and the ensuing prolific phone calls pretending eager friendship, asking what he was up to, where he was going, where he'd gone. The two men were transparent as glass. They made poor spies. And now they were very, very drunk. They'd been so anxious not to lose him again, they hadn't noticed him switching their fast-emptying glasses for his full ones, they'd just drunk whatever was at hand.

Now he watched with almost amused affection as the two men slipped gently together on the banquette seat opposite his on the home-going ferry, until their heads met and rested, propping up each other in drunken slumber.

Neil had lurched aboard with the best of them, raucously belting out the rebel songs, cheering again and again the finest details of every well-recounted goal. But even as he'd followed the match and even as he'd joined in the revelry, the glory, the story-telling, the jokes, the singing and the drinking, Neil, the professional observer, had been watching, prepared for his contact.

Feigning sickness, he pushed his way out onto the open deck and sensed someone fall in behind him. Without turning he continued the charade. He staggered away from the bright lights to a sheltered area hidden from the general view of the saloon and leaned out over the ship's rail.

He was conscious of someone standing close by and a match being struck. The pungent smoke of a Gauloise drifted past him.

'OK. Let's have your report. It's been a long day. I couldn't get near you for those bloody idiots and I hate football.' Randall was extremely tetchy. Neil smothered a smile.

'Couldn't I just phone?'

'With today's technology? Too easy to be tricked. Last time was once too many. I like to see who I'm talking to, it's safer. Did you deliver what they asked for?'

'Tonight, when I get back, but I don't bloody like it.'

'Whatever it takes, soldier, "Hearts and Minds", sometimes souls. Remember that. Now, what else?'

Neil's report was brief. 'Too slow, too slow,' was Randall's exasperated response. 'The longer you're there the more vulnerable you become. That was you, wasn't it, in the car-park shooting?'

Neil was staggered. 'How did you know?'

'I read the report. There's no hard evidence but before the explosion, ground control thought the trooper said something, as if he'd recognized someone. Mentioned no names, thank God, but when I saw your van number listed, I guessed it might be you. Gault researched the rest, made the Falklands connection. No one's pursuing it. Case is closed. I suggest you forget it too.'

Randall coughed and drew deeply on his Gauloise, before continuing. 'The Rah will certainly make use of you but it'll be a long time before they totally trust you. The daughter is your only way to get to McAuley quickly. Stay close to her. There may be a way you can be of service. We've information she could be heading for trouble.'

'I know she's on bad terms with her father but the Rah would never touch her.'

'Not the IRA, the other side; UDA, UVF, one of those. Craiglea is a heavy Loyalist estate. After that last bombing, they'll not take kindly to McAuley's daughter living in their midst.'

There was a sudden blare of noise. Three drunken football fans fell out onto the open deck. Gulping in the fresh air, they reeled about, grasping at whatever support was available. John Neil stood up and looked round but Randall had already melted into the shadows. Randall's urgent last message was conveyed in a disembodied whisper from the darkness. 'Look out for Hogan. Dangerous player. Very involved. Goes under a number of aliases – notably "Saoirse" after far-left splinter group Saor Eire. Record of armed robbery. Convicted on a number of charges, including murder. Jumped gaol '85. Linked to various jobs all over Europe. Last seen in New York two months ago, now we don't know where he is. Gault's on the trail but could be anywhere, even here.'

'Thanks a lot, Boss.'

'Sorry, John. He's still got family in Belfast, brothers and sisters, living in the Bone, off the Crumlin. He might make contact there. Keep alert. Don't like the sound of this one.'

It was late by the time Neil reached the Clonard bar. He drew up on the opposite side of the street just as

Gerry Hughes sauntered out, his arm slung around the titian-haired beauty, Sinead. Neil also recognized the man following behind him; he'd been with Hughes in the back room bar that last time. It was the mean ferret-faced man. Neil noted he walked with a limp.

Hughes shrugged off the girl and with a curt word to his sidekick, crossed the street. He came reluctantly, as if disappointed that Neil had shown up, and snarled at him for being late.

'You didn't set a time. Do you want it or not?' Neil said sharply.

'You have everything?'

With a hard stare, Neil held out the holdall. Hughes looked inside, but from his face it was obvious he had no idea what he was looking at.

'Would you like me to fit it up?' asked Neil, selling his soul for good measure.

'If you can,' said Hughes sourly.

'I can.' Neil threw the bag back in the van. 'Tomorrow night, then.' He accelerated away fast, making Hughes jump back, then waved casually through the window, enjoying the sight in his mirror of Hughes' furious face.

CHAPTER EIGHT

Eilish had felt apprehensive all day. She couldn't say why, there was nothing specific, nothing she could really pinpoint as a reason. She paced the immaculate living room, plumping a cushion here, straightening a picture there. She'd been doing that practically all day, anything to divert her mind. She'd finished all her paperwork for the Centre, done her household accounts, ironed, tried to read: attempted anything to divert herself from the feeling that something was terribly wrong.

She went over every little incident again. Was it her imagination or had eyes turned away too quickly when she'd walked along the street? Had greetings been a touch too abrupt? Had a neighbour deliberately rushed indoors as she'd passed the house? Were there less people on the street?

She went to the window yet again and looked out. Usually there were people working in their gardens on a fine autumn day like this but then, she reassured herself, the light was fading and they could have finished, be inside having tea. But it was quiet, unusually so. She almost regretted having those idiots removed who'd been parked across the street. She'd guessed at once they'd been ordered to watch over her by her father. She'd been so furious she'd marched across and threatened them: either they left or she got the police. She'd recognized them immediately, the acned youth and the man with the limp. They hung around with Gerry Hughes and were well known at the Centre for being enthusiastic members of the punishment squad. They disgusted her.

She wished Michael was home. He was out playing football with some friends, one of the parents was bringing him back. No need to worry. She flung herself down in a chair and picked up the newspaper. The pictures glared back at her. The grieving faces stared out in bewilderment, still uncomprehending of their losses.

In the aftermath of the latest bombing, a tragedy made even more epic by the very mundaneness of the setting, a fish and chip shop, Belfast was shaken to the roots. The people mourned as one.

At times like this Eilish wanted to die. The guilt she felt because of her family's involvement in the violence was sometimes too much for her to bear. Even though this time she knew the murders had been committed by the INLA, it made no difference. The remorse was there and it consumed her. As did her grief for the families in their bereavement. How could they bear the loss?

Sometimes, she thought, if it wasn't for Michael . . . The distant beat of a drum penetrated her consciousness. She leapt up and rushed to the window. Perhaps it was a radio. A car had stopped. Michael was getting out. That must be it, the car radio. She opened the door and waved her thanks to the driver. He didn't even look but drove off quickly, almost too quickly, as if he was embarrassed to see her or afraid. And the drumbeat was still there. She stood poised, her ears straining to catch the sound. Now, she could hear voices raised in anger. Fear clutched at her heart. 'Michael!' she called urgently, 'Michael, come on in!'

'Look, Mammy. Watch this. Look what I can do!' Michael, plastered in mud, was valiantly attempting to bounce a football from knee to knee.

'Stop that now and come in,' she shouted, her voice straining with anxiety.

He looked up in surprise. The ball bounced away into the road. He started after it.

'Michael!' she screamed. She ran out and caught her son by the arm, roughly propelling him back towards the house.

'My ball!' The boy broke away, collected his ball and came trotting back, his face pale, creased with concern. 'What is it, Mammy? What's the matter?'

'There's . . .' She stopped. Michael was staring up at her, his eyes wide with fright. 'Nothing, darling.' Above all else she must keep calm. She smiled, dispelling his fear. 'We're going round to Billy's house. Have tea there. Now I want you to bath, clean up quick as you can. I'll call his Mammy.'

She tried to tell herself she was worrying unnecessarily, that it was just another march, but the ominous feeling in the pit of her stomach warned her it was something else. The noise was still distant but getting louder.

'Answer. Please answer,' she begged the phone. A child's voice came on. Eilish desperately tried to lighten her tone. 'Billy, sweetheart. Can I speak with your Mammy? Quickly now.' It seemed forever before she heard the casual greeting of her friend.

Loathing himself for so doing, John Neil placed the holdall on the table in front of Gerry Hughes and the McAuley brothers who were lounging in the back bar snug, watching the television mounted in the corner.

Gerry Hughes leaned back in his chair, a sardonic sneer twisting his mouth as his eyes flicked from the bag to Neil and back again. He twitched his head. The man with the limp leapt to his feet, grabbed the bag and peered inside. He checked the contents and nodded.

'It had better work,' Hughes said. 'How much for the job?'

'Have it on me,' Neil answered in a bitter tone.

Hughes nodded his acceptance. 'We have something very special in mind,' he said. 'If this works we'll call you again.'

'And if it doesn't,' Brendan McAuley said, 'we'll still call.'

There was a sudden newsflash. A hiss of drawn breath whistled round the room, all eyes fixed on the screen.

Scenes of angry crowds marching purposefully, their banners held high, flashed out into the half-lit room. The red hand of Ulster waved threateningly, the roughly inscribed legends 'Taigs Out' and 'No Provos Here' leered out above the pent-up violence bubbling in the stream of heads below. But it was the newscaster's voice that made their pulses race. Colum turned up the volume.

'The promised retaliation following the IRA bombing of a Protestant-owned fish and chip shop in which five people were killed has resulted in more outbreaks of sectarian violence in North Belfast, with attacks on houses in the largely Protestant housing estates of Killyglass and Craiglea.'

'Christ, Eilish!' Colum blurted out.

'Tonight security forces have been drafted in to cope with the prospect of further violence following this evening's Loyalist parade, marking the anniversary—' Colum snapped off the sound, his face pale.

'Who the hell's looking out for her?' he demanded.

'I left the lad, circling round past her house. She made us move on. I told him to call . . .' The man with the limp blanched guiltily.

'You bloody fool. Christ! And McAuley's back tonight.' Hughes scowled, looking round, desperate to lay the blame.

'We'd best get over there.' Colum started for the door, then stopped. 'God! We left the car at the house.'

'My van's outside. I'll take you.' Without waiting for a reply John Neil wheeled round and was gone. For a stunned second the men hesitated, then bolted after him.

The light was fading fast and already the street lamps were beginning to glow. Eilish tore at the curtains, drawing them together, frantically trying to shut out the pounding of the Lambeg drums which was getting louder, the shouting and chanting of the crowd getting closer. Only a few streets away, she guessed. 'Michael,' she shouted up the stairs. 'Are you ready, Michael? Hurry, let's go!'

She raced round the house securing doors and windows. At the bathroom she stopped. There was the sound of splashing. She burst in. Michael playing happily in his bath looked up in surprise.

Panic-stricken, she stared, then screamed, 'For God's sake, Michael, I said no messin'.' She heaved the bewildered child to his feet and dragged him from the bath.

'But Mam—'

'No arguing. Hold still!' She threw a towel over his head, stifling the now querulous whimper, and rubbed hard, then pushed the frightened boy towards his room. 'Now dress. Fast. I'll get your bag.'

The noise outside seemed to swell. She stood breathing deeply, trying to quell the thumping of her heart. She could hear loud-hailers warning the crowds to disperse.

Michael came clomping sulkily down the stairs, his shoelaces dragging behind him. He plonked himself down heavily on the bottom step and started to tie them. Eilish yanked him to his feet, thrust his overnight bag into his arms and launched him through the open front door.

Outside all was bedlam. From nowhere RUC men in riot gear plunged about on horses, their shields raised as they manoeuvred into battle formation, while the chanting, the beating grew louder and louder. Other officers, weapons at the ready, mustered their inadequate forces, radioed urgently for reinforcements, shouted out warnings and ordered the residents to stay indoors.

Ignoring them Eilish dragged Michael towards her car.

'Get back in your house!' A senior officer stormed over. At the same time the angry mob turned the corner. Trapped, Eilish stood rooted. The first banner waved. 'Provos Out!' Her worst fears realized, she knew it was meant for her: the sins of the fathers . . . The RUC men, greatly outnumbered, spread themselves in a thin barricade just short of her house.

'Get back inside, woman! Do you want to be killed?' The voice broke through to her. Terrified, Eilish rushed her son back inside.

There were too few RUC men, she could see that, and the crowd was swelling, the roaring of their anger filled the air. Frantically she began hauling furniture across the door, screaming at Michael to hide behind the sofa, already pushed tight against the far wall.

Isolated shouts assailed her ears. 'No Pope here!' 'Murdering Papists!' 'Provos Out!' She heard the booming warnings of the megaphones. 'Please go back! We want no trouble here!' Calm at first, growing in urgency as the crowd swept on regardless.

'We call upon you to disperse. If you ignore this warning batons will be used!'

Cradling Michael protectively in her arms, she hunched down behind the sofa, praying the nightmare would end.

A volley of firing rattled out. Like one giant creature the crowd hushed in shock, then broke into a howl of fury, as the impact of the plastic bullets felled the few at the front. Maddened, frightened, the masses surged forward, forcing on those who had tried to halt the panic. The first stones smacked hard, and a horse gave a high-pitched scream. The clatter of hoofs dancing back in retreat, wheeling, spinning, charging, added to the chaos as the crowd hell-bent on revenge closed in on Eilish's house. The thin band of defence, the police – many now streaming with blood – fought to regroup, to hold at bay the mob that surged and broke and jostled to surround the house. Backed up to the fence, the police stood their ground, dodging the hail of missiles, stones, rocks and bottles that flew around them.

Quaking, Eilish and Michael wriggled further down, their heads together, hands over their ears, trying to block out the clamouring rage of the rabble.

A rock smashed through the window and clattered into the room. Mother and son, too terrified even to cry out, gasped. Their breath coming fast and shallow in quick pants, they cowered, desperately covering their heads with their arms against the onslaught of glass and rubble that pelted down on them.

It was the petrol bombs that made them scream. They smashed through the windows, exploding and flaring, splattering petrol everywhere. Flames burst up the curtains, the sofa roared into life, clothing, cushions blazed, the carpet spurted a river of fire. Eilish and Michael leapt up, choking and coughing in the billowing smoke, their eyes streaming.

'Upstairs, Michael,' Eilish yelled. Holding him tightly in front of her, she pushed for the door just as a petrol bomb smashed against the wall. Flames leapt between them, driving them apart. Blinded, Eilish flung up her arms, losing her grip on her son. She screamed out. Through the smoke she glimpsed Michael, fire licking at the petrol spattered up his legs, sobbing terrified and bewildered, frantically calling for her from the foot of the stairs.

'Go, Michael. Upstairs now!' she screamed, starting after him. Then there was a sudden roar, and the door blazed into a wall of flames, cutting her off completely.

They could hear the howl of the crowd from a distance. Even as they approached the estate, they guessed from the streams of dishevelled people running chaotically, the sirens, the security reinforcements ploughing through the crowds, the ubiquitous television crews assembling, that the rabble had got out of hand. Fear gripped all of them. John Neil drove like a madman, plunging down side streets, across gardens, along pavements until they could go no further. A mass of people and barricades blocked their way. Abandoning the van the four men hurled themselves into the throng, tearing it apart, thrusting their way to the front, the smell of burning adding strength to their determination to reach Eilish. For a split second all four stood staring at the burning house, petrified, then with a scream of fury, Hughes and the brothers hurled themselves at the police line. The police forced them back.

John Neil did not move. He no longer saw the house. Images of the blazing circus tent filled his head and in his imagination the screams of his dying wife and child rent the air. Then it was gone. Steeled, he saw the futility of following the men. He raced across gardens, battered down gates, hurdled hedges and fences to the back of Eilish's house. Smoke was seeping and curling under the kitchen door. He threw himself at it. Hopeless. He stood back. An upstairs window was half open and beneath it was the sharply angled roof of a flimsy lean-to. It was his only hope, he prayed it would hold. With every ounce of skill, finding the smallest footholds, he pulled at the adjoining drainpipe and began to climb. Gingerly he stepped onto the roof. There was the crack of tiles breaking but it held.

'Eilish! Michael! Here! The back window!' He listened intently. Nothing. No answering cry, only the roar of the flames and the battering as police tried to break through the front door. He called again. Nothing. Dreading what he might find, he hauled himself up to the window ledge and slithered inside, falling onto the floor. Smoke filled the room, his nose, his lungs. Choking he called again, keeping low below the rising fumes, blinking his streaming eyes. He could make out vague shapes, bed, wardrobe, but nothing stirred. Then he heard the shout, the hysterical screams of 'Michael!' coming from below.

'Michael!' The wild sobbing cry came again.

Neil lifted his head to the window. 'Where?' he shouted.

'Upstairs! I don't know! Find him – please. Find him!'

He crawled across to the door, reached up and opened it carefully. Flames leapt at him. He slammed it shut and turned back. Dragging at bedding he wrapped himself in a sheet and with a pillowcase shrouded his head against the searing heat, then edged open the door. The stairs were already an inferno. Cobwebs of deadly burning material floated gently in the air, sparks flew, fire blossomed where they fell. Hugging the wall he crawled along what remained of the burning timbered landing, into the next room. In the suffocating darkness, Neil was bombarded by debris falling from the smouldering ceiling which even now crackled into flame. There in the sudden flare Neil saw the outline of the crumpled boy, lying beneath fallen beams, deathly still across the bed. In two strides he was there. Hurling aside the covering of wreckage he lifted the limp body, smothered it with the sheet and with no thought for himself, ignoring the sparks smouldering in his hair, the flames caressing his skin, he ran, crouched protectively over the boy, back to the room and the open window. He kicked back with his foot, slammed the door on the spreading inferno, and bellowed to the men below for help.

Colum was already there, standing on the sloping roof, his arms held out ready to pass on the boy to Brendan, waiting below. Eilish, distraught and grief-stricken, cried out as the blackened rag-doll figure was lifted from hand to hand. Neil slithered down from the roof and collapsed. His scorched throat gulped at the cooling air, his lungs wheezed in pain and his head streamed blood. Ambulance bells were the last thing he heard.

They bandaged the gash on his head, dressed the burn on his arm, made him promise he would rest and discharged him. John Neil had superficial wounds. The boy did not.

Neil closed the door to the small private room softly behind him.

Eilish started. 'Michael! Michael!' Frantically she struggled to lift her bandaged head.

'Ssh, ssh, calm yourself, Eilish. It's only me – Jackie, Jackie O'Connell. Can I come in?'

'Where's Michael? What's happened to him? Will no one tell me?'

She fell back exhausted, tears running down her cheeks.

Neil stood close to the bed where she could see him. Her dark eyes were enormous in the pale translucent skin, their dilated pupils evidence that she was still in shock. She stared up at him fearfully.

Gently he touched her hand. 'You know who I am, Eilish? I'm Father Fergal's brother.'

'Where's Michael? I want to see him. Please let me see him.' Her eyes implored, her body trembled with stress.

'He's going to be all right, Eilish,' he said soothingly, 'but he needs to rest. And so do you. You'll see him soon, don't worry.'

'Then why won't they tell me what's wrong?'

'Just time. There's many were injured in the riot. They're working flat out. I stopped by his ward. The sister told me to tell you he was . . . comfortable.'

Neil hesitated. There were other things the sister had spoken of: 'internal scorching, burnt tissue, signs of infection, a critical state'. Words to terrify.

'You have to understand he's badly injured – third-degree burns, both legs fractured – but he's young, there's nothing that won't mend. He's lucky to have his life.'

'Will they let me see him soon?'

'Soon.'

She lay there, her face turned away, quietly digesting what Neil had said. There were dressings on both her arms, her hands were cut and scratched, the nails broken and torn where she'd fought to reach Michael. The black stain of an enormous contusion spread across her shoulder and her neck, a blue vein fluttered weakly in the whiteness of her throat.

There was a rustle of movement on the crisp linen, her hand reached out. He took it gently, folding it in both of his, aware of its fragility.

'I have you to thank for that. You saved his life. Gave me back my son.'

The savage pain of his own loss suddenly over-whelmed him. He wanted to cry out. Instead he bowed his head, cutting off the agonizing scream rising in his throat, willing it to pass, stifling the memory, obliterating the past. He felt her fingers lightly touch the wound beneath the dressing, tenderly caress the bruises on his face.

'Does it hurt?' she asked, misinterpreting his pain.

He shook his head, unable to speak.

'I owe you everything,' she said. 'Strange, I hardly know you. Are you a friend of my brothers?'

Neil looked up in surprise.

'I know you're Father Fergal's brother but are you . . . with Brendan and Colum?'

'I left Belfast before they were born!'

'But,' she persisted, 'are you involved?'

Neil shook his head. 'I happened to be there. My van was outside.'

Relief lit her face, a tiny smile broke on her lips and her eyes, heavy with tiredness, began to close.

'Sleep now,' Neil said. Impulsively he leaned over and kissed her gently on the forehead.

She smiled up at him. 'I won't forget what you did.' She hesitated. 'Please, Jackie . . . will you call in again?'

'I'd like that.' And John Neil realized he meant it.

Without warning the door opened. Liam McAuley strode in, followed by his sons, filling the small room with his overpowering presence. He stopped short when he saw Neil.

'I'd best take my leave. You take care now,' Neil said to Eilish and moved to the door. As he did so, the big man reached out, grasped his hand and shook it fervently. His eyes glinted with tears but for once he could find no words.

CHAPTER NINE

The call from McAuley came the following day. Fergal took it. Bristling with irritation he called to Neil who was strolling in the garden, breathing in the cool fresh air, exhaling the smoke fumes still clogging his lungs.

'I said you should be resting. That you couldn't drive and I was too busy. He said he'd send a car. The man doesn't listen – a law unto himself. I'll tell him you're not up to it.'

'Fergal.' Neil laughed, stopping the priest in his tracks. 'It's fine. What time?'

'This afternoon. Three o'clock.'

'Tell him to send the car.'

Fergal's mouth clamped tight. Vexed, he marched back into the house. Neil followed him in. He paused outside the study and heard Fergal's terse delivery of his message and noted the way he slammed down the phone. Neil walked in. Fergal, deep in thought, was sitting on the edge of his desk, his raised foot twitching nervously in the air.

'What you did was very brave, Jackie. And Eilish is a fine girl, but Liam and the boys are something else and I don't want you getting close to them,' he said without looking round.

'I'm sure he only wants to thank me.'

'And what else?'

'I thought you and Liam McAuley were friends?'

The priest had been expecting this. He crossed to the

window and stared out, his back to Neil. 'His wife was a rare woman. She was very kind to me, Jackie, when you'd all gone. Young then and beautiful, you know. Almost made me wonder about the priesthood...' There was a smile in his voice at the memory. 'God knows why,' he went on, 'but she loved the man, despite what he did. She hated that. When she died she made me promise to look out for him and the family, especially Eilish. She knew the trouble between them. Eilish is a lot like her but stronger. She also knew how much Liam loved the girl and how it pained him they'd grown apart. She made me promise I'd get them back together...'

Neil broke the long silence, 'I'll take care, Fergal. Promise.'

Fergal said nothing but as Neil left, he lifted his hand as if in blessing.

Joseph O'Shea collected him. Neil followed the close-shaven, bullet head to the car where Maguire was waiting, his blond curls even longer than before.

'Haven't seen you two since the funeral.' Neil spoke affably but his gut was curled tight with apprehension.

'You haven't seen McAuley either.'

'Come as a set, do you?'

He saw their shoulders stiffen and could have bitten his tongue. 'Only joking, fellas. Any news on Eilish and the boy?'

He knew already, he'd phoned that morning but he observed them relax and they answered sympathetically.

'Eilish is fine, the boy's not good. You OK?' Maguire's baby-blue eyes glanced at him through the driving mirror.

O'Shea, constantly surveilling, called back over his shoulder, 'Orange bastards. They'll pay for it, don't you worry!'

111

Faces at the upstairs window checked their arrival. O'Shea waved in acknowledgement then led Neil through the back door into the kitchen.

Gerry Hughes was there. He put down the girlie magazine he was reading, his face curled in a sneer. 'The hero returns,' he said sarcastically. 'That was some show you put on, O'Connell. You climbed that there house like a rat up a drainpipe. Amazin'.'

McAuley's voice roared through the house. 'Bring him in here. I want to see him.'

John Neil had been expecting a formal meeting across a desk, a show of power. Instead Liam McAuley was sunk deep in an armchair in the sitting room, his huge frame folded down into the frail form of an old man. His stockinged feet rested on a worn leather footstool. Black circles underlined the dark eyes and his drawn face, deeply etched with lines, spoke of a sleepless night. He waved his huge bony hand for Neil to sit down and barked at the hovering O'Shea to get out.

With slow deliberation he placed his elbows on the arms of the chair, linked his hands and fingers together, pressed them ruminatively to his thin lips and stared thoughtfully at Neil. 'Well now, Jackie O'Connell,' he said finally, 'you've placed me in quite a position.' He paused for the words to sink in. 'I owe you, and I owe you a lot.'

Neil started to speak. McAuley held up his hand.

'You saved my grandson's life, and I can never repay that.'

'I wish I'd got there sooner. Any more news?'

'Bad, son. Bad.' Unable to go on, his face haggard, he clenched his hands to his mouth.

'It's amazin' what they can do now,' Neil comforted.

'It's the infection. The burns go deep.' The old man shook his head despairingly. 'Bastards! The boy could lose his legs. Eilish doesn't know. Not yet. I won't let the doctors tell her. She's not strong enough herself. I thought maybe . . .' He struggled for words. 'She doesn't want to know me and the boys. Blames us, you see? Her brothers are there now – but outside. She doesn't want them in. She likes you, Jackie. Trusts you. I thought maybe you could stay close to her. Make her understand that she must come back to the bosom of her family. She'll be safe here.'

'Where else would she go?'

'My sister, maybe. But she's on her own, tied up with a business to run. Besides, there's no way she can protect them. I want Eilish and my grandson back here with me, where they belong.' His voice rose petulantly.

'I'll try, Mr McAuley.' He spoke modestly, suppressing the eagerness welling inside him. 'I'll talk to her, of course, my pleasure, she's a lovely girl but she doesn't really know me.'

'None of us do, Jackie. But you're Fergal's brother and I trust him. His word is good enough for me.'

There was a cunning gleam in his eye. 'Pour me a drink, Jackie.' He indicated a cabinet behind Neil's chair. 'And take one yourself. The old gout is plaguing me today. And the arthritis. Too many years in a cold, damp cell.'

Neil opened the cabinet to an array of malt whiskies. 'Quite a collection you have here, Mr McAuley,' he said easily, his senses alert for the trap intuition warned him was set. 'What'll it be?'

'A drop of your daddy's favourite.' The trap was sprung.

'Do they still make that?' He stalled, his fingers turning the bottles, checking the labels. 'I haven't seen it in a long time.'

He could feel the big man's eyes burning into his back, hear his breath rasping in concentration.

'Are you sure you have it?'

The breath caught in the old throat and held.

'God in heaven, here it is. Right before my eyes. I'll take the same, if you don't mind?' Neil teased on, knowing the Irishman was beside himself waiting to catch the name. Neil turned. McAuley was craning forward in his seat, his head cocked, his ear turned to Jackie, his eyes bright with curiosity. Neil walked over and handed him the brimming glass.

'To Eilish and Michael.' Neil made the solemn toast.

McAuley, outplayed, with a baleful look, threw back the tot.

John Neil did the same. 'Nice drop of Black Bush that. Haven't had it in years.' He smacked his lips and grinned at McAuley.

McAuley's face lit up like a grotesque Hallowe'en lantern. He smiled back.

John Neil blessed Gault silently.

Gerry Hughes stuck out his leg as Neil walked back through the kitchen, effectively barring his path.

'You may have fooled the old man,' he said softly, 'but you haven't fooled me. You and me's got talking to do.'

'Any time. Whenever you're ready.' Neil eased him aside.

'And keep your hands off Eilish. She's not for you,' Hughes spat after him.

Neil stopped at the door. 'I seem to remember you saying the same thing about Glorie Maguire when we were at school together.' He shook his head. 'I don't think I listened then.'

It was a bluff but from the astonished look on Hughes' face, it had worked.

Eilish, drawn and pale from stress, reached out for Neil's

hand as soon as he walked in. She grasped it to her like a lifeline, squeezing it tightly as if she'd never let go.

'They've told me, Jackie. About Michael.'

'I know. I've spoken with the doctor,' he said.

'I insisted, it was my right. I have to know, I have to be strong for him.'

She was holding on but he could hear the panic rising in her voice. He stroked her hand soothingly, speaking gently but firmly as he had in the past to men seriously wounded in battle.

'Michael is going to need all the courage we can give him, Eilish,' he said, deliberately linking himself with her, 'but it's a long haul and we have to be positive. Just his seeing you has helped. I popped in just now. He's being very brave and responding well, better than they'd hoped. If they can hold the infection, the fractures will have a chance to mend. He's young, the bones will knit quickly. What he needs is rest and care.'

He could sense her hysteria beginning to ebb. 'Once he sees you well and out of here, a lot of his fears will disappear and you'll be amazed how quickly he'll recover, mentally that is. Physically it will take time. You are going to need help. Just lifting him up and down stairs, to the bathroom, in and out of the car; it will all take a lot of strength.'

Hope held her enthralled. Her trust in him was unquestioning. What Neil was saying was true but his motive was that of a deceiver and it sickened him.

'Michael needs the love and support of family around him.' He felt her hand quicken in his; he plunged on. 'For his sake, Eilish, you must forget your quarrel with your father . . .'

'No! No!' She stared at him in horror. 'You don't know what you're saying.'

'Listen, Eilish, think with your head not your heart. Think about Michael.'

'That's all I do think about. That's why I left!'

'Fergal told me. He understands but even *he* agrees that for a while, until Michael is fit and well, until you've found somewhere to live, the most sensible plan is to go home. I'll be with you as much as you want. I'll visit you, I'll help you, we'll take Michael out . . . build his strength, get him walking again. After the trauma he's been through he needs to feel safe. Your father cares deeply for you both. He's destroyed by what has happened! Tell him you'll go home, on one condition – you set the rules. Believe me, he'll do anything you ask.'

Muffled against the biting wind blowing across Parkhead stadium, Neil watched the soccer match without his usual enthusiasm and though he lifted his arms to cheer or jeer along with the rest of the fans, his attention was focused on the man at his side. Randall, swathed in a Celtic scarf with matching woollen hat, did not succumb to the sway of the mob. It was only when Neil nudged him for the 'compulsory' Mexican wave that he deigned to raise his arms.

'Sorry to hear about the boy,' Randall said curtly.

'Almost lost his fucking legs.'

'Damn bad luck that. Not enough security. Still, at least you were on the spot.'

The crowd roared and so did Neil, venting his pent-up fury with a violent jab of his clenched fist, longing to smash at least a sign of repentance into the cold impassive face of the Intelligence man standing next to him. But Randall did not notice.

'And very much persona grata with McAuley now, I take it?' he asked smoothly.

'Oh yes.' Neil gave in. 'I'm in all right – but not with everyone. Gerry Hughes is very wary. Could be just jealousy over Eilish but somehow I doubt it. Keeps warning me to watch out. Has he heard anything? Anything he might have found out?'

'Certainly nothing that we know of.' Randall frowned. 'Not getting too involved with the girl, are you?'

'She's my passport in there. Without her there'd be no reason to visit the house.' Neil bristled.

'Mmm . . . Still, time's pressing. Concentrate on the father. He said anything?'

'Lots, but nothing we want to hear. He can be quite a charmer, friendly, even warm, especially since I've persuaded Eilish to go home. But we – he keeps me firmly on the social side. I daren't rush it, I have to wait for him to come to me—' Neil stopped short, his attention caught by the game. 'Oh great shot! Good man!' he exploded, then went on, 'There is one thing. There's talk of a Christmas truce. Pub talk, not McAuley.'

'Yes, not unusual. Gives them time to regroup. The Army Council time to replan. Still, it does fit in with what we suspect – a major shipment around Christmas ready for a big campaign in the New Year.' He waited for the roar of the crowd to subside, then asked casually, 'McAuley talk about going away at all?'

'Leaving the country?'

'The country, Belfast . . .'

Neil shook his head. 'Not since he came back the night of the fire.'

Randall looked thoughtful. 'Listen out. If this shipment is as big as we suspect, it's going to take heavy funding. We're talking big business here, not local "donations". He and the Army Council have got to be dealing with someone. Note who he talks to, any visitors – don't take anyone for granted; bankers, lawyers. Get me names. Someone's buying and we don't know who. Money's coming from somewhere.

'Could even be your friend, Hogan. He's proving to be a very bad boy. Our cousins in America have quite a record on him. Very connected with the drug world, a big player, apparently. Travels extensively, Colombia, Middle East, mid-Europe . . . even Russia. No trace of him over here as yet but you never know. I've a gut feel about him. Could be a link we've been looking for for a long time.'

'You think they're using drug money?'

'We *know* they're using drug money. So are the Loyalists. But they'll raise money any way they can, from pirate videos to business fraud, even the KGB.' Neil raised an eyebrow.

'Oh yes. Right from the start of the Troubles way back in '69 and the early seventies the KGB negotiated with IRA communists to supply German machine guns, rifles, pistols. "Operation Splash" was the code-name then. It's still going on with the Moscow Mafia even now. Iran, Japan; wherever there's a terrorist group, organized crime, or ruthless businessmen, there's a deal to be made.'

There was another roar from the crowd. Neil joined in automatically but Randall had retreated into his own thoughts, his face buried in the folds of his scarf. Neil roused him for the Mexican wave.

'The festive season is coming up. McAuley's a social animal – well connected. There'll be house parties, dinners, both sides of the border. We believe they'll use something like that as a cover for a meeting and you have to make sure you're there. It's a long shot but it could be a weekend house party at an estate near Dundalk.'

'Nothing else?'

He shook his head. 'As we know, so will you.'

Somehow Neil doubted it.

CHAPTER TEN

'Michael is progressing far better than anyone dared hope,' the doctor reassured Eilish. 'The infection is almost gone and the bones are knitting well. A few more days, if he goes on like this, and you can have him home.'

Unconsciously Eilish had grasped Neil's hand for support, now she fell against him with relief, tears falling between the fingers of her hands, pressed to her face.

'I thought you two would like to be the ones to tell him.' The doctor smiled, treating them as a couple.

Hand in hand they broke the good news. Michael was overjoyed. 'Will you and Mammy come and fetch me, Jackie?'

'Of course. We'll put the wheelchair in the back of the van.'

'Will I be out for bonfire night, d'you think? We could go together like we did with Daddy?'

Eilish, suddenly embarrassed, withdrew her hand from Neil's. 'Hush, Michael. I'm sure Jackie's a busy man and you'll have to rest, remember? It'll be a while before we can do things like that.'

'If the doctor says it's all right, we'll go. That's a promise. Only if you're well enough, mind!' Neil winked at the boy, remembering another time, another little boy, a similar occasion; Tommy in bed with measles, desperate to see the fireworks. He'd said the same thing then.

Neil bent swiftly and kissed the boy on the forehead.

119

'You get better now,' he said. 'I'll wait for your Mammy outside.'

By the time Eilish came out the lump in his throat had gone. 'I think a celebration is called for,' he said, his arm slung around Eilish's shoulders as they walked out of the hospital. 'How about dinner tonight?'

'I'd love that, Jackie.'

'Great. I'll drop you off at the house and pick you up around – eight?'

'Could I look in to work first? It's just across the street there.'

She pointed across the Falls Road to a row of shops. 'That's it, near the end. It used to be a shop, now it's a parent–youth group for kids in trouble with the Rah.'

'Like young Kevin?'

She nodded and led the way into the reception.

An agitated young man appeared from a door at the back. He held out his arms in welcome. 'Holy Mary, thank God you're back, we're going mad. I've just had Mrs McLoughlin on the phone. The Rah were round again last night.'

'Not Declan again? This is Jackie, by the way. He—' But the man was too fraught to be civil.

'This time he has to be out,' he said.

'But he's only fifteen!' Eilish cried. 'My God! Does he know anyone across?'

'He has an auntie lives in Liverpool. I have to get on, make the arrangements now. He only has until tonight. I'll have to call on—' he stopped himself with a hesitant glance at Jackie, 'our contact, OK?'

Eilish nodded. 'Good luck!'

'Sorry. Nice to meet you, Jackie. See you again.' And he was gone. Eilish sank down on the edge of the desk, wearily pushing back her hair. 'Fifteen! And if we don't get him out . . .' She aimed two fingers at her head like a gun.

'What did he mean about a "contact"?' Neil frowned.

She dropped her hand, examined her nails, then shrugged in an offhand manner. 'Just someone who helps us. We're getting more and more calls like that. Kids of thirteen and fifteen told to get out. We have a route for the older ones but this age . . . We even have little kids of eight joy-riding in Divis Valley.'

'Jesus, if they kneecapped them there'd be nothing left!'

'That age they punish the parents. We have to counsel them too. It's the drugs making things worse, I know it.' She spoke softly almost to herself.

'It's that bad now?' Neil asked, suddenly alert.

'We never had it before. Alcohol abuse always, from the cradle to the grave.' She smiled. 'But when the world was suffering the drug problem, we were clear. The Rah kept it out. It was the Loyalist paramilitaries brought it in. Now its big "fund" money for all of them.'

'With all the security, how the hell do they smuggle it in?' he said and noticed the stress lines tighten around her mouth. It was obvious she bore her father's guilt, he guessed her work for the group was her way of paying recompense. How far could he push her, Neil wondered, how much would she give? If it came to the test, where would her loyalties lie? With her father and the Rah or the saving of innocent lives? He dreaded the day he'd have to find out.

'Are you all right, Jackie?' Eilish, aware of the intensity of his expression, touched his face gently in concern.

Neil, fighting his emotions, pulled away, unintentionally abruptly.

Eilish pretended not to notice but, hurt at the rejection and shamed at her spontaneous show of affection, she jumped down from the desk with a false display of energy.

'Right, let's go! Sorry, Jackie, I've taken up enough of your time,' and with that she headed for the door.

Neil caught her shoulder, turned her to face him. 'Eilish, I didn't mean that. My mind was elsewhere, I'm sorry.'

'Great news, great news about Michael.' McAuley greeted him warmly when Neil called in to pick up Eilish. The big man was beaming. 'I can't wait to have him here. We'll soon have him on his feet.'

'Not too soon, Daddy. The fractures have to mend first.' Eilish, specially made up and groomed for the evening, was coming down the stairs. In a slip of a dress that showed to perfection her long slim legs, she looked beautiful. She acknowledged Jackie's appreciative appraisal with a cool smile.

'Michael's a McAuley, remember? We breed 'em tough.' Her father winked at Neil.

Eilish was not amused, she tilted her chin defiantly. 'My rules, Daddy, or not at all. Remember?'

'Ah, get on with you, girl! Take her out, Jackie. Give her a good time, she deserves it,' he said fondly. 'Go on now, I've work to do.'

He pushed open his study door; before it closed, Neil saw Gerry Hughes sitting there relaxed in a chair, a drink in his hand. He stared boldly back at Neil. There was a light of triumph in his eyes.

'What work's your daddy doing this time of night?' Neil asked casually as they drove along.

Eilish froze and looked away. 'He's still involved in business – calls to America. I don't ask.' She spoke coldly.

It took dinner and a bottle of wine for the atmosphere between them to thaw. Neil found himself saying things to make her smile, his hands itching to touch her, and the harder he tried to maintain indifference, the more aware of her he became. Conversation between them was easy, the laughter spontaneous and the pleasure they shared in each other's company undeniable. Neil felt sick at the prospect of betrayal.

'I haven't enjoyed myself like this for years,' Eilish said as if reading his thoughts. 'I feel I should feel guilty. After all you're the first man I've had dinner with since Chris . . . but I don't.'

John Neil wanted to say the same. Instead he took her hand in his and kissed it.

'Let's dance on it.' He pulled the delighted Eilish to her feet. The disco music which had been playing all evening was suddenly replaced by a ceilidh band. The vigorous young musicians leapt on to the tiny stage, their pipes and fiddles alive in their hands, and broke into a spirited Irish jig. Neil looked helplessly at Eilish.

'You've been too long away, Jackie O'Connell,' she remonstrated mockingly. 'Come on, I'll teach you.'

Neil learned fast. Laughing, they whirled and spun and tripped the traditional steps and patterns of the various old Gaelic reels and jigs. Sometimes they collapsed against each other, breathlessly, wordlessly holding each other for support, until the music urged them on, each very conscious of the other, both clinging a little longer than was necessary. When the tempo dropped and the soft music played, they folded against each other without hesitation, the lengths of their bodies fitting together as easily as the last two pieces in a jigsaw. And when the music stopped, though neither said a word, both knew that from then on their lives were inextricably entwined.

They drove back through the streets of Belfast, their stream of light-hearted chatter punctuated by moments of cosy silence. In the glow of passing street lamps, they stole glances at each other, trying to make sense of the senseless, fathom the unfathomable. It was a complication Neil did not want, knew he could not afford but when he thought of Eilish, looked at her, he knew he was involved and there was no going back.

Security lights flooded the night as they pulled up in the drive outside the McAuley house. They knew eyes would be watching.

'I'll walk you in.' Neil surveyed the area before walking round to open the door for Eilish. Neither could stop smiling.

The house was quiet. Eilish looked round in surprise, commenting on the darkened rooms leading off the half-lit hallway.

'Daddy's usually up at this time. Maybe he's being discreet.' She smiled impishly, wrapping her arms around Neil's neck as he pulled her to him.

Neil drove slowly back through the deserted streets. He wanted time to himself, to hold on to the warm glow of love that held him in thrall, to pretend for a few precious minutes that what he wanted could be – that the harsh reality did not exist.

The car came out of nowhere. It slewed across in front of the van, blocking him. Automatically, he swung the wheel and swerved up onto the pavement. Iron bollards raced towards him. He stamped on the brakes and jammed to a halt, slamming his head forward against the steering wheel. Dazed, he lifted his eyes. Black-hooded men swarmed over the van. The door was wrenched open, hands reached in to haul him out. A knife flashed, the safety belt snapped. Head down, he half fell against a tangle of legs, a mass of bodies, all struggling to restrain him. He relaxed, biding his time, waiting for his vision to clear, his balance to be restored, all his training, all his instincts preparing him to lash back. There were five of them. He stood up slowly and lunged. Like lightning his knee jack-knifed into the crotch of one, the heel of his palm smacked up into the nose-bone of another. He wheeled round to screams. There was a loud crack, a searing pain and blackness.

Water brought him round, a freezing bucketful thrown on his face. He kept his eyes closed.

'For Christ's sake, he said "bring him in", not fucking kill him!'

It was Gerry Hughes, he recognized the voice.

More ice-cold water splashed across his face, making him gasp.

'He's coming round.' It was a woman this time. Sinead, maybe? He'd never heard her speak.

'We should've done it while he was out.' Another voice, tremulous, anxious. Colum McAuley, perhaps?

'He'll talk more if he's threatened.' That had to be Brendan.

'I want to see the fear in his bastard eyes when he knows we've found out.' Hughes again. 'Douse him again!'

Water poured down from a height. He blinked furiously and shook his head, trying to clear his nose, his eyes. The pain was crucifying. A circle of faces stared down at him. They started away nervously when they saw him looking back. He was lying on what felt and smelt like straw, his hands and feet tightly bound. His whole body ached and throbbed. He waited for them to speak. Confused by his silence they looked at one another, not sure who should start the interrogation. Neil guessed from the agitated glances that they had already overstepped the margins of their brief. With the light behind them, he could see the four above him were still masked. By turning his head he could see a fifth nursing his crotch and a sixth, holding a bloody cloth to his nose. He guessed they must be the ferret-faced man with the limp and the acned youth.

Neil struggled to pull himself up into a sitting position, then waited for the shooting pains in his head to calm down before he shifted his position so he could rest his back against a bale of hay. Still they said nothing. He surveyed them slowly, one at a time, then looked directly at Hughes.

'OK, Hughes, what's your problem?' he said.

Irritated, Hughes snatched off his hood. Shamefaced, the others did the same.

'Ah, very clever,' Hughes sneered, struggling to regain the upper hand. 'But it won't serve you for long. You think you've taken us all in. Jackie O'Connell? Father Fergal's long-lost brother? The prodigal son returned! You've even tricked McAuley with your play for Eilish. The brave hero saving his daughter and grandson from the fire.' He turned his back, allowing the words to sink in, then wheeled round.

'Well, you haven't fooled me,' he said dangerously. 'I don't like you, O'Connell, and I don't trust you. You came too easy out of nowhere. You remember things we've all forgotten and you look too much. Your eyes are everywhere!

'The Craiglea Estate wasn't even built when you left but you knew every back double to Eilish's house. We didn't have to say a word. Not one direction. Did you notice that, boys?' He didn't wait for an answer. 'You didn't even try to follow us through the front. Why? Afraid the black bastards would say something we'd overhear?

'How come they didn't stop you going round the back? How come they weren't there? Arranged it, had you?' Now he was in full spate. He strutted arrogantly, convinced of the validity of his argument. 'And the way you climbed up that wall, none of us could do that! And the way you attacked us tonight. You've been trained, I knew it, from the moment I clapped eyes on you. You're a bloody tout, a spy. A four-square laundry job. You're no more Jackie O'Connell than I am!' he finished triumphantly.

'Is that what this is all about? Your paranoid meanderings?' Neil asked disparagingly.

Hughes frustrated, kicked him viciously in the ribs.

Neil grunted, doubling up with pain. He heard Colum shouting, Brendan cursing and the girl, Sinead, ordering them to 'get on with it'. Whatever they had uncovered they were obviously sure of their evidence. Playing for time Neil kept his head down while his mind raced, assessing and discarding facts, looking for pointers, indicators as to what they had found out. Something must have prompted Hughes to dare this display of strength. But what made Neil's gut recoil was the suspicion that the 'he' they had referred to was McAuley himself. Had his warm greeting early in the evening been a sham? Had he already agreed the ambush? And had Eilish been part of it?

Without warning a hand grabbed his hair from behind and yanked back his head. An open cut-throat razor waved before his eyes.

Brendan loomed over him. Sadistically he forced back Neil's head, pinning it down onto the top of the bale, exposing Neil's throat to the teasing silky swish of the blade.

'Hold it! Not yet. I want to hear what yer man here has to say. Who are you? Who're you working for, you bastard?' Hughes' closed fist slammed hard across Neil's face. Head locked, unable to move, his jaw juddered at the impact of the blow. Neil clenched his teeth but before Hughes could swing again, Colum grabbed his arm.

'For Christ's sake, Gerry, lay off! Do you want to break his bloody jaw or do you want him to speak?'

'Why don't you just get on with it?' Sinead joined in.

'I'm in charge of this, not you!' Hughes snarled.

Brendan yanked viciously at Neil's head and stuck his face close in against the pinioned man. 'Talk!' he growled.

'What do you want me to say?' Neil bluffed. 'You know who I am. Jackie O'Connell . . .'

'Liar!' Hughes' boot thudded into his thigh.

'Let him talk!' Colum shouted.

'Who do you work for? Who sent you?' Brendan held the blade threateningly against his throat.

'You know who I work for. Myself. And nobody sent me. I came home because I was born here, arsehole! I know Craiglea because I work there, dummy, as I do all over Belfast. I went round the back of the house because the front was barricaded, as any damn fool could see. And I know how to climb and how to fight because I was a fucking sailor. Eejit! Now if you're going to kill me, fucking well get on with it because there's nothing else to fucking tell, for Christ's sake!'

His anger silenced them.

Hughes flushed and aimed one last vicious kick of frustration. 'Right. You've had your chance.' He turned on the others. 'OK? I've given him his chance. Right?' He looked round questioningly, holding out his hand for verification, demanding their allegiance for when he made his report to McAuley, Neil guessed. Sinead and Colum nodded distractedly, their eyes glued to the captive.

'I'm going to enjoy watching you die . . . slowly,' Hughes hissed.

The open razor flashed. Relishing the terror he was about to inflict, Brendan twisted it above Neil's face. Neil did not flinch. Instinct told him they were playing, that they knew nothing, were only bluffing.

128

Brendan smiled down at him. 'Sure you have nothing to say?' Silence was Neil's only chance.

The blade whipped down to his throat. His head was cruelly strained back, forcing his bound body to rise until it arched like a bow.

He could feel the razor glide across the stretched surface of his skin, the first drops of blood beginning to bubble, seeping in warm thin lines down his throat. Strange how painless it was. Then there was a rasp, the rough-hewn stroke of blade on stubbled skin, the painful snag of the razor snatching mercilessly at his beard – Brendan was shaving him.

Sinead moved into his line of vision, drawn close, fascinated by the mundane operation. She was panting lightly. Neil realized she was excited. They were all holding their breath.

Brendan hacked carelessly at the beard, grumbling under his breath, 'Hogan better be right.'

Neil jumped at the name.

'Want to talk now?' Hughes jeered. 'Thought you were smart growing a beard? Thought we'd never find out? Well now, Sinead's brother has been asking a few questions. He's well connected. Travels a lot. Same places as Jackie O'Connell. Hong Kong, for instance. He phoned us up last night, he'd an interesting story to tell. Stop me if you've heard it.' He sniggered and looked round at the others for approval, then went on. 'Seems as how Jackie O'Connell got into a brawl, a knife fight, was left with a deep scar on his face. Strange now if it should not be there . . .' He stopped suddenly. There was an audible gasp from Sinead.

John Neil glared at them much as he'd glared at Gault's anxious face, watching it harden into resolute lines when at first he'd stubbornly refused the deliberate scarring. Now the imposed knife wound, streaking from

129

ear to chin, was no longer a stigma but the blessing Gault had foreseen.

Brendan let go his grasp, his face pale. Everyone stepped back, their eyes cast down or darting guiltily from one to the other, looking to place the blame. Neil relaxed his taut body. Every inch of him ached.

'Will you look at the state of him. You could have been more careful, Brendan. Untie him. Colum, get some water. Let him clean up.' It was Sinead who was the strong one. She stood calmly in front of Neil, challenging him to complain. 'We had to do it, you understand. We had to make sure. You're getting too close for us to take risks.'

Hughes had dropped down sullenly on a straw bale. He glowered across at Neil, suspicious and unrepentant. 'I still don't trust you, O'Connell,' he warned. 'I'm on your tail, remember that!'

Neil stood up slowly, rubbing his wrists and ankles, feeling the veins throb back to life. He stamped his feet and shook his hands and arms to revive the clogged circulation. He dipped his head and held his face in the bucket of cold water Colum held out for him, enjoying the sting of the cuts and nicks of his 'shave', glad to be alive. He shook his head, then pushed back his wet hair with both hands, flat against his head. And all the time they watched him, waiting for his reaction, willing him to anger.

'Let me tell you something.' Neil leaned confidentially to Brendan. The others perked up attentively. 'Forget being a barber. You haven't the knack.'

Brendan glowered, ready to spark back, but Sinead stepped between them. 'Leave it!' she snapped sharply. Between long lashes she glanced obliquely at Neil. 'You're a fine-looking fella, Jackie O'Connell,' she said softly. 'I'd hate the world to see you looking like this and sure we don't want to upset Father Fergal. Why don't you sit down and I'll tidy you up before we go. I've shaved men before, you'll not be the first. It won't be the cleanest shave you've ever had but it'll stop any questions being asked.'

Expertly she removed the tufts of beard left after Brendan's hacking. Aware of her body pressing against his, Neil struggled to keep his senses alert. He could feel her fingers probing the scar.

'It's still very red,' she muttered.

'Red raw it feels after Brendan's treatment,' he growled back.

'A dock-side brawl, my brother said. What happened?'

'Just helping out a friend.' Neil shrugged.

'And you went to jail for it? Well now, you sound like a good friend to have around. Maybe we'll call on you some time, you certainly know how to fight. Then there's that other little job you did for us. If that works, you could be quite a useful fella to us, Jackie O'Connell.'

Gently she dried his face. Then with the same cloth she blindfolded him. 'Until we know you better, Jackie,' she said.

They drove back in sullen silence, Neil squashed between Colum and the girl in the back. They pulled off the blindfold when they reached his van and pushed him out.

'Tell McAuley I passed the test,' he called after them as the car sped away.

He stopped at a call box on the way home. It was three in the morning. Randall answered, his voice weary with sleep.

'Our friend Hogan is in Hong Kong. He's been checking on me.'

'Any problem?'

'No. I think I convinced them but I don't want to

meet Hogan face to face. He's not over there for fun,
I'm sure of that.'

'We'll get on to it now. Anything else?'

He wanted to say, 'I think I'm in love with Eilish.'
Instead he said goodnight.

CHAPTER ELEVEN

Father Fergal stood shaking his head in disbelief. 'God in heaven, the power of women!' Critically he stared at the clean-shaven chin. 'Well now, if you were going to shave it off, you might have made a better job of it. Will you look at the cuts and nicks all over you. I don't think Eilish will be very impressed. And where on earth did you get that scar, or shouldn't I ask?'

'That's right. Don't ask.' Neil was already irritated with the number of comments on his new appearance and he hadn't as yet faced Eilish.

'Had a day of it, have you?' Fergal quizzed. Neil nodded.

'Getting serious with Eilish, is it?'

John Neil slung himself into a chair. At least he could admit the truth to Fergal.

'I don't know,' he conceded. 'I like her a lot, an awful lot, but it's early days.'

'Then walk away, Jackie, before it's too late. They'll have you involved before you know it.'

Neil shook his head. 'I can't walk away. I promised Michael I'd take him to bonfire night. Stop worrying, Fergal, I'm a big boy now; besides McAuley never talks to me about anything political. Neither do the others, except . . .' He left the sentence suspended tantalizingly in the air.

'Except who?'

'A girl, hangs around with Gerry Hughes and Brendan McAuley. Sinead, I think her name is.'

The priest huffed angrily. 'Sinead Hogan. Where did you meet her? She's a bad lot, that one, just like her brother. Not to be trusted at all. Don't tell me McAuley had her in the house?'

'I met her in the bar. Her brother's out in Hong Kong, she was saying.'

'Well, he certainly wouldn't dare show his face here.'

'Why not?'

Fergal's face darkened. 'Because the Rah would have him if he did. He's a fanatic, a fervent Communist, with a price on his head, him and his cousins. A while ago they came up with some foolhardy plan to kill Cabinet ministers. The Army Council rejected it. The fools wouldn't listen, went ahead anyway. But someone grassed on them to the Council. Just as they were about to carry out the plan, the Provos ambushed them. They shot two of them dead. Hogan and the cousins escaped, but everyone knows Sinead was part of the unit doing the shooting.'

'Meaning she let them go?'

Fergal grimaced. 'Meaning she was the one that grassed on them.'

Neil was puzzled. 'But she's still close to her brother. She was speaking to him only recently.'

'Quite possible. She twists with the devil, that one. That's why McAuley doesn't trust her. She's after power and she'll get it. Hughes is nothing, a cheap gangster, McAuley knows that, he keeps him close where he can watch him but Sinead is another animal altogether. She's well educated, clever, understands the way things are going, knows how to handle herself in the outside world. She's on her way to being a big player and God help anyone who gets in her way.'

134

'And yet she still stays in touch with her brother. Doesn't make sense,' Neil mused.

'I don't know. She comes and goes. She worked in finance at one time, still might – City, London stock market. But she was involved even then.' He shook his head cynically. 'Her brother was always abroad, gunrunning, drugs, who knows? Maybe they're in business together. Whatever it is they'll be up to no good, you can be sure of that.' He looked at his watch and jumped. 'God in heaven, you've got me here enjoying the crack and look at the time.' He rushed to the door then poked his head back. 'Just remember what I said. Keep clear of all of them!'

The call on Jackie O'Connell to make bombs came soon afterwards. Since the night of the kidnapping, other than a passing word when they'd met in the hall or as McAuley was going in or out of his study, John Neil had seen little of the big man. McAuley greeted him affably enough but his mind seemed on other things. He made no reference to the missing beard. He welcomed Neil to the freedom of his house and there seemed no suspicion, no wariness, no hint of ulterior meaning in the polite social context of his words. But that was all there was, that was the full extent of any conversation before the old rebel disappeared into his study, the one room into which John Neil was not invited.

The constant ringing of the phone indicated that 'business' was hotting up but when he mentioned it to Eilish it was obvious from her contemptuous shrug, the angry tilt of her chin, the frozen hostile glare, that whatever her father was doing, she did not want to know.

He took to calling in at odd hours with little presents for Michael, hoping to catch sight of a secret visitor or surprise a covert meeting. He'd pause unduly long outside the study door, to tie a shoelace or to look for a dropped coin, anything – his ears straining for a hint, a clue as to what was going on. Once, hearing the study phone's incessant ringing going unanswered, he almost made it through the door. He'd actually turned the lock when the restraining voice of McAuley called to him from the stairs, ordering him to 'Leave it!' 'Sorry, thought it might be important', had been his excuse but he'd felt the Irishman's piercing stare following him down the hall.

Frequently, on the pretext of getting Michael used to his wheelchair, Neil would wander with him in the garden. From there he could see McAuley at his desk, his face heavy with a concentrated scowl, studying papers or speaking on the phone. Often Gerry Hughes or the brothers would be there. From the way their bodies were directed towards McAuley, their attentive attitude when they listened, the intensity of their response, it was obvious something heavy was going down.

It was on one of these occasions, when they'd almost overrun the kitten Michael had been given to console him, that the boy let in a hint of light.

They were at the far end of the garden, where the mowed lawn merged with the long wild grasses under a small copse of trees. Dusk was falling rapidly and Neil was sitting on a log enjoying a cigarette while Michael cuddled his kitten. Lights were beginning to come on in the house, their glow spilling out across the grass, leaving the copse in shadow. Michael was chattering, Neil barely listening, concentrating instead on the lit study window where McAuley was standing looking out. It was obvious from the way he yawned and stretched and scratched his head that he had no idea he was being watched. Suddenly there was the sound of a car pulling into the drive. Immediately the big man smoothed back

136

his hair, checked his appearance and prepared to greet someone.

'That's Grandaddy's banker come from America,' Michael said suddenly. 'Sometimes he comes in a helicopter. Not here. He couldn't land here. When we go to the big house. Do you think they'll let me take my kitten there this year, Jackie? 'Cos Grandaddy says we go soon and my kitten will still be very small, he might get lost if I'm not here.'

Neil was suddenly very attentive. 'I'm sure your kitten will be able to go, Michael. Which big house is that then? Is it yours?' he said lightly.

Michael laughed. 'Don't be silly, Jackie, it's ginormous. The biggest house you've ever seen. It's got a river and a huge lake with lots of fish and . . .'

'I don't believe you. Where is it then? I bet you don't know.' Neil's heart was beating at the double.

'I do too, 'cos Mammy showed me on the map. It's near Dun . . . Do . . . Dundalk! And we have to go over the border. And we have fireworks there too but it's not bonfire night, it's a special American sort of day, like Christmas 'cept it's not Christmas.'

'You mean Thanksgiving.'

'Yeh, that's it. Will you come with us, Jackie? Mammy would like it and you and I could go fishing. I'll ask Grandaddy. I'll say . . . I won't go unless you can come.'

'And is it Grandaddy's banker owns the house?'

'I think so. I don't know, there are so many people there.' He wriggled in his chair, bored with the questioning. 'My kitten's getting cold, Jackie . . .'

'We should go in. I love fishing. What sort of fish do you catch there, Michael?' Neil tried to prolong the conversation.

'All sorts. I want to learn fly fishing. Could you teach me, Jackie? Promise you'll come?'

'I'd love to. I've a great fly rod. I promise I'll teach

you, but you'd better ask your Mammy and Grandaddy. It's not up to me. Now let's go inside.'

Keeping to the shadows they drew closer to the house. Neil had observed a tall slim upright figure in a dark suit enter the study, ushered in by McAuley. Both men chatted easily, heavy tumblers of whiskey in their hands. The American moved about the room familiarly, sat on the edge of the desk or on the windowsill. At one point he looked out into the garden but with the light behind him it was impossible to make out any features before he turned back, picked up a briefcase and sat down out of sight. Business was about to begin, Neil presumed, anxious now to get into the house.

Eilish was preparing supper in the kitchen. 'What were you two up to out there? I thought I'd have to send out a search party.' She hugged Michael, delighting in the healthy glow the brisk autumn air had brought to his hospital pallor.

'OK, big boy, let's smarten you up,' Neil said, helping Michael out of his anorak and scarf. 'Looks as if we might be having a visitor for supper.'

'No, no!' Eilish retorted, too sharply. 'He won't be staying.'

'Fine,' Neil said lightly. 'I'll just take Michael's things out to the hall.'

He closed the door quietly behind him, checked the deserted hall and that Eilish was still chatting with Michael, then slipped along to the study. He could hear the murmur of voices but only odd words were clearly audible. It seemed to be legitimate banking talk – of bonds, letters of credit, stocks and shares.

'And this new broker. Can we trust him?' It was McAuley's voice.

'Oh yes. A top man, reputable firm, good contacts . . .' The voices dropped low again as important confidences were exchanged but Neil caught the words, 'construction company', 'East European bloc' and he thought 'Hungary'.

There was the sound of a chair being pushed back, papers rustled, a case clicked; signs the meeting was coming to an end.

'So we'll finalize everything there.' He heard the American's voice close to the door but it was McAuley's response that set his pulse racing.

'I'll have the delivery ready. I'm also looking forward to the day. I just hope young Michael's up to it. He had such a great time around the estate last year.'

Swiftly Neil threw Michael's coat over the stair banister and made it back to the kitchen before he was discovered.

He'd carried Michael up to bed and was coming downstairs when McAuley, who had not put in an appearance at supper, opened his study door. 'How're y'doing, Jackie?' He rubbed his eyes wearily. 'Michael gone to bed?'

Neil nodded. 'Eilish is enjoying cosseting him. She's reading him a story now.'

'Come and take a drink with me, then.' And he threw open his study door.

It was the pictures crowding the walls that startled Neil. Naively drawn and crudely painted, they represented a history of 'heroic' actions executed in the name of the IRA, in the ongoing battle for freedom. Images of young men staring boldly out, dressed in paramilitary fashion, their Armalites at the ready, the tricolour flying, their particular deed imposed as a back-drop behind them. Colourful versions of exploding British Army tanks, trucks and helicopters highlighted with hurtling, dismembered, khaki-clothed bodies. Pictures of RUC stations or army barracks, bomb blasted or consumed by fire, or simply young men standing proudly on the barricades or resolutely staring out from gaunt faces with starving eyes.

'Billy Sands, God bless him,' McAuley said, following the direction of Neil's gaze. 'Brave lads, all of them,' he added, fiercely proud, 'from Michael Collins to our Sean.'

'So many years, so many dead,' Neil couldn't help saying. 'Will there ever be peace?'

'Not till the British get out. Not till this country is one. Gerry Adams and his lot can hold as many secret meetings with the British Government as they like but it will be the gun will end this war, not politics. Have you any idea of the number of peace initiatives I've lived through, Jackie? And all the time the British Government, the preachers and the politicians are talking peace, the British Army is here, imposing the will of its government by oppressing the people with violence. And as long as they do that then every man, woman and child has the right and the duty to take up arms in defence of this nation's sovereignty.' He sank back wearily in his chair. 'It's up to the young ones now, my sons and grandson, young Michael there, whatever his mother says, to carry on the fight. I'm getting too old, Jackie. Done too much, all those years living on the run, moving from one safe house to another, never seeing my family, my children growing up . . . That last time, when was it now? Two, three years ago, we only just got out in time. Germany it was, pretty town, not far from Munich. Nice area that, the Black Forest, Bavaria. Be nice to go back for a holiday. You know it, Jackie?'

John Neil had stopped listening, the blood had frozen in his veins and his heart had stopped beating. Yet even as the intensity of the emotion threatened his very consciousness the professional undercover man found himself shaking his head, a polite smile plastered on his face.

'So you've retired then, Liam,' Neil managed to say, amazed at the normality of his voice.

'From active service: never from the fight! No, no, I'm on a different side now, back to being a businessman, using my brain not my brawn, though I've still plenty of that.' He winked at Jackie, man to man, and flexed his arm muscles.

'How're you making out with Eilish? Looking after her, are you? And my grandson, Michael?' He spoke rhetorically, answering his own questions, nodding his head as old men do. 'That's good. He needs a man about him. Eilish watches everything I say and she doesn't like the brothers near him, especially not Brendan. Colum's not so bad but he's weak. Sean was the one she was close to. A bit of a dreamer, like herself; fancied himself a poet, until I knocked some sense into him. It was his first time, you know. I don't think he even fired a round. It doesn't matter, he did his duty, shed his blood, gave his life . . .' The voice faltered and cracked; his eyes misted, their piercing light had gone, even their darkness had faded. The macho warrior had lost, the patriotic rebel had given way to the father grieving for his son.

Neil looked at the man who had murdered his family. All his feelings of bloody vengeance had gone, replaced by a deep, gnawing sadness for them all, for everyone, Catholic, Protestant, soldier, involved in the tragedy of Ireland.

McAuley hardly noticed his leaving, barely raised his hand to wave him away. When Neil left, for both men, the tears were falling.

That night John Neil contacted Randall again.

'The big fella's opening up. I want to call off the meeting.'

'Why? What's the brief?' Randall did not waste words.

'Nothing specific but I think he now trusts me. He's started telling me things, confiding in me. Family things mostly but I'd be better staying close than coming over there.'

'And the girl?'

'She's my passport. I told you. There's a meeting being planned, I need to be there.'

Tersely Neil went over the events of the evening, passing on names and snippets of conversation for Randall and the team to analyse and investigate.

'I may not get over for some time, things are hotting up,' he concluded. 'I'll be in touch.'

They arrived at the top of Cave Hill just as the bonfire was being lit and joined the throng of families crowding round, eager for the fireworks to begin.

Following Eilish, Neil manoeuvred Michael in his wheelchair to where a group of his schoolfriends were already positioned at the front. Below them lay the city, lit like a crystal cobweb spun between the surrounding hills, everywhere fireworks rocketed and blossomed into a myriad colours, hanging like exotic blooms in the sky, before falling to earth in glittering showers.

'Isn't it fantastic,' Eilish said in a hushed voice. 'Look, Michael!'

Michael, wide-eyed and eager, was lit up with excitement, his cheeks bulging with sweets, his lap full of goodies. Delighted to be back among friends, he gazed in wonder at the distant show.

Eilish hugged Neil's arm. 'There was a time I thought I'd never be this happy again.'

The bonfire suddenly flared up with an enormous whoosh. Flames leapt up filling the air with crackles and cracks, and at the same time the firework display began. The night was alive with explosions and whistles, fire and light and colour. The mass of upturned faces, rosy with heat from the fire, joined in with a chorus of approval as the night erupted with stars and spangles and gunpowder.

John Neil with his hand protectively on Michael's shoulder felt the child stiffen and shiver. He looked down quickly. Michael's face was frozen with fear. His eyes wide and panic-stricken, he stared hypnotically at the leaping flames, living again the trauma of that horrific night. Alerting Eilish, Neil stepped swiftly in front of him, blocking out the scene. 'You're safe, Michael.' He smiled reassuringly into the boy's face, taking him firmly by the hand. 'See Mammy's here and all your friends.' Neil drew Eilish by his side, encouraging her to touch her son's face, drawing him gently out of the nightmare memories back to the security of the present. The boy clung desperately to both Neil and his mother but gradually as the compassionate voice of the man reassured him in quiet even tones, they watched the fear fade.

'Should we go now, Michael?' Neil asked, allowing him the belief it was his own decision. 'I've seen enough if you have?'

Michael nodded, and Neil pivoted the wheelchair away into the crowd.

By the time they reached the house, Michael was talking about the evening as if he'd thoroughly enjoyed the entire event. It was only as Neil was leaving his bedroom that he heard the lingering note of fear in Michael's anxious voice talking to his mother. 'Will Jackie be there for the fireworks at the big house?'

'I'm not sure if we should go there this year, Michael. Let's see if you're well enough.'

'But Jackie could teach me fishing.'

'Let's wait awhile, Michael. If the doctors say yes, then you can ask him,' was Eilish's diplomatic reply.

Neil paused at the foot of the stairs where a light was

showing beneath the study door. McAuley, seemingly unaware of their early homecoming, was talking on the phone, his voice raised as if speaking to someone far away.

'Shimna on the twenty-sixth then,' Neil heard him say, 'and will we see you on the weekend? At Thanksgiving? Good, we'll talk then.'

A door slammed. Someone had come into the kitchen. Swiftly Neil slipped into the living room, timing his reappearance at the door to look as if he was coming out to investigate the noise, just as Gerry Hughes and the brothers stepped into the hall. Each man carried a similar holdall. They were startled to see him.

'Off on your holidays then, boys?' Neil joked.

'What are you doing here?' Brendan said, caught off guard. 'Eilish said you were taking Michael up Cave Hill to see the fireworks.'

'We had to come back early, it upset him. Reminded him of the fire.'

They all nodded but Neil could tell they were annoyed rather than sympathetic. Without another word they pushed past him to the study. Noting Colum's relaxed hold on the bag, Neil knocked it from his grasp.

'Sorry, Colum.' Beating Colum to it, he picked up the bag and handed it back. From the way the young man snatched at it and hustled after the others it held something special, something reasonably heavy. Drugs was Neil's first thought, it certainly wasn't heavy enough for arms. Semtex maybe?

The door was firmly closed against him but he could hear them whispering and McAuley growling at them to keep calm.

It was too risky to hang about in the hall, so Neil slipped into the kitchen and out into the garden. The murmur of voices in desultory conversation and the sound of feet kicking at gravel reminded him of the constant presence of McAuley's minders. Tonight they were round at the front of the house relieving the boredom of their surveillance by talking to Hughes' men. He listened carefully, identified there were indeed four voices, then keeping close to the wall, approached the study window. The sound was muffled but Neil was sure he heard the clump of a safe door being shut. McAuley was speaking.

'I want it all in now, lads. Discreetly, mind. We don't want you upsetting people. Hughes, remember! But we have to have it ready for the pick-up which doesn't give us much time now.'

'We'll have it. We've two or three weeks to go,' Brendan replied. A shadow loomed across the light, someone was looking out of the window. Neil flattened to the wall, hardly daring to breathe.

Whatever had been in those bags was in them no longer. But where was the safe? Neil drew fruitlessly on a mental picture of the study. The shadow disappeared. Time was running out, he daren't be discovered looking in. Swiftly he moved to the shadows on the outer edges of the garden where he could look back without being seen. He could make out the younger figures but the big man was out of sight. Frustrated, he made his way back.

'That you, Jackie?' O'Shea stepped out of the shadows.

'There it is!'

The minder froze.

Using sleight of hand assisted by the dark, Neil ducked down and pretended to retrieve his lost lighter from almost beneath O'Shea's heavy foot. 'Great. I'd almost given up. I guessed I'd dropped it somewhere here, wheeling young Michael.' Neil grinned companionably at O'Shea.

'I saw you come back early. He enjoy the fireworks?' O'Shea asked.

He chatted amiably enough but John Neil was shaken. He had been completely unaware of the man's presence. What else had the man seen? O'Shea gave no hint of suspicion but that was no guarantee. Familiarity and acceptance in the McAuley household was blunting the edges. He was getting too comfortable, Neil warned himself and that way danger lay.

He found Eilish in the sitting room kneeling in front of the fire, deep in thought. She looked round as he came in and her face lit up with pleasure.

'Michael gone to sleep OK?' Neil sat down in the armchair next to her.

'He's fine. I never even thought . . .' she said in a troubled voice.

'If not tonight, it would have happened at some time, just be thankful we were there to help him through it. He'll be fine next time, you see. In fact,' he said carefully, 'the sooner he's exposed to something like that again where we can be on hand to reassure him, the better.'

'You think so, Jackie? You don't think it will upset him again?'

'As long as we're there. People he can trust.'

'In that case . . .' She hesitated. He watched the reflection of thoughts fleeting across her face, saw the warmth and the trust and hated himself for using the two people he least wanted to hurt.

'Michael really likes you a lot. He wants to ask you something.' She smiled teasingly, 'I hope you say yes.'

'For his sake or your sake?'

'Both.'

Neil was drowning in her eyes. He pulled her to him and kissed her. She sighed happily, nestling closely against his legs, her head on his lap. Gently he stroked her hair.

CHAPTER TWELVE

Neil waited for something to be said about the incident in the garden, a slanted question, a curious remark hinting at suspicion or mistrust, if not from the father at least from one of the sons, but 'That the lighter you lost?' was McAuley's only passing reference.

Even so he sensed a new tension about the house, a feeling of things gearing up. Neil, desperate to search the study, was frustrated at every attempt. The house was rarely without visitors, the room never unattended. The boys were round more often, closeted with McAuley. Frequently they carried the same holdalls making their deliveries and O'Shea and Maguire seemed more in evidence too. From the kitchen Neil observed their routine, their constant checks and searches, inside and out, on both house and cars. It had to be for evidence of bombs or bugs planted, he guessed. Now too, at night, he noted the glow of a cigarette in the garden where one of them guarded the study window.

After much self-vilification, and cursing Randall, John Neil had handed over his home-made bombs to Hughes. No words had been exchanged with Liam McAuley concerning the matter but the following day, in the kitchen, McAuley's hand had squeezed Neil's shoulder warmly, as a sign of his grateful acknowledgement.

Eilish had witnessed this and flinched and when on another occasion, her father said, 'Glad to have you with us, son,' she'd looked openly hostile. The old rebel had noticed and laughed. 'I meant with the family, Eilish. Michael tells me Jackie's with us for Thanksgiving. I was worried how the boy would cope. I didn't want him disappointed, he loves it there so much. But with Jackie here to look after him . . .!' The craggy features softened when he spoke of his grandson.

Eilish waited for him to leave the kitchen. 'I can't wait to get away from here, Jackie!' she said as soon as her father was out of earshot. 'To be in the countryside. To have some peace.'

Neil caught the strain in her voice. 'You're never alone here, I'll say that. Something special going on?' If he hoped to provoke a comment from Eilish he failed. Instead he witnessed the closed expression, the blank eyes, the same determined rejection of anything to do with her father's affairs.

Belfast itself seemed under a hush of anticipation. There were rumours of peace talks, of Gerry Adams and Martin McGuinness meeting with the British Government. Rumours which created dangerous rumblings from the Loyalists who suspected they were being sold out. Rumours which endorsed Fergal's earlier warnings that this was a bad time for Jackie to have come home.

All over people talked nervously of the violence escalating, feared the resulting indiscriminate tit-for-tat of sectarian killings.

Working as an electrician in the Catholic ghettos, Neil was aware of a growing unrest among the business community, where the call on 'donations' to the Cause was suddenly more pressing, and the amounts disproportionately increased. Those that could not pay were being heavily leaned on and those that complained were punished. Accepted as one of their own, called into their houses or places of work, Jackie O'Connell was the recipient of confidences, some indiscreetly revealed over a cup of tea, others overheard. All pointed to the fact that the network of small businesses that fronted the IRA's fund-raising, the drinking clubs, the pirate video and audio shops, the fleets of black taxis, were under pressure to come up with the cash.

It didn't take him long to deduce that the content of the various holdalls being ferried to the McAuley safe was 'dirty money'. And the American banker, could he be the laundry man? Doubtful, Neil told himself, the man wouldn't be that visible. He was more likely to be the legitimate intermediary.

What was becoming obvious was the importance of the impending weekend. Not only was it destined to be the pick-up location for the money but it seemed more and more certain that among the guests gathered to celebrate Thanksgiving, some would be major players in the IRA's financial structure and that the main agenda at the meetings would be the funding of the prospective heavy arms deal.

'Learn what you can but don't risk anything,' was Randall's response to his report. 'Most of the players you'll see there will have iron-tight fronts of respectability. Trust none of them. Listen hard. But remember this is not the big one. These are just the money men. We want the strategists. And we need you for that.'

'What about Shimna on the twenty-sixth? Any idea what that might be?' Neil queried.

'No, nothing at all.'

The house stood at the end of a long avenue of trees; magnificent, white and Georgian, its pillared classical beauty enhanced by spreading specimen trees in neat lawns that became one with the rolling parklands that stretched on for ever. Master of it all was the American banker.

Irish American, Neil corrected himself when they met. The accent still retained more of the old country than the new. In his late forties, Paul Heaney had the confident air of a man not only born to money but whose life was one of personal success. His elegant American wife, Patricia, was every inch the professional hostess. She had practised charm. She was also fervently Irish, even though fifth-generation American, to the bottom of her bleached roots.

Guests arrived and gathered for an informal buffet lunch which was served in the conservatory, which led from the dining room out onto the terrace, overlooking the lawns, the parterre gardens and the lake. Supposedly a 'family' gathering, there were no young children present other than Michael, but three teenagers who had met Michael on a previous occasion took him away to join them for lunch, leaving Neil and Eilish to socialize with the other adults.

Eilish knew them all. They were part of the set of wealthy high-flying Irish families who travelled the country from one social event to another, one house to another, partying as only the Irish can party. The Heaneys' Thanksgiving was but one of the highlights of their calendar and signalled the start of the Christmas social round.

'We have a lot of family living in the Free State,' Eilish explained. 'We were down here a great deal when I was young.' What she did not add was the number of times they sought refuge in the South, living in safe houses until things had cooled down or while her father planned his next 'job'.

Neil joined with Eilish in the round of social chatter, his face attentive to the conversation in hand, his ears straining for snippets of a more confidential nature. All the time he observed McAuley; noted his body language, who he leaned towards, the intimacy of his speech, the play of light and shade in his eyes. But if the old rebel was there for ulterior motives, he gave nothing away. Neil saw only Liam at his charming best, flirting with the ladies, entertaining and conversing with the men, and though the undercover man eavesdropped as much as he dared, he heard nothing suspicious at all.

The young people had returned with Michael. They were off to the stables, to saddle up for a hack. Michael was desperate to go fishing. The teenagers had excited him with tales of a giant fish said to lurk in a deep pool where the small river tumbled over a series of shallow waterfalls on its way to the lake. This, he insisted, was where he would start his fishing career.

Enjoying the bright autumn weather, Eilish sat well away from the two fishermen, thrilled to see the expression on Michael's face as he concentrated on his throw, teasing and flicking the 'fly' on the surface of the pool, watching it drift and flow. She did her best not to laugh when the fine line looped around Jackie or tangled in the mechanics of Michael's wheelchair but looked down at her book or away to the distance, marvelling always at Jackie's patience and her incredible fortune in meeting such a wonderfully kind man. Sometimes, feeling the warmth of the late sun on her face, she closed her eyes, listened to the murmur of their voices and dreamed of a life with Jackie, the three of them together, walking the hills, playing on a beach. Then her heart would contract, her eyes snap open and she'd see Michael in his wheelchair and all the pain and anger at what had happened to her child, her husband, her brothers would come surging back. Life had taught her not to dream. But Michael adored Jackie, she told herself. She watched the two of them, their heads together as Jackie leaned over Michael's shoulder, showing him how to pull and let go of the line, how to tempt and tease the fish, saw it in the trusting way her son looked up at him. Jackie should have a son . . .

As if reading her thoughts, Neil came running up the bank and threw himself down beside her.

'He's happy enough whether he catches a fish or not,' he said.

'He loves it here,' she said simply. 'Especially being with you. You're so good with him, Jackie.'

'He's a great little lad. A credit to you.'

'I'm proud of him. He never complains, you know, and it's hard for him seeing his friends running around. But . . .' She hesitated. 'I have to get him away from my father's house, Jackie.'

'Why? Has something happened?'

Eilish shook her head. 'I'm frightened, Jackie.' Neil sat up and held her to him, stroking her hair reassuringly, encouraging her to speak.

'Brendan's been talking to him about the people who burned our house, how they're going to make them pay. How he'll get his revenge. I don't want that, Jackie. I don't want him to grow up with hatred in his heart. He's a little boy, I don't want him indoctrinated with the glories of the Cause. Not ever!'

Neil remained silent, hoping she would reveal something about the increased activity at the house.

'I warned Brendan, but it's when I'm not there. I can't watch all the time. As soon as Michael's well . . .' She paused. 'It's so wonderful being here. With you I can relax. Thank God I have someone I can trust.'

Neil kissed the top of her head. 'Your dad will be upset if you leave. He's very fond of you, you know.'

'I know. Despite all the rows. At least we don't fight any more. We just don't speak, not really. We have nothing to say to each other. He knows I despise everything he stands for. It wasn't always like this. When I was little I adored him. I remember holidays at our summer house, riding on his shoulders. Him teaching us all to swim in the river, Colum and Brendan, me and James and Sean . . .' Her voice faded dreamily. 'No killing, no violence. Or maybe there was and I was just too young to understand it.'

Eilish shivered. The sun had dropped low and a chill was nipping the air. They called to Michael to draw in his line and headed back to the house.

'Are your brothers not joining us here?' Neil asked as he pushed the wheelchair up the long lawn leading to the terrace.

'Later,' Eilish answered shortly but Neil detected that same dismissive note she adopted when the subject matter was closed. He felt a flutter of apprehension. He was sure they were timing their arrival to deliver the money directly to the pick-up, which meant whoever was collecting had not yet called. Without realizing it Eilish confirmed his suspicions.

'There's many more will be here for tonight. People come in from all over, especially for the fireworks. The Heaneys are noted for them.' She glanced anxiously at Michael but his mind was on other things.

'I did see that big fish, you know, Jackie,' he said. 'I nearly caught it too! It came right up to my fly and sniffed at it. It was as ginormous as this.' He held out his arms as far as they would stretch.

Both Eilish and John Neil burst out laughing.

'Fishing stories already,' Eilish exclaimed. 'What have you been teaching him, Jackie O'Connell? And I said I could trust you!'

They entered the house just as McAuley was coming down the stairs from his afternoon rest, dressed and ready for the evening. He helped Eilish with the wheelchair, while Neil carried Michael upstairs to his bedroom. From the way he glanced at his watch, Neil

153

realized he was preoccupied with more pressing matters than Michael's fishing stories.

'Could I have a word with you, Jackie?' he murmured, indicating the door. Eilish, who was helping Michael out of his clothes, looked up suspiciously.

'I'll see you later then, Jackie,' she said frostily, hating to see her father and Jackie sharing confidences. 'In about an hour. Ready for the barbecue.'

Outside the room, McAuley closed the door behind him and drew Neil away down the hall where they could not be overheard.

'Michael be all right tonight? With the fireworks and all?' he said, his face creased with concern. 'Eilish told me what happened last time.'

'I hope so. The more he faces his fear the better, I—'

'Good, good! You take care of them both now. Look after them. Make sure they have everything they want. I may not be around. There's a . . . business meeting, the people involved are quite sensitive, if you know what I mean? Just, ah, don't say anything about it to Eilish or anyone else for that matter, you know?'

Neil waited until McAuley had disappeared into the bar, then slipped down the stairs and out to the front of the house where the evening guests were beginning to arrive, muffled in warm clothes ready for the barbecue which even now was being prepared out on the terrace. There was an assortment of cars, most of them expensive, many of them four-wheel-drive luxury vehicles fitted with every optional extra, personalized in every possible way. Toys for the rich rather than working jobs. Sitting in Eilish's car, pretending to search for something, he made a note of the numbers.

He'd seen the helipad when they'd first arrived and in fact had taken Michael to look at the Heaneys' helicopter, a Bell Jet Ranger, parked there. Now he saw it was missing. A couple of estate workers were organizing the parking. Seeing them standing idle, awaiting the arrival of the next visitors, Neil meandered over.

'Seen anything of the McAuley brothers yet?' They shook their heads, taking the cigarettes he offered.

'Their nephew's worried they'll miss the fireworks; maybe the helicopter's gone to pick them up?' he joked.

The two youths laughed. 'No, it's been put away, to make room for another one that's coming in later.'

'Who's that then?'

'Friends of the boss, but they're not staying long. They're on to somewhere else.'

'Sure, must be lots of parties going on tonight. Oh well, back to work, lads.' Neil nodded a greeting as another group of young people tumbled out of a car, all set for a good time.

Enticing aromas were wafting from the barbecue as they pushed Michael out towards the terrace. It was a fine clear night, the conservatory doors were opened up and people were milling inside and out. Neil spotted McAuley at once, standing with a group of older people, a drink securely tucked against his body in the crook of his arm; sign of the professional drinker pacing himself, Neil thought. Occasionally McAuley checked his watch but from his easy stance, he seemed set – at least for a while. Of the brothers there was no sign.

Outdoor gas heaters spread light and warmth over the assembled guests seated at the long trestle tables out on the terrace. In the background, near the lake, people bustled about, preparing the firework display.

'I hope this is a good idea,' Eilish murmured as her son, now with his teenage friends, glanced anxiously back at them – except this time he waved – at Colum and Brendan who had suddenly appeared in the conservatory. They waved back briefly before cornering their father. Neil saw him nod then check his watch and look across

155

at Heaney. Then he offered his sons a drink. Whatever was happening was not happening yet.

Excusing himself before the fireworks began, Neil quickly checked the front drive and saw Brendan's car parked close by the helipad in a space that had hitherto been marked as reserved. Leaning casually against the back of the car, guarding the boot, were O'Shea and Maguire.

At the first whoosh of fireworks lighting up the sky, Eilish and Neil moved close to Michael but it was clear that at this distance from the action, and with no bonfire to remind him, he was going to be fine. They sat on the balustrade, looking out across the grounds to the lake, relaxed and easy with each other, enjoying the evening and Michael's pleasure. At least that was how they appeared, but John Neil was coiled like a spring, positioned to observe, ready for the first sound of blades whirring down from the skies.

It came camouflaged by a particularly long, noisy and extravagant display of Catherine wheels, golden showers and exploding rockets that deafened the ears and drew the eye. A clever piece of timing, John Neil decided, as his trained ear distinguished the sound and his keen observer's eye noted the disappearing backs of Heaney and the McAuleys.

He had his plan prepared. Without a word to Eilish, he ducked down by Michael and whispered in his ear.

Michael shook his head vigorously. 'No, no, I want to stay. I'm all right, Jackie, really.'

Neil stepped back to Eilish and squeezed her arm. 'He's just cold, don't worry. I'll get him a blanket. Keep your eye on him.' And before she could say anything he'd gone. He exited the house on the opposite side from the helipad and keeping to the shadows crept through the gardens and shrubbery surrounding the drive, approaching the helicopter from behind. It was a French craft, he noted, a Squirrel built for speed and distance and not readily available in Ireland.

Three figures, two men and a slim young woman, all carrying briefcases, were walking across to the house, where McAuley and Heaney were waiting to escort them inside. Neil stared after them; there was something familiar about the assured bearing of the girl, the way she swung her hips, her short hair, and when, in the light, she turned her face to receive a warm greeting kiss from the two men he knew he was right – it was Sinead.

A fourth man, obviously the pilot, was already working with the brothers. Assisted by O'Shea and Maguire, they were loading four large holdalls from the car to the helicopter. The 'dirty money' was on its way to the laundry. Looking back at the house, Neil could make out the shadows of the visitors in the windows of the library. He was about to retrace his steps when a sudden shiftiness in the way the men looked round caught his attention. He waited. The pilot seemed to be unscrewing a panel from the body of the craft. Neil watched as a secret compartment was revealed and what looked like a bulging plastic shopping bag was handed over and quickly thrown in the boot of the car. Did McAuley know about this? Somehow from the way the men looked towards the house, Neil doubted it.

Keeping low, Neil raced back the way he'd come. Picking up the blanket he'd hidden earlier in the evening, he walked into the hall. Everyone was still outside watching the fireworks. Dropping down as if to retie his sports shoe, he positioned himself close to the library doors.

Someone was speaking in a halting foreign accent, answered by a man with a smooth City voice, something about a company being undercut and a take-over of shares.

'We'll also have letters of credit and documents in the bank's name.' That was Heaney speaking.

'And our friend in Spain. He's organized it all?' McAuley asked.

'With my brother. He's also handling the Hong Kong end.'

'Good. OK, Sinead, this is the last document, then you've signed everything,' the city man said. 'That's it I think, Milos.'

'Yes, that is all. Now Sinead, when she comes to my country, will have the account. She can sign for any-thing.' There was a nervous ripple of laughter at the man's tease.

'So the deal goes through, Hogan checks the delivery and . . .' McAuley paused.

'Everything will be in place, on time,' the smooth man assured him.

'And the big meeting is . . .?' Heaney demanded.

'St Stephen's . . .'

Suddenly there were footsteps, someone was coming from the kitchen. Quickly Neil jumped back, mounted the bottom stairs then walked briskly down, holding out his blanket. 'Getting chilly out there,' he said and smiled at the maid.

Neil was buzzing with what he'd just heard. Sinead and her brother were playing a clever game. Presumed outcasts, the two radicals were deeply entrenched and well-trusted power players in a sophisticated financial operation.

Eilish, engrossed in chatting to a friend, looked up as Neil handed her a glass of champagne he'd retrieved on the way. 'You're a darling man, Jackie, but Michael's not going to need that.' She indicated the blanket. 'He's as warm as toast. I think the shivering was just excitement. He's loving it, Jackie.'

Her face glowed with happiness, so different from the

woman he'd seen when he'd first arrived. Now he dreaded the day he'd wipe that smile away.

The fireworks were coming to an end when he heard the sound of the Squirrel wheeling away. There had been no further opportunity to learn anything more without arousing suspicion but at least he now knew there was a meeting at St Stephen's.

But St Stephen's – what? A church? A hospital? A school? He had no idea.

He left Eilish helping Michael to bed while he went down to the bar for a quiet drink. He needed time on his own to think and assess the evening's events. There were few people about, some had gone home, some on to other parties, most across to the barn for the dance.

McAuley spotted him as soon as he walked in. He was with a group of men lingering over their drinks, deep in conversation. The big man, in ebullient mood, called him over, indicating an empty chair next to him.

'And where's my beautiful daughter?' he said jovially.

'With your handsome grandson, putting him to bed. She'll be down soon.'

'Good man, good man, Jackie.' He patted Neil affectionately on the knee. 'Great to have you with us, son!'

Throughout this exchange, a lively discussion was in progress. The politicians at the gathering were being probed about the possibilities of impending peace in Northern Ireland. The view of the man at the front was McAuley's contribution. History was called upon in terms of dates, names, actions, the Troubles, the violence, the intransigence of Catholics, Protestants, Brits; the sad anthem of divided Ireland.

The American businessmen listened intently. From the questions they asked and their knowledge, Neil realized not only were they of Irish heritage themselves but important representatives of Noraid, sent over by Washington to assess the current situation. But what made him really prick up his ears was that all the rumours abounding of the British Government meeting with Sinn Fein here were being pronounced by the politicians as fact.

Paul Heaney was listening carefully. This was no random choice of guests, Neil realized, but an informal meeting to explore the initial stages of a momentous deal.

'Washington is very keen to assist in any way it can, of course, especially if the talks are progressing that well,' was the Americans' diplomatic proposal. 'Not only that, but if a cease-fire – a permanent cease-fire that is – can be agreed, we are ready to guarantee substantial investment in Northern Ireland.'

'It would need clever orchestrating. We'd have to get everyone around a table, not just government and trade officials, we'd need assurances from the IRA as well. Which would mean both Sinn Fein and the Army Council being represented. But if we could pull it off . . . what a coup!' Heaney enthused.

It was the following morning when all the house guests were strolling back from early Mass in the exquisite private chapel belonging to the estate, that McAuley surprised him. A wintry sun was etching long black shadows across the frosted lawns and a low mist hovered, shimmering with the opalescence of dragonfly wings, above the milky lake. It was a morning of such ethereal beauty that the worshippers coming out of the darkness of the chapel drifted back spellbound, in silence.

Eilish was clinging dreamily to Neil's arm; even Michael for once was hushed by the spirituality of the setting. As they approached the house, McAuley caught up with them. He drew Neil to one side and with a jestful wave of his hand shooshed Eilish away, telling her to walk ahead with Michael, he needed to talk to Jackie alone.

Eilish, not amused, strode off burning with curiosity and anxiety, terrified at what she saw as a growing involvement between her father and Jackie O'Connell.

'I've been watching the two of you this weekend,' McAuley began, his noble head raised like an old wolf sniffing the air, his hands linked behind his back. 'And I tell you, I haven't seen my girl so relaxed and happy in a long while. I've a great deal to thank you for, son. You've brought my daughter back into the bosom of her family and my grandson to where he belongs, where he can learn the traditions of his heritage, his birthright. I love my daughter, you know, Jackie. I gave her the best; school, college, university – she had it all. But on the way I lost her. She had her own views and I respected them but since her mother died . . .

'She won't listen to me, Jackie, doesn't want to know. Has she said anything to you about leaving?'

The question caught Neil off guard. 'I don't think she's thinking of anything except Michael walking again,' he answered diplomatically.

McAuley understood and laughed. 'Oh, she's right to trust you, son. You're a good man, Jackie. But I want you to explain to her, I need her to understand, she belongs with her own people. Maybe you'll succeed where I failed.' He walked on deep in thought, then shaking his head continued, 'All this talk of peace going on. There's a lot will happen between the talking and the doing. The British Government has to know this time we mean it. We have to create such fire, we'll have them begging for peace. And that won't be done round a table. The Loyalists won't take this lying down either. There'll be war, Jackie – precious blood spilt before there's peace. You make Eilish understand that, now. I want her and my grandson with me where they can be safe.'

The words he spoke chilled Neil. For all the reasoning charm of last night, McAuley spoke with the rhetoric of a fanatic; for him his uncompromising dogmatic belief in the glory of the Cause was paramount, the sacrifice of human life and suffering but a stepping stone to its achievement.

'There's something else I want you to do for me, Jackie.' The big man put his arm around Neil's shoulders in fatherly fashion. 'Before long I have to go away for a few days – me and the boys. I want you to take care of Eilish and the child, look after them for me.'

Neil's pulse quickened. 'Fine,' he said, hardly daring to speak.

'There's not many I can trust, and none Eilish would. I need you to keep them safe while I'm away.' And McAuley squeezed his shoulders.

'When will that be, then?' Neil asked casually.

'St Stephen's Day.'

'St Steph . . . When's that?'

The Irishman glanced at him curiously. 'You've been too long away, Jackie O'Connell. They call it Boxing Day across the water. St Stephen's Day, the twenty-sixth.'

''Course. I haven't heard it called that in a long time.'

It was a bad mistake and he knew it. 'Shall I tell Eilish or will you?' Neil forced himself to continue the friendly tone but McAuley's arm had dropped from his shoulder and when he next glanced at him, there was a glint of cunning in the fierce dark eyes.

'You, I think, but take your time,' he said enigmatically. 'A lot of things can happen . . .'

'I hate to see you two getting too close,' Eilish said passionately when Neil returned. 'Are you sure that's all you talked about, me leaving the house?'

'He worries a great deal over you, Eilish, you and

162

Michael. That last incident really shook him. He's nervous you'll want to go back to Craiglea.'

Eilish stared confrontationally at him, her chin tilted at the stubborn angle he now knew so well. 'He's a very convincing man, my father, he knows how to charm and manipulate people. He's a man used to getting his own way. I hate to see him drawing you in, confiding in you, getting you involved. I'm terrified you might join them, Jackie, because if you did – I'd never want to see you again!'

'There's no danger of that, Eilish. That I can promise you. I never want to do anything that will stop me from seeing you again.' If only she knew how he meant it, he thought, as he held her close and kissed her.

CHAPTER THIRTEEN

'Interesting, interesting,' was Randall's comment when John Neil relayed his report of the weekend. 'We've had evidence for some time that the IRA have a sophisticated route for laundering terrorist money from Northern Ireland through the stock market. This just confirms it. We also know they've joined up with organized crime both here and in America. Intriguing they mentioned the contact in Spain.'

'You know of him?' Neil enquired.

'Mmm, could be. Our American cousins have informed us of a big fraud case they're investigating involving a bogus bank issuing fake letters of credit, bank drafts, etc. Seems they've uncovered evidence that the fraud is linked to a huge fund-raising exercise by the IRA. Your man in Spain could be at the centre of it. Intriguing! But that's not crucial for your investigation, Neil.

'What it does mean, however, is that the arms deal is about to be finalized. Sinead will sign the bill at an account set up by your friendly bank manager some-where in Europe and Hogan will dispatch the arms cargo. But from where, by what means of transport and to which destination? That's what we have to find out.

'The meeting on Boxing Day has to be the big one. You have to be there.'

'I've been requisitioned to look after Eilish and the boy, but I'll be there, wherever "there" is. "Shimna" on the twenty-sixth must surely be the location. Any more ideas on that?'

'Drawn a complete blank, I'm afraid. Unless—' Randall paused. 'Unless it refers to the name of a ship? The date the arms cargo sails?'

'Or arrives?'

'We'll check all shipping sailing in the Far East in the next few months. Worth a try. We'll be in touch. I may need to contact you urgently. I'll use the name Brian. If I have to leave a message, call me back immediately.'

'And if I need *you* urgently?'

'This line will be open for your calls twenty-four hours a day.'

The traditional huge Christmas tree was in position in front of Belfast City Hall. John Neil, sitting at a window table in the tea-room opposite, did not want to think about Christmas. It brought too many painful memories of the past and too many forbidding prospects for the future. Preoccupied with such thoughts he didn't even notice Eilish striding along, her coat flying, until she was there, her face pressed comically against the outside glass, blocking his view.

She pushed her way through the crowded tea-room, apologizing for her lateness with a radiant smile. He didn't need to ask her news, everything about her shone. He stalled, letting her savour the telling.

'Coffee, tea?' he asked deliberately.

'Nothing thanks. Jackie, it's great news!'

'Tell me.'

'They're taking off the plaster.'

'For good?'

'They hope so. The grafts have taken, knitted together really well . . .'

'So he can walk?'

'He'll have to take it slowly. Start all over, but yes.'

'Fantastic!' He reached for her hand. 'What a Christmas present. Just, don't get too . . .'

'I know, I know. The doctors have already warned me not to be too eager. I know it's going to take time but who cares? He's going to walk again, that's what matters.'

She pushed back the chair restlessly, animatedly she tugged at his arm. 'Let's get out of here. I'm too excited to sit.'

Outside they joined the crowds listening to the carol-singers grouped around the Christmas tree.

John Neil drew her away. 'Eilish, I've news for you, too.' His voice was unintentionally harsh.

She looked at him, anticipating the worst. Deliberately he lightened the tone.

'Your father. He's going away. He's asked me to look after you and Michael.'

'When?'

'St Stephen's Day.' Neil took her shoulders, gently turned her to face him and looked enquiringly into her stormy eyes. 'Do you mind?' he said tenderly.

'It's not that – I love being with you, Jackie. So does Michael,' she added hastily. 'It's just . . . I don't like my father using you. This is his way of tying you close, getting you involved. You don't know him.'

Neil shook his head, bemused. 'Then if that's what he's doing, I'm all for it. The more closely involved with you I am, the better.'

'I'm serious, Jackie. I meant what I said. You get involved and we're finished.'

'Hey, hey. Look at me, Eilish. I meant what I said. Trust me!'

She smiled up at him a little tremulously. He kissed her reassuringly and hugged her to him.

'You're an amazing woman, Eilish. I sometimes wonder, after all you've been through, all the hurt. James, was it? Sean, Michael. Do you never feel the need for revenge? Do you never want to lash out for all the pain—'

'And add to the killing?'

'But don't you hate those—'

'I hate anyone who uses guns and bombs to get what they want. The paramilitaries and the Brits.'

For a moment they stared at each other. Eilish broke away. 'Oh come on, Jackie, let's not talk about it. I don't even want to think about these things. I just want to talk about Michael.'

She walked determinedly ahead, her hand linked to his pulling him along. Suddenly she turned and started walking backwards, smiling back at him with an exaggerated grin, urging him to 'lighten up', to smile back . . .

'You know what I'm going to do soon as Michael can walk? I'm going to take him back to Shimna. We'll walk in the Mournes, we'll go swimming in the Annalong and we'll go riding again. Oh, he used to love—'

'Where did you say?' Neil interrupted, his heart pounding.

'The Annalong? It's the river . . .'

'No, the other name?'

'Shimna? That's the house I told you about, remember? Our summer house, in the Mournes.'

'I didn't realize you still had it.'

'Oh yes. We used it a lot when Chris was alive. It belonged to my mother's family, did I tell you? When she died she left it to me. Her wedding present, her way of making up.' Eilish fell into step beside Neil. 'Daddy wouldn't let her come to the wedding, you know – in fact, soon as he knew of my relationship with Chris he forbade her to see me, to have anything to do with me, Chris being a Proddy, of course! I think it was the only time in her life my Mammy went against him. We used to meet in secret at my auntie's house. One time, when

Daddy was away, she came to the Mournes, with Chris, me and Michael. She loved Shimna!'

Neil barely listened, his mind was racing. 'So you don't use it now?'

'Shimna? No, not since Chris died. I hadn't the heart, you know.'

'But your family still use it?'

'Never, no!' she said adamantly. 'It's mine now.'

'So why don't we go?' He struggled to keep his voice normal.

'To Shimna? You mean it? You, me and Michael? Oh Jackie, that would be fantastic! But when?'

'Well, summer's a long way off, and as we're together anyway, how about Christmas?'

Eilish, her eyes shining, squeezed his arm. 'Oh God in heaven, Michael will be over the moon. But what about Fergal? Is he not expecting you?'

'Can you imagine, Fergal and me sitting with funny hats on, pulling crackers? Besides, it's his busiest time, remember?'

'Of course. Oh Jackie, it'll be wonderful! We'll take a turkey and a Christmas tree, light a big fire. Oh, I can't wait!'

Eilish was still planning, as John Neil drove along the Falls Road to drop her off at the Centre.

'Stop a minute,' she cried out suddenly. 'That's Kevin's sister. She looks upset.' She threw the door open even before the van had come to a halt and jumped out in time to catch the young girl, who flew into her arms, crying hysterically.

'It's our Kevin, Miss. You have to come. Now! They're out to get him this time. Please, Miss!'

'Calm down, Bernadette. Tell me quietly. Where's Kevin now?'

'At home with Mammy. She's real upset . . . they're goin' to kill 'im this time. She said you had to come.'

168

Eilish glanced across at John Neil.

'Get in, I'll take you.' He helped the sobbing child into the van, easing her between himself and Eilish in the front, then drove off at speed. The girl was terrified and confused. All they learned was that the men had warned them Kevin had to be gone before nightfall.

The mother was barely more coherent but in between screaming abuse at the silent youth, who was slouched defiantly in his chair, and hysterical weeping, she managed to convey that the punishment squad had issued the final ultimatum. She had no idea why and Kevin refused to explain.

While Eilish strove to calm the mother, Neil helped the youth into the kitchen. Kevin, still bandaged and incapacitated by his recent encounter with Provo 'justice', stared sullenly and silently at the floor.

'What's it all about then, Kevin? You'd better tell me. There's no way you're going to get out of here without my help and unless you do get out, there's no way you can fight back.'

'You won't like it,' the boy sneered unrepentantly. 'I saw him – him with the limp, trying to make my brother sell drugs. He'd tried it before. Tried to blackmail him. Threatened him they'd kneecap me again if he didn't do what they wanted. I warned him then, that bastard! I told him I'd tell the police if he tried it again. I warned him!' The tears were starting in his eyes, he looked suddenly very vulnerable.

'So what happened?' Neil asked.

'There's a new lot of drugs about. I don't know what they are, but I caught him this morning with our Seamus. He's only a kid. Eleven, for Christ's sake! What does he know? I told the police there and then. There was a patrol. The bastard must have seen me . . .'

'Who?'

'The dealer. The man with the limp.'

'Did the police get him?'

He shrugged hopelessly. 'The phone call came dinner time. They told our Mam I was a tout. I had till midnight to get out. I don't care, I'd do it again, so I would too!' He spoke with all the arrogance of righteous youth but his clenched fists trembled at the prospect of the consequences.

'That took a great deal of courage, Kevin,' Neil said admiringly, putting his arm about the boy's shoulders. 'Your Mam's frightened now, but one day, she'll be proud of you for that. However, there's no glory in waiting here to die. You have to get out, build a new life. That's the best way you can help your family now. I'll talk to your Mam, you talk to Eilish.'

'Thanks, Jackie.' The youth held out his hand gratefully. Neil shook it, man to man.

When Eilish came out with Kevin there was a new determination in his bearing. His mother noticed it. She too had calmed down. She'd packed his few belongings in a bag, resolutely dried her tears and now stood by to watch her eldest son leave the family home for ever. She'd listened to Jackie but not really understood; all she knew was she was losing her son. Life had beaten her again.

The light was fading, there were no watchers, no friends to cheer him on his way, only his mother and sister saw him go.

He looked back once. They turned the corner.

'You haven't told me where we're going,' Neil reminded Eilish.

'There's a house, a contact. She'll take over from there.'

She directed John Neil to the Antrim Road, to a place he knew; the hotel where he'd first stayed, the night of his arrival. Eilish had phoned ahead. The owner was waiting. She stood as John Neil had first seen her, an imposing figure in a crisp white shirt, peering over glasses slipped halfway down her nose.

'You again?' And she looked at Jackie with that same humorous mock severity. 'A bad boy again?'

Eilish looked shocked. 'Close your mouth, Eilish dear. It doesn't become you looking like that,' the woman said.

'But . . .' Eilish stuttered.

John Neil, enjoying her confusion, introduced Kevin. 'This is your guest for tonight. I'm just the delivery man this time.'

'That's a pity, Jackie O', I enjoyed your company. Is there something the matter, Eilish dear? You're very quiet for you. Is Michael all right?' The woman was suddenly concerned.

'He's fine, Auntie Annie.' Now it was Neil's turn to be surprised. 'But how do you know Jackie?' Eilish pursued.

'Sure he stayed with me once, isn't that obvious? You were here, in fact, the night before Sean's funeral. Jackie O' was a guest.'

'But you never take guests.'

'If they're as good-looking as this one I do. A good man is hard to find, haven't I told you that, Eilish? And this one is not only a good-looking fella, he has beautiful arms. Did you not notice the strength of them?' She laughed wickedly. 'Now, young man, Kevin is it? Let's find you a room and something to eat. The bastard bullies been up to their kneecapping games again, I see. What is it now? The hanging judge calling, I suppose? They have a lot of misery to answer for, those bastards! My brother's one and I know. Don't you worry, my darlin', we'll have you out of here safe, you see. Now hold on to me, we'll take it slowly.'

She looked back from the stairs. 'Off you go, you two, I've got a lot of organizing to do for this young man.

But call round again, I enjoy a good crack. And Jackie O' – you take care of my girl now. She's very special, very precious to me. Don't you do anything to hurt her now, or you'll have me to answer to!'

As they left Neil heard her continue, guiding Kevin up the stairs, 'Now, young fella, you'll stay with me until you're fit and your legs are strong. You'll be safe with me. My brother knows better than to let his bully boys come sniffing round here. Then when you're ready we'll get you across, set you up with a job. A new life. You'll see, things will be good.'

John Neil sensed the atmosphere as soon as he walked into the house. McAuley met him at the door and with a quick glance upstairs, where Eilish was saying good-night to Michael, led Neil into the study, closing the door quietly behind him with exaggerated care.

'I need to call on your help again, Jackie.' He pointed to the chair for Neil to sit down, at the same time pouring him a tot of Black Bush from the bottle already waiting in anticipation of his arrival.

'I hear you're joining us for Christmas.'

Neil looked surprised. 'I didn't realize . . .'

'I would be at Shimna? No. Well now, the fact is, I had no idea Eilish would be going there either and I've made other arrangements which she doesn't know about and which she must not know about or there'll be all hell to pay. This is where I need your help. I've a few friends arriving Christmas night for dinner. Eilish doesn't know them. She thinks they're just old family friends. They're a bit more than that. They're there for a special business meeting, a bit like the last one, set to begin the morning of St Stephen's Day.'

'I see, so that's why . . .?' Neil said with a grimace of complicity.

172

'Exactly! I have to have Eilish and Michael away from there first thing that morning. Make any excuse you can but get them away. I'd hate Eilish to think you're in any way involved. If she knew or guessed that you'd helped us out . . .' The sentence was left hanging but the sinister implications were clear.

'You also have to understand the full extent of the confidence I'm placing in you and that if you ever mention these people or anything about this meeting to a living soul, your life is forfeit. And not only will I not be able to do anything about it, I will be the first to sign your death warrant!'

Impulsively John Neil held out his hand. McAuley for a split second was thrown – then with grave faces the two men squared up to each other and shook hands on the pledge.

Eilish was furious. She stormed into the study, even further enraged to find Neil sitting there, drinking with her father.

Her Irish temper was in full flow, Neil allowed her complete range. By the time he guided her down Victoria Street into the Crown bar, her anger was subsiding. But it had been an impressive display and Neil told her so. She laughed.

'Now,' he said as they toasted each other, 'can we talk about it reasonably? I believe it was Michael who insisted your father came?'

'So he says!'

'Even so, whether you like it or not, Eilish, there is a special bond between them. Michael loves his grandfather and it's not so surprising they both want the family to be together for Christmas Day.'

'I know, I know, but it's him taking over I hate, asking

173

along all his friends. Besides, I wanted us to be together, on our own.'

'Then let's go down a day early?'

'Christmas Eve? Oh, that's a great idea!'

'Except . . . Your father. What'll he say?'

'Who's to tell him?' Eilish smiled wickedly, leaned over and kissed Neil long and lingeringly. It was a kiss full of promise.

'This is most probably the last time I'll be able to contact you,' Neil informed Randall. 'Things are moving fast. McAuley has been forced to take me into his confidence – why, doesn't matter. I'll tell you later.

'So the brief is this: the meeting is set for Boxing Day, the twenty-sixth, possibly set to last two or three days. The location is Shimna. Shimna is a house near the Annalong River, in the Mournes, County Down. Could be in the name McAuley or Eilish's married name, Byrne.'

'And you'll be there?'

'Of course. The main players' ETA Christmas Day evening, that is the night of December twenty-fifth, ready for the meeting proper on the twenty-sixth. Whatever happens I'll be looking for transport on the twenty-sixth or twenty-seventh, probably at short notice. I'll let you know. So for Christ's sake don't let me down.'

Slowly Randall replaced the receiver.

'You didn't tell him?' an incredulous voice asked.

Randall said nothing.

'Don't you think you should at least have warned him?' Gault's worried face glared at his boss's bowed shoulders. Randall straightened resolutely and turned to confront the questioner.

'He's too close – why risk unnerving him? A few more days and the operation will be over. Besides, what would I tell him? Something's made McAuley suspicious? He's initiated further investigations into O'Connell's background?'

'It's gone further than that,' Gault sparked back hotly. 'Hogan's interrogated O'Connell's closest friend. God knows what he's found out!'

'A friend out in Taiwan. Believe me, if Hogan had discovered anything to merit concern, no way would McAuley allow Neil anywhere near those players or that meeting.'

'Unless it's a ruse, so McAuley doesn't let him out of his sight?'

'For what purpose? The only way there could be a problem is if the friend confronts Neil personally and as far as I can see there's little danger of that. If you're that worried, have the man held in some way until this is all over.'

'I've tried. He's disappeared. So has Hogan. Our contact lost track of them both.'

'This operation is too important to be aborted on a premise, Gault,' Randall barked decisively. 'Hogan is no doubt on his way to dispatch the arms shipment; obviously we don't know from where. Hopefully Neil will find out from the meeting. The "friend" could have gone anywhere. It's all too . . . nebulous. No, until you have something more positive to report, we do and say nothing that will distract Neil from concentrating on this mission.'

Randall grunted irritably, sat down bolt upright at his desk and swung round in his revolving chair, presenting his ramrod back to Gault's accusing face.

Had John Neil been forewarned, he might have been

more apprehensive when he overheard McAuley authorizing the travel arrangements for someone he referred to as 'the close friend'. As it was, Neil simply interpreted it as yet another euphemism for one of the dangerous power players coming in for the St Stephen's Day meeting.

CHAPTER FOURTEEN

Snow was frosting the high peaks of the Mournes as John Neil's van snaked down the tortuous mountain road leading to Shimna.

'There it is! There it is! Look, Jackie!' Michael shouted excitedly as they veered off down a rough track leading to the sturdy white house and its surrounding outbuildings hugging the fold of the hill.

'Hey Michael – this is fantastic! And is that the river I can see?'

'Don't be an eejit, Jackie!' Michael giggled. 'That's just a wee stream! We couldn't swim in that!'

Despite the hard core of uneasiness deep in his gut, John Neil could not help but be infected by the elated spirits of his two companions. All journey long they'd sung, joked, pointed out favourite landmarks, gasped at the incredible beauty of the mountains and planned their Christmas holiday as if it would go on for ever.

They pulled up in front of the rambling old farm-house, Eilish jumped out stretching wide her arms to embrace the view. She breathed deeply, drawing in the sweet mountain air.

'Oh this is my favourite place in the whole wide world,' she cried. 'Look, Michael, even the windows are twinkling. Mrs O'Leary's such an angel, will you look at the way she's got it all ready to welcome us. See, d'you see the holly wreath on the door, Jackie? Oh God in heaven, and look, just look at the pile of wood O'Leary's cut for us. There's enough for a lifetime!'

John Neil lifted an impatient Michael into his wheelchair. 'You're a real featherweight without that plaster,' Neil teased. 'We'll have to watch you don't float away. You'd better pack some food into this young fella, Eilish, or one puff of wind and he'll be gone.'

The boy, eager to share his world with his new friend, urged his mother into action. 'Come on Mammy, I want to show Jackie where we saw the baby foxes and that sheep's skull I found. Remember? There were all maggots crawling through the eyeholes, Jackie!' He wrinkled his nose and wriggled his fingers.

'Ah don't, you disgusting child,' Eilish cried, pretending horror, delighted to see her son so happy. 'Come on, let's get into the house first and unload everything. Leave the presents in the van,' she whispered to Neil.

The heavy wooden door swung open, flooding the wide stone-floored hall with pale wintry sunlight, revealing the gleam of old polished wood on the handrail of the broad sweeping stairs. Eilish sighed with pleasure then started back with a scream of terror.

A man stepped out of the shadows. In his hand was a gun. It was only when his face came into the light that they recognized him. It was Gerry Hughes.

Speechless with rage Eilish stared at him. 'Don't you dare point that gun at me,' she spat. 'What the hell do you think you're doing in my house?'

Open-mouthed, Hughes stared at them all incredulously. 'Well fuck me! What are you lot doing here?' he croaked.

'What are we doing here?' Eilish's voice rose in pitch and decibels. 'This is my house, for Christ's sake! And you are trespassing.'

'I have orders from your father to make sure the house

is safe.' Gerry Hughes twitched his shoulders and neck defiantly. 'That no one gets in that shouldn't!'

'I'm sure we'll all sleep better knowing that.' With an angry thrust she pushed him aside and stormed into the house.

'Well, as you're here, you might as well help,' John Neil said brusquely, thumping a heavy box of food at Hughes' soft stomach.

'Does the big man know you're here?' Hughes grunted with a vain attempt to regain his dignity.

'That's none of your business,' Neil snarled. 'I'd keep well out of the way if I were you.'

By the time everything had been unpacked and put away, the Christmas tree set up in a corner of the living room and Hughes dispatched to a room in one of the outlying buildings, Eilish had recovered her humour.

They spent the afternoon exploring the land and collecting holly with Michael perched on Neil's shoulders, reaching up to cut the highest bits – more often pelting Eilish with berries. Of Gerry Hughes there was no sign. No doubt McAuley, whom he must have called, would have warned him to lie low.

Michael could hardly contain his excitement as the evening drew to a close. He'd had tea an hour early, helped decorate the tree, then abandoned it, restlessly awaiting bedtime. Conspiring together, Neil and Eilish had encouraged him to sing carols, told stories round the fire, played board games, even completed a jigsaw; done anything in fact to keep him from going to bed too early, desperate to prolong the night, to avoid the inevitable dawn rising on Christmas Day morning.

Finally, laughing, they gave in.

'Now don't wake too early or the presents won't be there,' Neil warned as he carried Michael to bed.

'Put the pillow case where I can reach it!' Michael ordered. 'What time do you think Father Christmas might come?' he asked slyly, with a glance at his bedside clock. 'Six o'clock?'

'Definitely not before. Those reindeer have a lot to do just covering Belfast. They'll not pass this way until they're on the home run.'

'And if they see you awake, they won't stop by at all,' Eilish joined in.

Michael lifted the curtain for one last look through the window; he had long given up the belief in Father Christmas, but like all young children he clung to the legend for his mother's sake, and just in case.

Cocooned in the loving warmth of this little family, Neil struggled to concentrate on the job he was there to do. He left Eilish with Michael and set about marking and discovering the territory, preparing for the operation that was about to begin. He had already explored most of the house, noted the various entrances and exits, the position and contents of the outlying buildings and barns.

It was obvious from certain precautions he'd taken that whilst they'd been out, Gerry Hughes had searched through his belongings in the bedroom. He'd expected nothing less. Now Neil unlocked his van. Nothing in there had been touched. Aware that Hughes was probably watching him, he lifted out a pile of wrapped Christmas presents, locked the doors behind him and carried them back to his room. Hidden amongst the genuine presents was a box containing bugging devices, micro-transmitters in various guises from thirteen-amp twin plug adaptors to fountain pens. He had no idea in which room the meeting would take place but there was one he suspected – one he'd discovered was locked.

'What's in here? A dead body?' he asked Eilish, who was coming down the stairs.

'No, Chris's study. How odd it's locked. Or is the door jammed?' She shook the handle hard.

'No, it's locked all right.'

Eilish stared at it perplexed, then shrugged. 'Maybe it was locked when the O'Learys secured the house. The key's probably in a drawer somewhere.'

She seemed rather subdued. Playfully Neil put his arm around her waist and swung her round to kiss her under the hanging mistletoe.

'Come on now, it's grown-up time,' he said in a mock-seductive stagey voice in an effort to lighten her mood. 'Let's drink and be merry. Tell you what – you get the drinks and I'll finish young Michael's artistic tree décor.'

A log fire was blazing in the living room, reflected in the Christmas baubles still scattered across the small table near the tree. Music played softly in the background. Neil joined in, humming along while he plugged in the lights to one of his bugged adaptors and finished decorating the branches already laden with tinsel and lashings of mock snow. Pleased with the effect he stepped back, calling on Eilish to admire his work. When she didn't answer he looked round and saw her, kneeling on the rug, staring sadly into the fire.

'Hey, what's all this?' He sat down beside her and gently turned her face to his.

'Why so sad, sweetheart?' he asked tenderly.

'Sometimes it just gets to me. Seeing him lying there. He's only a little boy, it's so unfair, you know!'

'Of course. But he's one of the lucky ones, Eilish. Look how happy he's been today. At least you know he's on his way to getting better. Come on now. You've both got a lot to be thankful for.'

'Thankful!' She turned on him, her eyes flashing tearfully. 'Have you any idea what it's like to see your own child burning up in flames right in front of your eyes? How can I be thankful for that?'

181

'He could be dead,' John Neil snapped and turned away quickly before she could see the pain in his face, the grief that would never be done.

That night lying in bed, awash with moonlight, he allowed himself to remember another Christmas; Tommy and Julie. He tugged at the memories, summoning them to his consciousness, dwelling on each one. He could feel his son's arms, round and firm about his neck, the peach skin of his cheek rubbing his face, the tousled silk of his hair. And Julie. How he ached for Julie!

Suddenly he started. There was a soft knock at the door. Eilish came in.

'Are you awake, Jackie? Do you mind . . . holding me awhile?'

He pulled back the covers and she slipped in beside him. He drew her to him. For both of them, past, present, future fused into one, there was only the moment, their bodies clinging together and their love.

John Neil eased his arm from beneath Eilish's head. He could hear her soft breathing, see the slight smile that had not left her lips since she'd whispered goodnight. For a long, long time he studied her sleeping face, the flutter of her eyelids, the pulse of life at her neck. Last night he had truly loved her. Today or tomorrow he would betray her.

Silently he slid from the bed and monitoring the rhythm of her breathing dressed quickly and left the room. Swiftly he descended the stairs and by the light of a narrow beam from a miniature torch held in his mouth he picked the lock of the study door. Inside the dark was dense but he could make out the bulk of the desk and the outline of a reading lamp angled over it. He was wary of using the torch lest Hughes should spot its light from the building opposite but by running his fingers up the brass lamp-stand, he managed to position the miniature transmitter under the glass shade, up tight against the bulb.

Light blinded him, flooding the room. Then his sight cleared. He spun round and saw the gun pointed at his chest and behind it, the grinning face of Gerry Hughes with his hand still on the light switch.

'Gotcha!' he jeered triumphantly. 'I knew it! I knew I didn't like you. What are you? MI5? Police? SAS? Well you're not so fucking special now, are you?' And he swaggered towards John Neil, waving the gun, his finger toying sadistically with the trigger. It was then the phone rang. A harsh shrill blast that momentarily distracted him. It was enough for the trained killer. Two fingers knifed into the windpipe; the Irishman dropped like a stone. Neil caught him before he hit the floor, heaved the body to the centre of a rug, and gently let it fall, slumping it down without a sound.

There was the rustle of silk. Neil whirled round, gun in hand. Eilish stood there, drowsily yawning, rubbing her sleepy eyes with the backs of her hands, while a satisfied smile still played on her lips. With half-closed eyes, she drifted into the room, stretching lazily, her arms above her head. She draped them around Neil's neck with a sigh, undulating the length of her body against his, luxuriating in the aftermath of a night of love, nuzzling her lips against his.

Puzzled at his lack of response, she moved back. The cold grey glint of his eyes frightened her. He reached up and drew her arms from around his neck, standing tall and distant, dreading the moment she would see the body of Hughes, half-hidden by the desk.

'Go back to bed, Eilish,' he commanded.

Bewildered, her eyes wide, she stared at her lover

who was suddenly a stranger. 'Jackie? Jackie? What's happened? Tell me. You're frightening me.'

She looked round frantically and Neil saw the dawning horror in her eyes. Drawn to the body, she pushed Neil aside, her hands smothering her mouth, while all the time her broken voice chanted over and over, 'Oh my God! Oh my God! Oh my God!' louder and louder until she stood over the lolling head, the bulging eyes of Gerry Hughes.

Neil moved to protect her. She cringed away staring at him with abhorrence. 'Don't touch me!' she whispered hoarsely. 'Who are you? What devil are you?'

Comprehension blazed from her eyes. It was as if a light had come on.

'You're a tout! A spy! . . . What are you, SAS? Come to . . .' She backed away and flung herself at the door.

Neil lunged and caught her, holding her firmly. He drew her back. 'Eilish,' he said, 'you have to understand . . .'

She shook her head, uncomprehending, her face contorting with impossible questions. 'And me? Michael? It was all part of the job. Oh God! All part of the job. And the fire? Was *that* part of the plan?'

With fierce strength she broke away from his grip, only to hurl herself at him, pounding and punching and scratching and kicking until he felt her energy ebb and he held her close, pinioning her arms to her sides.

He could feel her whole body throbbing with deep anguished sobs, feel her struggle to suppress them, her body rigid and unforgiving in his arms.

'Whatever you may believe and whatever may happen I want you to know that loving you was not part of the plan. I did that all on my own.'

She lifted her head and stared at him with contempt. 'And loving me moved you to this,' she spat, indicating the body.

184

'I had no choice. I have a job to do, Eilish, and I intend to finish it.'

'And now I suppose you have no choice but to kill me and Michael . . .'

Tormented, Neil pushed her away. 'Don't you even want to know what it is? Don't you want to know why I'm here?'

'I don't want to know anything about you.' There was that same defiant tilt of the chin, the same blank ice-cold stare but this time it was directed at him.

Furious, he seized her wrists, holding them tight while she fought, forcing her to listen. 'Oh no Eilish, that's too easy! It must be wonderful up there in the rarefied air on the pedestal with your principles. But to make those principles happen some of us have to scrabble in the mud. This time, girl, I'm calling you into the arena.

'These so-called friends your daddy's expecting . . . you don't really think they're here to celebrate Christmas, do you? You know exactly what they're here for? It's not peace and goodwill to all men on their Christmas list, is it? *Is* it, Eilish?' he shouted. 'And when they stand round the table and pray, "For what we are about to receive," believe me it doesn't refer to Christmas dinner.'

Brutally he forced the struggling young woman to look at him. 'No! Shall I tell you what is on their list? What they are about to receive? Guns, arms, explosives, rocket launchers; everything you despise. Things that kill, Eilish! The biggest shipment of arms in the history of the IRA.

'And they've gathered together in this remote farm-house – your summer home – to plot murder and violence. To tick off names on their death list, to decide which targets to hit where they will have most effect, and to hell with the innocent people and children who will be killed and mutilated in the process. That's what

185

your daddy does, Eilish. That's his business. He lives his life planning death.

'You know it and you do nothing about it. And in my book that makes you as guilty as he is!'

'No, no . . .' She shook her head violently, tears streaming down her face. 'It's not true . . .'

'OK. So tell me, Eilish – you're the one proud-mouthing how much you hate the guns and the violence. Tell me what we should do. Walk away and say nothing? Cry and beat our chests when we read about the dead? Or do what I'm trying to do which is to stop them?'

'With more killing and murder? You're just as bad as they are.'

'And you think by doing nothing, you're not? Come on then, you're the one with all the high principles, the moral certainties. Tell me, what should we do?'

'You wouldn't understand,' she sneered contemptuously.

Wounded by her words, enraged at her contempt, Neil threw her onto the sofa. 'Is that right!' Struggling to hold on to his fury, his face ashen, Neil glared at her. Eilish was shocked at his anger; his whole body trembled with its force. She drew back, expecting at any minute his clenched fists to lash out. Instead she saw them uncurl, his body forcibly relax and when he spoke his voice was chilling in its subdued precision, awesome in its control.

'You think you are the only one that has suffered and that somehow that gives you the right to understand . . .' Neil hesitated, fighting to maintain his control.

'Let me explain my position. Today is Christmas Day. By rights I should be enjoying it with my wife and my little son. This would have been his sixth Christmas – except your father and his friends killed them both. Blew them sky high while they were watching the circus!'

Eilish, appalled, stared up at him in shock. He continued, his face expressionless.

'Tonight you told me that I could never imagine what it would be like to see my own child in flames. Well believe me, I am *consumed* with imagining it. By the time I found my son and my wife the flames had died down and they . . .' Neil was silent for a moment. 'I was too late to do anything about it then. I am not too late now, and no one – not you, not Gerry Hughes, not anyone – is going to stop me this time. You can join me or not as you wish.'

'What do you intend doing?' Eilish said faintly.

'I intend to stop that shipment ever getting into the hands of these people. I intend to report back to my superiors every scrap of information I can gather that will enable them to intercept that shipment and those responsible for it.'

'And what would happen to them? What would happen to my father and brothers? The same as him?' And she pointed at the body.

'Those are not my orders. I am here to get information.'

A halo of light was streaking the Mournes, time was running out. The undercover man looked at his watch. 'Well, Eilish, what are you going to do?'

'Do I have a choice?'

'You do. I don't. You could try and stop me. You could do what you normally do – turn your back and say nothing. Or help me.'

'And you could kill me. After all it is your job.'

John Neil did not respond. It seemed an eternity but finally she said, 'There is no choice. I'll help you.'

Relieved, he reached out to her. She held up her hands to shield him off. 'Don't, Jackie . . .' She broke off. 'I suppose that isn't even your name?' Dejectedly she shook her head. 'I know nothing about you, do I? And now . . . there's no point.'

'When it's all over . . .' Neil said.

'No! There's one thing – please, Michael's suffered enough. Please don't hurt Michael!'

John Neil flinched. 'You didn't have to say that.' With a bitter smile he turned away.

The body of Gerry Hughes prompted him to action. Quickly he pulled the rug over the corpse, enveloping it in its folds, then with a huge effort heaved the dead weight up and onto his shoulders in a fireman's lift. Without a backward glance he left the room and the house and crossed the yard to the barn where he hid the body deep within the stacks of hay he'd already noted on a previous reconnaissance.

What he did not see was the twitch of the curtain at an upstairs window, where Michael, who'd awoken to discover his pillow case was full, hearing a noise outside, was looking out, hoping for a final glimpse of a disappearing Father Christmas.

Even when Neil left the room Eilish did not move. She felt utterly exhausted. All she wanted was to sleep, for the nightmare to end.

Michael's call pierced her consciousness.

'Mammy, Mammy, come and see. Father Christmas has been!'

CHAPTER FIFTEEN

At Larne Ferry, Colum McAuley searched through the tide of disembarking passengers and waved to the three people he was there to meet, two men and a woman, all in their early thirties. 'We'll be driving direct to Shimna,' he informed them as they shook hands. 'The others are coming in through Dublin – they'll be on the road now.' He looked round. 'Where's the other fella, the close friend? We thought he was coming across with you.'

'He was,' one of the men answered with a shrug, 'but we got the message – he'd missed his flight. He'll be in later now – he'll need someone to meet him at Aldergrove.'

John Neil was ready. He stood at the window of his room, mentally checking every detail in preparation for his mission. Every micro-transmitter was in place; he'd checked his covert equipment was operating. From his examination of the study, it was apparent that McAuley had been using the property as a safe house for meetings: a pile of magazines and old newspapers, tidied up by Mrs O'Leary, gave away the dates and a used book of matches carried the name of a restaurant in Dublin which Eilish had never heard of, let alone could explain.

This revelation that her house had been used as a base to plan death roused in her such abhorrence that the fury she had directed at Neil paled in comparison to the disgust with which she now viewed her father. Neil felt her torment but could do nothing about it. It did not alleviate the cold distance between them or reassure him as to how she would act when the time came.

From his position at the window, he could see the mountain road and the track snaking down to the farmhouse. He checked his watch for the hundredth time. Too early yet for anyone to arrive. He could hear Eilish and Michael in the living room below. For Michael's sake, they had agreed to make the day as normal as possible. With one last look around the room, he picked up his bag and carried it down to the van.

Eilish, piling fir cones and logs on the fire, heard him. Her heart was thumping wildly, she felt physically sick with apprehension. If anyone looked in now, she thought, it would all seem so normal. They'd see a little boy sitting at the table playing with his toys, a mother dreaming before the fire, the lights, the Christmas tree with a mountain of presents beneath it.

There was a sudden gasp behind her. 'Mammy, Mammy . . . look, I'm walking!'

She turned round. Michael, unaided, was stepping tentatively towards a chair. He grasped the arm and collapsed over it, laughing.

'I did it, Mammy. I walked! I forgot I couldn't. I just got up like always and walked! Jackie,' he called out as Neil entered the room, 'did you see? I just walked. Watch. Watch me!' Gingerly he pushed himself away from the chair and on unsteady legs aimed for the table. Both adults, equally excited, hovered ready to catch him. They caught him just as he tumbled, their faces close together, hugging him and each other in the joy of the moment, their differences momentarily forgotten.

'That's wonderful, Michael,' Neil encouraged. 'The

physio said you could do it. All you needed was confidence.'

'Oh darling . . . Oh Michael!' Tears streamed down Eilish's face as she beamed at Michael.

'Don't cry, Mammy. Look, I'm going to do it again. Stand over there ready to catch me, Jackie.'

Thrilled at Michael's achievement, Neil held out his arms, but when he looked back to share the excitement with Eilish, her eyes were only for Michael.

Liam McAuley was ready. The operation that had taken months in the planning was now in its final stages. The old excitement was still there, the blood still fiery in the veins, the resolve to free the Six Counties as strong. Only the body had weakened, only old age had robbed him of the ability to act.

Impatiently his huge hand tapped the top of the telephone, ready to pounce as soon as it rang. He checked his watch; Colum should be on the road by now. The thought caused his frown to deepen. That friend of O'Connell's would be with them. They'd confront Jackie with him . . . then they'd know!

He couldn't believe he'd been taken in. Deceived by Jackie. He'd really liked the fella – trusted him with his daughter, for God's sake. Besides, Fergal would never lie and he was convinced Jackie was his brother. This so-called 'friend' was probably just after the free trip home. But how could someone forget St Stephen's Day? No matter how long you've been away? And what was it the friend had told Hogan? Jackie O'Connell was an inveterate gambler. Couldn't hold a job to save his life. That didn't tie in at all with the man he knew as O'Connell.

The phone rang, making him jump.

'Yes,' he said irritably.

'We're on our way.' Colum's voice crackled over the car phone.

'No problems?' he shouted back. 'Everyone through safely?'

'All except the "friend". He missed his flight.'

'What do you mean, missed his flight? Oh, never mind, tell me when you see me.' He slammed down the phone. 'Brendan!' he shouted. 'Get the car. I'm ready. I'll just call Eilish, tell her we're on our way.'

Michael was improving with every step. Encouraged by Neil and Eilish, he was practising walking from one to the other when the phone rang. Eilish froze. John Neil smiled coolly and caught Michael in his arms.

'You'd better answer it, Eilish,' he said quietly, as he lifted Michael onto the sofa.

'Hello,' she said hesitantly. 'Oh, hello Daddy.' She glanced at Neil. 'Yes it's me, Eilish. We came up yesterday . . .'

Neil held his stance, listening intently.

'Yes, Gerry Hughes was here.' She turned her back. Neil waited. 'I told him to go away. To come back tomorrow. We didn't need him here. We were safe enough with Jackie.' Her voice broke tremulously, but she went on, 'No, I'm fine, it's just . . . There's great news. Michael's started walking again . . . Just this morning. You'll see when you get here.' Slowly she put the phone down and smiled brightly at her son.

'Grandaddy can't wait to see you. He's on his way.' But her glance at Neil was one of resentful complicity. The painful betrayal had begun.

Neil was following the stream down the hillside with the boy on his shoulders, making his way back to the farmhouse when he heard the whirl of a helicopter over-head. It was an Army Puma, surveilling the area.

'I hope they're not thinking of dropping in for Christmas dinner, eh Michael? I'm starving, aren't you? I swear to God I can smell the turkey from here.'

The chopper veered away just as Colum's car turned off the mountain road and started down the track.

'Come on. Let's race it to the house. Hold on tight now, Michael!'

With much whooping and hollering, the two of them galloped down to meet the car as it turned into the yard and the visitors clambered out. John Neil noted the gleam of suspicion in the hard looks they shot his way before the social masks snapped into place and they waved and responded cheerily to Michael's exuberant calls of 'Happy Christmas!'

'Can I help? Carry anything?' Neil offered.

'We don't need your help!' Colum's response and its terse delivery was almost abusive. There was a new aggression in his manner. Colum was always the affable one; something had changed that! Neil felt distinctly uneasy.

He led the way into the house. Ignoring him, Colum pushed himself to the fore, assumed the role of host and authoritatively directed the guests to their rooms.

'Colum!' Eilish came into the hall. 'Don't you think, as it's my house, I should do that?'

'Daddy told me to organize the sleeping,' he answered rudely, flustered at the reprimand.

'Fine. Then I'll get on with the cooking.' Eilish, with quiet dignity, retired into the kitchen.

If Neil had suspected Eilish might have called for help in his absence this filial display of one-upmanship now convinced him she had not.

But Liam and Brendan's arrival did nothing to assuage his apprehension that something was wrong. Liam was as ebullient as ever, Brendan as arrogant and aggressive but there was an added watchfulness in both of them. Frequently he caught them scrutinizing him as if he were a stranger and when he spoke, which now he rarely did, they listened with more than careful attention. Over the weeks, Neil had become used to Liam's tactile manner, the familiar way he called him 'son'; now the big man kept his distance. John Neil's intuition warned him his time was running out.

The last guests drew up, just as they were opening Christmas presents around the tree. Brendan went out to meet them, to escort them to their rooms while the family sat around enjoying Michael's excitement as he unwrapped his gifts one after another. Now that everyone was together, Liam seemed to relax, or maybe the wine was beginning to have an effect. Colum too, enjoying the conviviality of the occasion, had resumed his easy-going manner. Only Eilish was tense and though she smiled and joined in the laughter, when the new visitors came in Neil noticed her fingers twitching nervously and the anger in her eyes at the familiar way they walked into the room. There were four of them, three men and a girl all in their late twenties, or early thirties. From the way they helped themselves to drinks and found glasses, it was obvious they'd been to the house before.

Liam, the genial host, was handing out the last few presents, those for the adult members of the family together with token gifts for the guests. All the presents from John Neil Eilish had kept to one side, unopened. Liam spotted them.

'You're not unwrapping your presents, Eilish! Come on now, join in the fun!'

'I like watching Michael open his,' she said as an excuse.

'Well I like seeing your face when you open yours,'

Liam answered craftily. It was as if she'd woken up to the game they were all playing. She opened the packages and for the first time that day, she smiled warmly at John Neil. The smallest box she reserved for after dinner.

'Which will be burnt if I don't move,' she said brightly and rushed out to the kitchen.

When Neil walked in a few minutes later, her cheeks were streaked where she'd been crying. In her hand was the brooch he'd given her that she'd admired one evening when they'd been walking together in the centre of Belfast.

'It seems like another lifetime,' she murmured, seeing his reflection in the window, standing behind her. 'I can't believe this is happening. I want to be back in that other life, Jackie . . . whoever you are.'

'We can't go back. But we can have another life, Eilish! Just stay strong a little longer.'

He wanted desperately to hold her but as if she read his thoughts, she whispered, 'Don't touch me or I swear to God, I'll not have the courage . . . I'll collapse.'

There were voices, people coming into the kitchen to help. The two of them made a show of serving dinner.

Liam, the grand patriarch at the feast, sat at the head of the table with his two sons, his daughter Eilish facing him, accompanied by Neil and Michael with the guests ranged on either side of the long refectory table.

Liam was in an expansive mood, a mood which grew more buoyant as the evening progressed. Highlights of colour glowed on his cheeks, the big lantern jaw cracked with a permanent smile. His good humour embraced all at his table; even John Neil seemed back in favour!

For her son's sake, Eilish made a pretence of joining in the merry-making but Neil noticed she deliberately made herself busy or confined her attentions to Michael.

Like all of them, John Neil's speech was starting to slur. But Neil had actually drunk very little and his trained eye had observed a great deal. There was a buzz about these people that had little to do with the wine, he reflected. Alcohol had merely released their suppressed jubilation at what was to come. This was the feast before the fight and in all of them the rush of blood and the fire of pre-battle nerves lit up the zealous passion in their eyes.

'Remember these faces,' Gault had warned. 'These are the major players. These are the ones we want.'

Neil had identified them all, mentally had matched person to picture, checked eye and hair colour, height and weight. The girl drinking wine had planted the bomb that killed four. The man strumming the guitar had mortar-bombed a barracks. That one had shot dead a father in front of his children, and so on. Murder, bombing, killing; they'd done it all. And now they were singing, in soft sentimental fashion, their voices rising sweetly, harmonizing the words of 'Silent Night'.

He felt a tug at his arm. Eilish smiled over to where Michael was curled in an armchair sound asleep. They left the room together, Neil carrying the child who even in the depths of slumber had curled his arm lovingly around his friend's neck. This simple act of trust ripped like a bullet through Neil's gut. Let him not hate me too soon, John Neil, the agnostic, prayed.

At the bedroom window, Neil savoured the tender scene as Eilish brushed back the hair from her son's face, tucked his arm beneath the covers and gently kissed him good-night. Tonight of all nights – it tore him apart. Neil turned away quickly, stared out of the window and concentrated his mind on the action ahead.

Eilish stole across to join him. They stood side by side in silence. Both knew there was no reaching out and no going back.

Finally Neil spoke, 'Do you know who those people are?'

Eilish shrugged. 'A couple of them were at my school. I knew their names, nothing more. The one man, I know, Terry—'

'Oh yes, he massacred two British soldiers, did you know that? Savaged them like hounds with a cornered fox.'

'They said they were spies.'

'They were still human beings — someone's child, someone's father. Listen to them. Hypocrites!' The last refrain was dying away: ' "Sleep in heavenly peace, sleep in heavenly peace."

'What will they do if . . . when peace comes? You saw them tonight, they're high just thinking about all the death and destruction, the havoc they're about to create. It's in their blood, like a drug driving them on. They've known nothing else but violence. Do you think they'll be happy in a mundane world, living as postmen or office workers, whatever?'

'You tell me, what's the difference between your life and theirs?'

'I'm not driven by hatred and fanatical idealism – they are. Listen!'

Songs of peace had given way to war. Downstairs the carousing had begun, the rebel songs, the old stories of dead heroes, the avenging legends of battles and insurrections – the constant reliving of Ireland's past.

'What will happen to all that hatred when there's peace?' Neil asked, knowing there was no answer.

He moved to the door and for a while stood there looking back at her. As John Neil, the man, the lover, he wanted to tell and ask her so much . . .

The night was black, the cloud-base low, sky and hills

congealed as one dark mass. Without being seen he left the house and secured himself inside his van. With luck they would think he was with Eilish. The singing was still going on. He winced as he fitted his earpiece. His micro-transmitter was working well. He made himself comfortable and prepared for a long night. He guessed from the clink of glass on glass that the rounds of spirits were slipping down well. He knew the meeting proper was set for the next day – what he hoped to catch was a comment or reference to himself. Despite the easing of the atmosphere, he was in no doubt that something had happened to arouse their suspicions but what it was baffled him. It surely wasn't just the St Stephen's Day slip. This was something new, something that had happened in the last few days, but whatever it was, it had not been confirmed or they would have shot him without hesitation by now.

The singing was beginning to fade, signalling that the evening was coming to a close. Liam McAuley's voice rose above the rest.

'We've a long day ahead; I suggest we get some sleep but before we do, I've some exciting news to give you. But I suggest we move to the study, we won't be disturbed in there.'

'Where's O'Connell?' Brendan demanded harshly.

'He went up with Eilish. Must have gone to bed.' Colum sniggered drunkenly.

'Enough of that!' his father snapped. 'When's this fella arriving? I'll be glad when this business is over. If O'Connell's not who he says he is, I want rid of him fast. Otherwise I want you leaving him and Eilish alone!'

'O'Shea's picking him up first thing. We'll know by noon, one way or the other. Hogan says this friend's been close to O'Connell for years.'

'Where's he coming from?'

'He's . . .' Neil fidgeted with the earpiece but the

answer was lost in the general hubbub as they moved from one room to the other. By the time they'd settled in the study, the topic was exhausted and Neil was no wiser. All he had now was a deadline, a witness coming in to blow his cover, unless somehow the man could be stopped.

From the expectant hush, Liam was about to speak.

'I thought before we all retire we should prepare ourselves for what lies ahead. Tonight has been a night for celebrating not just Christmas but the fulfilment of our plans. We've all worked hard and suffered some set-backs this year; the loss of that arms shipment from Iran for a start. And funds, as you know, are getting harder and harder to come by. Many of our sources have dried up and we've all had to use our imaginations to find alternative methods, sometimes in ways we don't like. But we've swallowed our finer feelings and done it for the greater glory of the Cause!

'And it has been worth it when I tell you the MV *Magdeburg* left Taiwan a few days ago – and set sail from Tripoli at 09.00 hours this morning, fully laden with some of the best weaponry money can buy.'

McAuley paused to allow the gasps and murmurs of approval to die down before he continued. 'With a fair wind and a following breeze, she should pass through the Straits tomorrow morning, some time around noon, and on to a rendezvous off St Nazaire, where two of our boys are waiting to greet her. Where it all goes after that is up to us. And that's what we are here to plan over the next few days. Therefore, ladies and gentlemen, our New Year offensive is not only on, but set to go with a bigger bang than ever!'

There was applause and cheers of approval which the Big Man sought to calm. 'Save that for the end of the meeting,' he instructed. 'We'll have even more to cheer about then. Now to bed, all of you, tomorrow is a hard day.'

At his watch in the van, Neil remained on alert. He heard the scrape of feet as people left the room and the soft murmur of voices fading as they climbed the stairs. Then McAuley very close, at the desk perhaps, warning them to go quietly, not to wake the boy, and his voice instructing Colum to turn out the light. Neil held his breath, there was an insistent scratching in his ear, as Colum's fingers fumbling for the switch almost dislodged the transmitter hidden there.

Then silence. Wrapped in thought, Neil removed his earpiece only to be startled by the sound of the front door opening and someone breathing heavily in the cold night air. He'd been so absorbed in the transmission he hadn't noticed a coil of wire hanging behind his head. He moved slightly, knocked against it and heard it clink against the side of the van, only once but in the stillness of the night, it sounded as loud as a rifle crack.

'What's that?' It was McAuley. 'Over by the van.'

'I didn't hear anything.' Colum yawned.

Neil froze. Heavy footsteps approached and stopped outside. He could hear McAuley breathing, listening. There was a light tap. 'Jackie?' his voice called softly, 'you in there?'

Colum moaned impatiently. 'Come on, Daddy. Let's get to bed. He's not in there! It was just a mouse, or something. He's with Eilish, I told you.'

There was a pause. The footsteps retreated, the farmhouse door slammed shut and there was silence.

For a long time John Neil sat unmoving. His mind made up, he looked through the window, checked outside carefully, then made ready the covert transmitter and prepared for contact.

Randall must have been sleeping nearby. He

answered, his tone scratchy with irritation, alarmed at the unscheduled call.

'Good God, what time's this? Is it an emergency?'

'I'd hardly call to wish you Happy Christmas. Get ready. Take this down.'

Fully awake, Randall barked, 'Ready.'

Neil began with the list of names.

Randall grunted at every one. 'Go on,' was his only remark when Neil had finished.

'The arms shipment on the MV *Magdeburg*, repeat, MV *Magdeburg*, departed Tripoli, Libya, repeat Tripoli, Libya, 09.00 hours, 09.00, Christmas morning, December twenty-fifth. Expected through the Straits of Gibraltar, noon today.

'There is a rendezvous arranged somewhere off the coast of St Nazaire. I don't know when exactly, late evening some time, I should think, you'll have to work out the ETA yourself.'

'Excellent! We'll make sure we're there to meet them.'

'You'd better. This may be all the information I can get.'

'There's a problem?'

'I think my cover's about to be blown. They're bringing someone in. Someone who knew O'Connell well.'

'Mmm, yes, we'd heard about that. We thought they might.'

Neil was shocked. 'You mean you knew and you didn't tell me?'

'I didn't think it necessary.'

'Jesus Christ!'

'There's been a change of plan. With all the main players assembled under one roof for the conference, we decided to safeguard our option . . .'

'As against me? Written me off, I suppose. Already shot dead in a ditch as a spy.'

'Pay attention, Neil!' But Randall was uncomfortable, Neil could tell.

'A combined air and land assault will move in on Shimna House at 08.00 hours this morning. That way we get both information and players and you, of course, out. There's a piece of high ground, north-east of the barn, hidden from view of the house. We'll look for you there. Be in position 08.00 hours precisely.'

Neil was icy with fury. 'And if I hadn't contacted you? Not necessary to tell me this either, I suppose?'

'Be there, 08.00 hours precisely.'

'Not so fast, Boss. What about Eilish and her son?'

'What about them?'

'I promised her there'd be no killing.'

'If they all come quietly there won't be.'

'But Eilish is innocent. She has no part in what's going on. She's done nothing but help me. I want her and her son protected,' Neil demanded, 'I want them brought out with me.'

'Don't be a fool, Neil. You know that's impossible. I'll make sure they're looked after, don't worry.'

'I want them out, Randall. With me!'

There was a long, tense silence, then Randall's voice, silky and slippery as an eel, said, 'Very well. Be in position 08.00 precisely.'

'I'll be in a blue jogging suit, don't miss me.' The line went dead.

John Neil had no idea if Eilish would come with him, all he knew was he had to try.

It was already six in the morning; he had only two hours in which to organize his evacuation. Quickly he changed into the jogging suit and with meticulous precision began preparations for his departure. Any incriminating electronic evidence he broke into innocuous parts; some he left in his tool box, other components he stuffed inside his suit and under cover of darkness carried them away up on the hill, where he buried them along with his covert equipment deep in convenient rabbit holes. If anything should go wrong, he did not want to be discovered with high-tech espionage equipment in his possession.

By the time he had jogged back and marked out the high ground behind the barn, his watch showed 07.40 precisely.

Inside his study, McAuley and his two sons were already preparing the day's agenda. They looked up at a tap on the door. Colum opened it. Michael stood there, a big grin on his face while Eilish, in the background with his wheelchair, looked on proudly.

'I walked downstairs on my own, Grandad!' he yelled excitedly. 'Mammy only had to help me a bit.'

The big man held out his arms but in his rush to impress, Michael slipped and fell, a hard fall. With a cry Eilish rushed to him.

'Where's the carpet out of this room?' McAuley shouted angrily, looking round.

'It wasn't there last night,' Colum said.

'It's all right, Grandad, Jackie took it.' Michael smiled, trying to appease his grandfather's quick temper, his mother's anxiety.

Eilish paled. 'Don't tell stories, Michael,' she said sharply.

'But he did, Mammy! I saw him carry it to the barn . . .'

'Oh Michael, how could you? That's a silly thing to say. It's not . . . it's not true . . .' she faltered.

McAuley didn't wait. 'Go and look, Colum,' he ordered.

'I'll go.' Eilish started for the door.

Her father stopped her. 'No! I said Colum. Colum and Brendan will go.'

Deliberately he closed the door behind the two men.

Eilish was trapped. 'Now Michael, let's see you walk again,' he said slyly.

After such a late night, Neil was surprised to find the house already stirring. He entered at the back and was about to go into the hall, when he saw Colum and Brendan leaving by the front. He waited for the door to close, then swiftly mounted the stairs to Michael's room. Time was running out fast but he knew if he gave Eilish the chance to think, she'd never agree to come with him. He stopped in surprise: the door was open and the room empty. He dashed downstairs. Her voice was coming from the study. He knocked and walked in. He could tell immediately something was wrong. Brashly, he bluffed on, swooping Michael into his arms.

'I thought you and I were set for a jog this morning, young Michael. Come on now, I thought we'd do five miles at least!' Neil said cheerily.

Eilish caught his arm. 'We should be off, Jackie. Let Daddy get on with his meeting.' He noticed her hand was trembling.

McAuley stepped between them and the door. 'No hurry. Your brothers will want to say goodbye,' he said.

'You go, Jackie.' Eilish was nudging him. 'Get ready. Go on! I'll wait for them.' There was an insistent ring to Eilish's words. He sensed she was warning him.

'We'll go together,' Neil said. 'Get Michael's things to the van, then come back to say goodbye.'

Before Neil could reach the door it opened and Colum and Brendan pushed their way in carrying the rug between them, forcing Neil back into the room. Swiftly he set down Michael with Eilish. She gasped at his flinty look of accusation, shaking her head in denial. Already the rug was unrolling. Neil stepped forward, shielding mother and son from the corpse of Gerry Hughes as it sprawled across the floor.

When they looked up, Brendan's gun was pointing at Neil's head.

'No! No!' Eilish screamed out and leapt at her brother.

That split second's distraction was enough. Neil moved, his elbow cracked McAuley's chest, his forearm chopped Colum's throat and he was through the door.

There was a roaring, a dust storm blowing and the helicopter rose up from behind the barn. Neil darted towards it. Bullets traced his flight, shells spat at his feet. Neil cut back, zig-zagging wildly. From every window of the house gunfire tracked his path. A bullet ripped past, he felt its heat. He flung himself behind the wood-pile. The vast expanse of the yard was now between him and the helicopter, hovering out of range, north-east of the house.

The Provos had him trapped.

He could hear McAuley at the door, bawling out orders, demanding his execution, no matter what, positioning his men for the kill. Suddenly, there was a volley of answering fire. Troops appeared out of nowhere, shooting hard, swarming towards the house.

'Jackie!' The scream rent the air. He poked his head out. Eilish had broken away from her father and was running wildly, trapped in the exchange of gunfire. Neil leapt out, sprinted across the erupting yard, grabbed her hand and pulled her along in headlong flight, dodging the bullets which even now were chasing him, forcing him away from the safety of the barn. Suddenly the helicopter reared up in front of him, the pick-up harness whistled across his path. He lunged at it and missed. Screaming at Eilish to stay with him he let go her hand and this time caught the swinging line. With one move, he attached it and turned for Eilish, but she was backing away, shaking her head.

'Come with me! Come on, Eilish!'

The chopper was beginning to rise. He looked up, signalling frantically. 'Wait! Eilish . . .' He stretched his hand towards her, urging her to reach out, willing her to take hold. She stood there, shaking her head, tears flowing down her cheeks.

'Mammy! Mammy!' The piercing scream rose on the air. Michael was stumbling from the house. Eilish and Neil looked back, they saw Michael, they saw him grab at his grandfather. And they saw McAuley, with his rifle aimed at John Neil, press the trigger. There was the blossom of fire.

John Neil knew what would happen – in that split second – time, the world, the noise, the commotion stopped. And Eilish fell . . . her body shattered by the bullet that was meant for him.

'*No!*' The bellow reverberated around the hills. Helplessly he clung to the line; the helicopter wheeled him away.

Chapter Sixteen

He was sitting in the dark corner of a small bar, on the Rue de Richelieu, nursing a glass of red wine, his third if he was counting, when he remembered . . . It had been a few years ago, Tommy had just been born, life couldn't have been better. He'd called round to see an old army pal, back from Belfast, a dedicated soldier, great sportsman, good-looking bloke . . . almost unrecognizable after stepping on a booby trap that had cost him his legs, one arm and almost, his life. John Neil had been shocked: 'You must be so bitter,' he'd said. Now he remembered his friend's answer. 'Oh, no!' he'd said. 'Bitterness eats you alive. That way the bastards win twice.'

John Neil looked up. An attractive girl had walked in; she joined an older man who'd been there for some time, chatting to the barman. As she lifted her face to be kissed, she glanced at Neil with interest. He looked away.

He'd kept himself together all through the debriefing solely in the belief that the job was done and at the end of it all, he'd be back in Scotland. Randall would have none of it. 'Now is not the time to bury yourself, Neil! Too many loose ends still to be resolved. Too many loose cannons! The operation's at a different level now. You have to follow it through. There's been a lot of interest in the information you've been feeding back. It's tied in with several investigations in progress at the moment, both here and in the States. There's been a specific request for your continued services and cooperation. It means handing you over to another controller but I think you'll get on. Rendezvous, twelve noon. Bar Juveniles, Rue de Richelieu, Paris. Lucky man . . . Try the Cornas. I had a very good bottle of '82 last time I was there.'

John Neil checked his watch, two minutes past noon. 'Fast. Your watch is fast,' a voice said, and an elegant woman in her forties, dressed in a well-cut black suit, slid into the seat opposite him.

Neil smiled. 'Well, well! I think a continental greeting would be in order, don't you? Especially between old friends.'

He reached across and kissed her on both cheeks.

'Colleagues,' she demurred, without affectation. 'I wasn't sure you'd remember me.'

'How could I forget, top trainee in the "Killing House"? You put most of us men to shame.'

'Balls,' she said coolly.

'What are you now? Colonel?'

'We don't use rank where I am now. But we do drink.' She turned the bottle label to face her. 'Ah, the Cornas? Randall recommend it?' she said, her eyebrow raised knowingly as she called for a glass.

She poured herself some wine, swirled it in the glass, enjoyed the bouquet and slurped it appreciatively in true wine-lover's ritual before she continued. 'What else did he tell you?'

'That the food here was good, and they did great tapas!'

'Business first,' she said briskly. 'What do you know about the Hogans?'

'Declan and Sinead Hogan? Apart from brief encounters with both, not a great deal. Randall left it for you to fill me in.'

'Let me give you a broad picture. First and most important, think of them as twins, not in age, but in character and outlook. Mentally and emotionally, each is the exact counterpart of the other. They are also both fervent left-wing radicals, devoted to the cause of international terrorism. They are fanatical Republicans but they see their ambitions of becoming major players in the IRA as mere stepping stones to their roles on the world stage. They are extremely intelligent, well above normal IQ, calculating, ruthless, have no scruples, no integrity, or moral codes . . . and they will use anything, any means, and anyone to get what they want.

'They have deliberately set their lives on two courses, Hogan the criminal course, Sinead the legit. Hogan has become high profile in the world of organized crime while Sinead has risen in the world of big business, finance and the City . . . Now they appear to be drawing the two sides together.

'Just how effective this collusion can be, you've already witnessed in the funding of this latest arms shipment, which thanks to your efforts we managed to intercept. However, for the Hogans this is but a minor set-back, their sights are already set far higher, and there are all too many regimes all too eager to fire, feed and take advantage of their ambitions, notably Iran.

'Iran, in its fanatical drive against American imperialism, is determined to make Europe pay a heavy price for supporting American policies in the Middle East. To this end they have befriended some of the most secret and feared terrorist organizations in the world, from the Japanese Red Army to the Hezbollah. Recently, a meeting was held in Tehran with leaders from each group. The sole agenda was the formation of an international terrorist movement; the objective unprecedented devastation in western European capitals – coordinated bombings and assassinations culminating in revolution in Europe.'

'And of course the IRA were represented,' Neil jumped in.

'By the Hogans, amongst others. Courted and seduced by the offer of state-of-the-art arms and funds. The IRA have been looking for a new supplier for a long time.'

'But why now? Iran's had close relations with the Rah for at least ten years, they even sent over a diplomat to attend Bobby Sands' funeral,' Neil said, frowning intently. 'Then that madman, Ghaffari. The "machine gun mullah", I think they called him?'

'The one who promised to blow up British factories and ships along with Mrs Thatcher?' The Controller raised an eyebrow. 'Oh yes, Sinn Fein have visited Tehran on a number of occasions as well as welcoming Iranians to their Dublin conference three years running; all in the name of politics.' She slipped an olive into her mouth and chewed reflectively, then continued, 'It also marked the beginning of terrorist contacts between the IRA and Tehran. We've monitored various negotiations for arms and cash, even supplies of drugs to generate funds, but it is this terrorist summit that is of most significance.' She spat out the stone into her clenched fist, frowning intently as she talked.

'Look at it in the light of what is happening today,' she said. 'For the first time, the different factions in Ireland are talking, albeit tentatively. If the peace initiative is seized and if it works, the main revolutionary vehicle in Britain comes to a halt. Iran daren't be seen to be conducting terrorism against Britain or Europe in its own name, or there would be war; it needs front men. What better than known terrorist organizations already in the field of operation?'

'So it's in Iran's interests to keep the Rah out there and active? And supplied with more devastating weaponry,' Neil said, appalled at the thought.

'Exactly, especially when there are hardliners like the Hogans all too willing to cooperate. But the Hogans are far too clever to be the puppets in the hands of one master. They intend to be world players but first they know they need to build, strengthen and finance their own army. To this end we believe they intend to take over from the moderates on the IRA Army Council and install themselves at its head. Sinead, we suspect, has been manipulating a certain financial house, Cottrells, in the City. It's a merchant bank, she's a partner there. We're convinced she's been compromising them with deals such as the recent one at Dundalk, in preparation for a far bigger operation set up by Hogan with his contacts in organized crime. We also know Hogan has made connections with the Triad and the Russian Mafia who have God knows what to sell; even plutonium is creeping onto the black market.

'Add to all this an ex-KGB agent with secrets to sell who the Hogans have been seen visiting, plus the murder of a Military Intelligence officer, Major Bob Turner, not only expert in Middle East affairs but just back from three years in the Gulf . . .'

'Seems like things are on the move,' Neil said.

'And I am thirsty. Another one?' She indicated the bottle.

'Why not,' said Neil with approval. 'When in France . . . Actually, why am I in France?'

'Not for R and R, I'm afraid. No, matter of fact, the KGB man is here!'

'Shit, that means the Hogans too, I suppose?'

'They've left. And without the secret information. The price too high, perhaps? But they could be back. We need you to go in, find out what he has to offer. Old KGB secrets don't have much value. It must be some-thing special for the price he's asking.'

Petrov, ex-KGB, was finishing a game of chess. He was a man in his sixties; once heavily built, his muscle had

211

wasted, his face become shadowed and haggard not just by age; there were signs of illness about him. Neil followed him from the bar and fell into step beside him. The man's pace did not falter.

'April in Paris, mmm?' The voice was extraordinarily deep.

'I prefer August. You get the place to yourself.'

He led Neil to a well-appointed building in the Rue Ranelagh, behind the Trocadero. The flat was large, comfortable, book lined, more the apartment of an academic than a KGB agent.

'I expected one of these young, straight-out-of-school, razor-brained, intellectual types,' he murmured, looking sideways at Neil with a glint of humour as he poured them both a shot of vodka.

'As against a trooper from the trenches?' Neil, declining to sit down, prowled about the room. It was meticulously ordered and neat. He pulled out a book on the history of the USSR and smiled at what were obviously angry, scribbled annotations in the margins, then snapped the book closed and replaced it.

'Glad it's all over?' he asked the Russian.

'Of course. Now the real, the true Communism can begin!' Petrov scrutinized the replaced book and with precision adjusted its position, raised his glass and threw back the vodka. 'This time we will get it right,' he said.

'But not with the information you wish to sell?'

The Russian shrugged. 'I need the money. My heart. I need triple bypass surgery. It is very expensive. I am not ready to die just yet.' He smiled casually and poured them both more vodka.

'Thirty-five thousand pounds is very expensive information,' Neil hedged.

'Compared to what?' Beneath beetling brows, the

chess player studied Neil with amused patience, already anticipating his next move.

'Since the Wall has come down, so has the going rate for information. There's a glut on the market,' Neil responded spiritedly.

The Russian shrugged nonchalantly and threw open his hands. Neil, not to be outplayed, strolled equally casually about the room, nodding with approval at pictures, the record collection and more books. Much as he warmed to Petrov, he suspected the man was bluffing.

'KGB secrets when the KGB no longer exists are hardly worth the keeping, let alone the buying. I think my boss will need a little more convincing before parting with that much money,' he said.

'The KGB guarded many secrets, not only its own. For you this could be a bargain.' Petrov splashed two more vodkas into the glasses. 'For me it is my life.' He threw back the spirit. 'But there are others,' he added with the hint of a tease.

'Maybe to exorcize the pain of the expense,' the Englishman parried, 'you should titillate the appetite with a little aperitif?'

'A free introductory offer?' The Russian bellowed with laughter, amused at Neil's audacity. 'Very well,' he conceded, 'what do the names Annie Shepherd or William Roper mean to you?'

Neil searched his brain. 'Nothing. Were they, are they agents?'

'You want more than the aperitif, you want the main course.'

'One more drop?'

The Russian smiled indulgently. 'They both went to Sussex University,' he said.

'Is that it?'

The Russian laughed. 'It is enough. You go to work,

Englishman. But first, now the Wall is down we will drink, compare our lonely lives in the field and tell each other stories . . .'

Controller Jane Black stood with her back to her office window with its magnificent views of the Thames and Westminster and frowned over the report in her hand, which was disappointingly short on information.

'Not much to go on here.' She began to read out loud for Neil's benefit, abbreviating as she went. 'Annie Shepherd, single, fortyish, civil servant by day, Department of the Environment. Language teacher three evenings a week, Adult Ed. Centre, German conversation. William Roper, married, no kids, fortyish, successful . . . own company, computer software, et cetera, international market, et cetera. No criminal records, no misdemeanours, in fact fairly ordinary, middle-class lives, seemingly no connection between them whatsoever, at least not since university. Both were quite active left-wingers in those days, but then everyone at Sussex was – is. It has a reputation for breeding young radicals.' She sat down at her desk and pushed the paper across to Neil.

'I suppose Petrov could be bluffing?' she quizzed.

'I did think so at first, but the more we talked the less sure I became. Besides, why would the Hogans be so interested?'

'Did he refer to them by name?'

'No, no, just as "others" but he did let slip they could be back. Even so, thirty-five thousand, cash? Takes some raising, even dirty money.'

'But Sinead does work at Cottrells Bank. And we all know how honest banks can be. Especially bona fide, old establishments, making up their third-world losses.' She raised a cynical eyebrow.

Preoccupied, Neil smiled briefly in response. 'Tell me

more about Major Bob Turner. I've looked through the details but apart from the fact that he was shot through the head at close range – while sitting in his car by the side of a run-down private airfield – the Military Intelligence report is not particularly forthcoming. Any more news on why he was murdered?' he asked intently.

'None. He was Military Intelligence, undercover – back after a three-year stint in the Gulf. And, usual form, after debriefing, while the experience was fresh, the Army were using him to instruct the next lot. His papers were in order . . .' She shrugged helplessly.

'You say he specialized in humint?' Neil pursued.

'Human Intelligence, please! I hate these American-isms,' she said pedantically. 'He worked undercover in Iraq, although Iran is the one to worry about.'

'Is it possible he knew more about Iran than he admit-ted in his reports? Learned something about the IRA involvement, perhaps?'

The controller shrugged. 'He was having an affair with a woman on his course, Liz Baker. Very bright, fluent Arabic, high career potential. She's obviously upset by his death but for all our questioning, we've drawn a complete blank. The Court of Inquiry did no better. Despite specializing in the same field, she swears he told her absolutely nothing about his work over there.'

John Neil pushed back his chair and stood up. 'Well, Boss,' he said with a grin, 'this has all been most enlightening. All I seem to have are addresses; I guess I'd better pay a visit all round.'

Knowing Major Turner's flat had already been searched by the Military Police, John Neil began his own system-atic investigation, looking for any information that could throw light on the Intelligence man's murder or link him to the terrorist plot being hatched by the Hogans.

Everything in the apartment was in meticulous order. A close examination of files, books, video and audio tapes, behind pictures, the personal computer, revealed nothing. Frustrated, Neil moved into the kitchen; he was examining the cards and notes pinned to a noticeboard when he heard the front door being tried. Swiftly he raced for the bedroom. Someone was in the flat. He peered through the door crack expecting to see Turner's girlfriend; instead he saw a man of medium build and height, in his early thirties. From the shifty way he looked and the stealth with which he moved, Neil guessed he was not there on legitimate business and was also no amateur.

Anticipating the man's movements, Neil tracked him as he searched the flat, in the same methodical, painstaking way as himself. The man stopped only to stare for a long time at the photograph of Bob Turner and his girlfriend, Liz Baker, taken in some Mediterranean resort. The sound of the lift rising startled them both. Swiftly, the intruder glanced round the room and left, almost immediately followed by Neil, who glimpsed the top of the man's head disappearing down the stairs. Neil leapt for the stairs leading up, just as the lift doors opened and Liz appeared, her ears plugged into her Walkman. Neil, realizing her hearing would be impaired, slipped past her while she wrestled with her key, raced down the stairs and out into the street just as his quarry jumped into a car, an Audi, parked at the end of the street. Neil's car was immediately opposite. He ducked low below his windscreen as the intruder roared past and noted his number plate. He followed at a distance, weaving around the London traffic, disguising his movements from the quarry who, Neil noticed, regularly checked in his mirror. They were in the City when the Audi suddenly swung into a private underground car park, heavily guarded by security gates and cameras. As

Neil drove past he gave a low whistle. The car park was for occupants of the office building whose nameplate in discreet lettering read 'Cottrells Merchant Bank'.

'Interesting,' Neil muttered to himself as he punched in his scrambler code on his cellnet radio transmitter.

'Interesting,' repeated his controller.

'I'll need to get in there. Find someone who can fill me in on City-speak.' He laughed at the annoyed 'humph' at the Americanism.

'The place is guarded like Colditz. I'll need a job of some description, something that'll allow me to move in and out, no questions asked. And find out what you can about that young hood in the Audi. "Hood" is a Belfast expression, by the way,' he teased, but the memories were suddenly too fresh and the pain too raw. He changed the subject quickly.

'I'm on my way to follow up on Petrov's names, Annie Shepherd and William Roper. See if I can learn anything from them. From the way things are shaping up, I think we should respond to Petrov fairly swiftly.'

His meeting with 'Bill' Roper produced nothing new. A smartly dressed businessman in his forties, he was obviously considered a leading expert in his field. Neil, purporting to be in the market for a big order of software, was surprised at the man's dismissive response. It certainly was not the aggressive attitude he'd have expected of a man who in ten years had built up a multimillion-pound international company. There was no edge to the man, no spirit, no hard sell – in what was after all a highly competitive field. It was as if he'd completely lost interest in his business. He did admit, however, that much of his dealing was now with the Eastern bloc.

Annie Shepherd was slim, dark, attractive, brisk and

business-like. She gave him a timetable, agreed his German was rusty, handed him an enrolment form and said she'd see him in class.

'Roper's a disillusioned man. Something's really bugging him. Annie Shepherd is locked up tight in her own brick walls, they'll take some knocking down. If anyone's going to break it will be Bill Roper,' Neil reported to Control, as he stood at her office window and watched a barge making its way downriver. 'I need time to work on them. What I don't want to do is lose Petrov. I've a strong hunch he's got more than just his memoirs for sale. Any more news on the Hogans? Declan? Sinead?'

'No, but we've tracked down your "hood",' Jane Black said gravely. 'Name's Jason Sturden, age thirty-one, Scot and ex-Commando.'

'That figures,' Neil commented.

'Employed at Cottrells for the last eight years as a chauffeur. That's all we know but we do have a contact who will fill you in on the City – Rose Herbert, a great source of information. You'll like her. I've booked you a cosy dinner for two. Don't plan on anything for afterwards – it will be a heavy night!'

In a City suit, John Neil followed a throng of baying yuppies down into the cavernous wine bar. He decided it must be the hours spent on the Stock Exchange floor that made them speak several decibels above normal, it certainly wasn't that their conversation merited attention. Wads in the wallet, broke in the brain, Neil decided.

Rose Herbert was a big lady with a personality to match. 'Hello, luvvie,' she beamed. Her eyes, two shining crescents, peeped over the mounds of her cheeks. 'What a treat! I don't often have a handsome man for dinner. I'm into the voddies but I ordered a couple of bottles of red to start with. You can have white if you prefer. I drink anything,' she guffawed. 'I'm also famished. Food here's pretty naff, but steaks're good. Shall we order?'

'Val!' she bellowed. A waitress responded, took the order and disappeared.

Rose was a mine of information, an institution in the City and a cornerstone of Cottrells. 'Chauffeur, gopher, rodent, rat!' was her dismissive opinion of Jason Sturden, ex-Commando. 'But his boss, Rylans, doesn't move without him.'

Brendan Rylans she spoke of in terms bordering on reverence. A senior partner at Cottrells, he had brought in hundreds of millions to the firm, navigating it skilfully through the recession by changing tack and initiating introductions in new markets, notably the now accessible Eastern bloc. He was a rare spirit in the City, she added.

'A rare spirit who needs a rat like Jason Sturden to do his dirty work perhaps?' Neil suggested.

'Luvvie, who knows?' Rose shrugged her massive shoulders and held out her empty wine glass for Neil to refill. 'Ninety per cent of deals would have to be clean, the rest . . .' she wiggled her hand expressively.

'If Sturden was doing something illegal would his boss, Rylans, know about it?'

She thought hard. 'Indisputably . . . I think,' she said with a wry smile, then brightened visibly at the arrival of two enormous T-bone steaks overflowing the outsize plates. 'And another bottle of red, Val, there's a good girl!'

Neil nodded in agreement. He was holding back on the wine, trying to keep a clear head. 'Sinead Hogan,' he began. 'What connection does she have with Cottrells Bank?'

Rose thumped down her knife and fork with a look of disgust. 'Oh God, don't put me off my food, luvvie! The "ginger rock" I call her. Hard as they come, sharp as a four-sided razor. I should know, I trained her. Before I knew it she'd slept, kicked and knifed her way up the ladder out of here into a top job on Wall Street.'

'She's back now, I understand?'

'Too bloody right! Turned up as a junior partner over a year ago. Had boss Rylans in her knickers before he knew it, poor bloke. Talk about sexual harassment. He might be clever with the business figures but with hers stuck in his face he didn't stand a chance. He's been walking around like a lost soul for months. All over now, though.' She winked knowingly and forked in an enormous mouthful of steak. 'Had a terrific row, in the office. Couldn't help but overhear,' she said innocently, her cheeks bulging.

'What about?'

'Money, by the sound of it. I heard him telling her she was asking too much. That he'd had enough. She stormed out, packed her bags and left. He was in a foul mood all day.'

'Gone for good?'

'Oh God no, luvvie, no. Off on business somewhere – Paris I think – out of the office a couple of weeks. No, no, Cottrells couldn't afford to lose her, too good at the job. Turns over a fortune. Got the golden touch,' Rose muttered begrudgingly, 'just like Rylans. Amazing! While everyone else struggled in the recession those two made a mint.'

'Interesting,' Neil said intently, relieved that the threat of bumping into Sinead Hogan had been removed. 'Now, about a job. Any chance of getting me in?'

'Oh absolutely, luvvie. Not with Rylans himself. He's got Sturden. Unlike most of the other banks, Cottrells still uses messengers for business they don't want to put through the computers.'

'The dirty ten per cent?'

'Could be,' Rose Herbert guffawed.

Neil arrived back at his rented flat in Bayswater to find

an urgent message to call Control. Someone had tried to run down Major Turner's girlfriend, she informed him. The girl was unharmed but frightened. It was possibly a warning – more likely not. Someone obviously believed Liz Baker knew more about Turner than she was admitting, someone who saw her as a threat. Liz still claimed she knew nothing. Police and military protection had been instituted, both at her flat and to and from her training course.

Neil reflected silently for a moment. 'Major Turner was shot in the head, right? That's odd. Why not do the same to the girl? Hit-and-runs are messy.'

'As I said, it could have been a warning,' Jane Black reiterated.

'Unlikely – if it merited murdering Major Turner, it must still be dangerous enough to merit killing the girl. More likely it was a different hit man using another method.'

'Whoever or whatever, maybe Petrov has the key. I suggest you fly to Paris tomorrow, contact Petrov. Make a deal.'

CHAPTER SEVENTEEN

John Neil was at headquarters early. Jane Black, together with a clerk from accounts, handed over the money. Neil signed the documents, picked up the briefcase and was at Heathrow in time for the first flight to Paris.

Petrov had advised him of his routine. At this time of day he would be home, at that time off for his walk, in another hour or so at the bar for his ongoing game of chess, a little lunch, back to his apartment, a little sleep.

'No need to call,' he'd said. 'Come when we have a deal. The vodka will be iced and ready, trooper from the trenches.'

John Neil climbed the stairs, surprised at the pleasure he felt at the prospect of seeing Petrov again. He'd enjoyed the old Russian's company. He knocked on the apartment door. At this time, Petrov should be reading the morning papers, keeping up with the world news. Neil smiled to himself and knocked again but this time he noticed the fine scratches around the lock.

He dreaded what he would find: he knew what he would find. The lock was easy to pick. He guessed from the fact that the safety chain was intact that it had not been attached, that Petrov had been out and the intruders had waited for him.

They'd left him propped in a chair, his eyes still open, a bottle of vodka by his side. Neil guessed he'd suffered a massive heart attack but the deeply scored red welts around his wrists and the bruising on his neck and jaw told Neil why. Petrov had struggled hard, been overpowered and tied in a chair, his hands tightly bound behind him while they pistol-whipped him for his secrets. Gently Neil closed the old Russian's eyes.

The room was tidy. Meticulously ordered – it was not. The book Petrov had positioned so carefully was now upside down and on a different shelf, the systematically arranged tapes and records were no longer in alphabetical order, but the very fact that the intruders had taken time to put the room to rights indicated to Neil that they were pleased with a job well done. Frustrated, their anger would have driven them to abandon the place in chaos.

He left quietly. Today or the next day, the concierge, someone, would notice the chess player was gone.

On the street, Neil took time to look round. It would have taken more than the two Hogans to overpower such a big man, there had to be others involved. Someone must have seen them go in. There was no way a British agent could investigate or be involved, he'd have to wait for the French police report. It was then he caught sight of a video camera monitoring traffic, mounted on the building opposite.

Back at Control he threw the briefcase on Jane Black's desk and slumped in a chair.

'So – the Hogans are out of the picture?' he asked, picking up the threads of the conversation they'd been having via his transmitter on the way back from Heathrow.

'Well, neither of them was in Paris, let's put it that way. Sinead flew into Dublin and Declan Hogan was in The Hague. We even had a picture taken specially for you.'

Neil picked it up with interest. The face of the Irish

boy was almost as he remembered from their youthful adventures in the Lake District. The years had scored their marks, of course; deep lines now cleaved his face from nose to chin and the once-sharp jawline was blurred with flesh but the hair was still dark, the complexion pale. It was the eyes that had really changed, tired, dull eyes, narrowed with suspicion, underhung with sagging skin and dark circles that spoke of sleepless nights, too much booze, too much excess of everything.

'Where was this taken?' Neil peered at the print.

'An apartment building in The Hague, home of an Iranian diplomat attached to the Iranian Ministry of Information. Hogan visited him last night.'

Neil dropped the print despondently. 'So who got at Petrov? If we could get our hands on that video film . . .'

'Done! A copy will be winging its way, soon as possible. If there is anything on it, anyone, we'll have blown-up copies made and sent to Archives for identity.'

'Good.' Neil stood up and pushed back his chair. 'Meanwhile, whoever they are and whatever they've got, Petrov's two names, Bill Roper and Annie Shepherd, will be on their list. I think I'd better call on those two again. How's Liz Baker, by the way?'

'Shaken but not stirred. Her instructors couldn't speak more highly of her and I must say I found her quite impressive. I don't think she knows anything of Turner's activities or work.'

Neil grimaced doubtfully. 'Two people in the same business,' he puzzled, 'knowledgeable old master and eager beaver young student, in the sack together night after night. And you're telling me he didn't try to impress her? Not one scrap of information? One itsy bitsy tiny secret? She's lying!' And with that he left the room.

Roper he met for a drink – called him at the end of the

working day and on the pretext of being in the area, arranged to meet him in the bar of a local hotel. Neil watched him walk in, noted the careful way he placed his feet, the rigid upright stance, and concluded he'd been drinking already.

The computer man ordered whisky, to add to the several already evident in his breath, and looked at Neil with morose eyes. He was at the self-pitying stage. It didn't take long for the story to spill. Neil looked concerned, sympathetic and learned all about his domestic problems. It was a common enough equation: wife drives husband on to success; success demands hours of work; successful husband equals neglected wife; neglected wife equals affair; affair equals disaster. The wife had left with the affair. Roper was the disaster. Without his wife, all his money, his business, and his success meant nothing.

He drifted through sorrow to bitterness to anger. Neil calmed him and drove him home. There Roper passed out but not before he'd proclaimed he was being punished – that he was a soul in torment and that his guilt was driving him mad. When Neil asked him to explain, Roper, with exaggerated care, put his finger to his closed lips, whispered 'Hush!' and collapsed. Neil made him comfortable on the sofa and began his search of the house. It was a big, impressive, neo-Georgian house in a country road of similar wealthy properties but it was apparent from the piled-up dishes and unmade bed that his wife had not been around for some time. Neil had not expected to find anything and he was not disappointed but instinct told him Roper was a man ripe with secrets ready to drop. Neil sensed the man's urge to talk, to confess, even, if not to himself then to someone who shared the same secret. That someone, Neil guessed, was his old university chum, Annie Shepherd. He bugged the phone, checked it was being monitored by Control and left.

Lights as always shone out across the Thames from the splendid green and cream building riding the South Bank like an old state liner at anchor. 'British Security, guarding the nation around the clock,' Neil mocked in the stiff British tones of a war-time newsreader. All it needed now was the music. He swung off Millbank and across Vauxhall Bridge.

Black was in her office impatiently waiting for him. Large blow-up prints covered her desk. 'There appear to be two of them,' she said without preamble. 'Not very clear, most of these prints. It was dark. However, I think we can see enough here' – she pointed with a manicured finger – 'and here to make some sort of stab at identity.'

Neil stared at the blurred images; two figures at the building entrance looked round furtively. One was caught full face, the other three-quarters. Both were men in their early thirties, medium height, slim, dark-haired . . . it was hard to tell. He recognized neither. He shook his head. 'Mean nothing to me.' He peered again. 'They're not Iranian, that's for sure. Could be Russian, from the new regime, sent to stop Petrov selling, or Irish, sent by the Hogans.'

'I'll get them to Archives. See if they have any luck.'

Neil started for the door, stopped and turned back. 'One thing's been puzzling me. The report on Major Turner. His flight back from the Gulf was routed Kuwait–Athens, Athens–Heathrow. I don't remember the exact dates but there's a missing three weeks in between his arrival and departure from Athens. Where was he? Do we know?'

'No. Either Military Intelligence is being very secret-ive or they don't know either. I suspect the latter.' Her face was stiff with irritation.

'And the girl?'
'Still admitting nothing.'

Neil checked into Cottrells Merchant Bank the following morning. Security was thorough but Rose Herbert had performed miracles and in no time he was directed to her office in one of the executive suites, opening off a vast central area of madly clicking computers and operators. She shared the same floor as Brendan Rylans and Sinead Hogan. Sinead's office was firmly locked. Rylans' voice carried through his half-open door clear as a bell. It was the one Neil had suspected he might hear, the one he'd overheard at the secret IRA financial meeting with Liam McAuley and Paul Heaney, that last Thanksgiving weekend in Dundalk. His memory sparked with images of Eilish – he blocked them fast.

'The name Paul Heaney mean anything to you?' he asked Rose.

''Course, luvvie, big financial family, one of the oldest established firms on Wall Street – branches everywhere. Sinead the ginger rock worked for him, in New York, of course. Still does, on the quiet.' She lowered her voice dramatically. 'I think that's why Rylans is a bit anti – doesn't like the man at all. Does business, of course, but under duress. You can see it in his face.'

'What makes you think Sinead Hogan still works for Heaney?'

Rose gestured to Neil to close her door and beckoned him to her. She shifted her huge bulk comfortably in her chair and settled into gossiping mode.

'I keep my eyes and ears open, and I work late. Well, nothing to go home for really, luvvie! It's amazing how careless people can be after lights out.' She tapped the side of her nose with her finger, leaned towards Neil and whispered confidentially, 'Believe me, she and Heaney have got quite a few deals going on, big ones too, especially in the Eastern bloc. Between you and me, I think they've put pressure on Rylans to risk a bit more over there than he likes, especially with all the unrest in Russia. I tell you, luvvie, he's under a lot of strain lately, not the man he was.'

There was a shout, followed by a shriek of girlish laughter from the computer pool.

Rose frowned. 'That'll be Jason Sturden, the rat, with another of his crude remarks. Can't understand it, the girls love him.' She sniffed primly. 'Little rodent!'

John Neil, City messenger, found his way down the emergency staircase to the car park. He hesitated before entering, peered through the glass pane set in the door and noted the static state and positions of the security cameras set at intervals around the walls. Sturden's Audi was parked in the far corner to the right. Keeping to the shadows, masked by the parked cars, Neil made his way towards it and with incredible force drove a needle-sharp bolt into the back tyre, muffling the sound of expelled air with his jacket, then swiftly, hugging the walls, he raced back.

Rose had advised him of Sturden's routine. Neil timed his first delivery accordingly. The rodent was already revving the engine when Neil appeared in the car park, wearing his official identification tab, carrying his parcel. Sturden roared out, forcing Neil to jump aside. The undercover man grinned, slid into his own car and waited for the roadhog to shriek to a halt. Sturden, humiliated and furious, leapt out and kicked at the flat tyre.

'Don't kick it,' Neil called out as he pulled alongside. 'Want a hand?'

Sturden scowled viciously, jumped back in the Audi, reversed at speed back into his space, slammed the door and stomped out, a thin envelope clasped in his hand.

Neil waited and introduced himself. 'Pat Beale, the new messenger,' he said. 'I saw you in the office. I'm off on a job. Do yours at the same time, if you want?' He smiled sunnily and clasped Sturden's hand.

Jason Sturden glowered. 'You know Mr Rylans' address?' he asked begrudgingly.

'Nah, just started, haven't I? You tell me, I'll take it.'

Sturden stared at him, then making up his mind, strode round to the passenger side. 'You drive. I'll direct . . .'

John Neil decided to impress. Deliberately, he chatted casually, his hands light on the wheel, his elbow resting on the open window, while with breathtaking audacity he manoeuvred the car through the traffic with all the skill of a rally driver steering a Formula One through a stock car race.

Sturden was in awe. 'Where'd you learn to drive like this, then?' he asked with growing interest.

'Here and there. I haven't got no record,' Neil answered cagily, playing him along, laying on the South London attitude.

Sturden nodded, a leery smile twisted his mouth. 'That right? Well you should 'ave, driving like that. Wheelman!'

'Listen, I really need this job, all right?' Neil played right into his hands.

They pulled up before an impressive house set at the end of a street of other large stockbroker-belt mansions. Before he jumped out, Sturden picked up Neil's parcel lying between them and checked the address. He looked back quickly at Neil.

'Know where this is?' he said.

'Yeah, I looked it up.'

'You could have walked there.'

'I was told to get it there quick.'

Sturden jumped out. 'Wheelman!' He grinned and walked off.

'I've scored with Sturden. I think I could be his new best mate,' he informed Black as he drove back into town. 'What are the chances of getting a look at Rylans' client list? I've a feeling he's into far more dirty dealing than we first assumed, possibly being blackmailed into it by Sinead Hogan. I'd like a look at her list too. Paul Heaney, the American financier, could also be involved. Do you have anything on him?'

There was a short silence. 'Did you get that, Boss?' he prompted.

'Yes, yes I did. I'll get on to it. There's a message just coming in from Control. Bill Roper's made the call to Annie Shepherd. They're meeting for lunch. Can you make it?'

'When and where?'

It was a country pub restaurant, up-market but quiet. Neil pulled into the car park with time to spare but Roper had beaten him to it. As Neil parked, he saw Roper walk into the restaurant and a waiter seat him at a table in the window. Neil, wary of Annie Shepherd's imminent arrival, skirted the building, plugged a minute radio transmitter to the corner of the windowsill below Roper's table, and was back in his car in time to hear the waiter taking Roper's order for Scotch. Even from afar he could make out the despondent droop to Roper's shoulders, and from the way the man downed his drink Neil guessed he was near to breaking.

Annie Shepherd parked with verve, steeled herself and marched briskly into the restaurant. Neil had the feeling she'd gone through this before, several times. He set his tape recorder.

They kissed as friends and ordered wine; food could

wait. Annie Shepherd dismissed the waiter. Evidently she'd guessed Roper's level of inebriation and decided to talk while he still made sense.

Neil settled down and prepared to wait, observing their body language from a distance. Roper bemoaned the betrayal of his wife; Annie offered advice but refused to indulge his self-pity or to be a shoulder to cry on.

Listening in the car, Neil grew restless; domestic troubles were not his line.

'You cried on mine,' Roper whined. 'When things went wrong I was there for you . . .' Neil struggled to concentrate.

'When the Irish boy stepped on the mine . . .'

Neil was suddenly listening hard.

Roper's voice was strangled with torment and guilt. 'I still see him running up the beach shouting, "Sare-sha! . . . Sare-sha!" Then boom! Up he went!'

Annie was looking round anxiously, snapping at him to stop.

'That's all I think about now she's left. The old guilt, that boy calling. Nothing to distract me, you see. Sometimes I think the only way is to go to the police and confess.'

'And spend the rest of your life in jail? Don't be a fool!'

'We all fooled ourselves then, Annie. You, me, the others. What the hell did we think we were doing? And those madmen? A real mine, for Christ's sake! – I know, I know – I should forget it. I know it's over but sometimes I worry it's going to come back to haunt us. Somehow we'll pay. Oh God.' He covered his face with his hands. 'I see that boy in my dreams, always yelling that cry, "Sare-sha". Boom!'

'You're drinking too much and getting maudlin. The only way we'll have to pay is if you talk.'

Roper seemed to get a grip on himself. 'Sorry, I don't

231

really mean it. Sometimes I have to let off steam. You're the only one . . . with you I don't have to hide anything. Listen, I'm fine now. You go, Annie, I know you're short of time. And thanks.'

Neil slid down in his seat as Annie Shepherd walked over to her car, her face clouded with concern. At the same time an urgent beeping on the transmitter returned his attention to Roper who was still at the table. He saw Roper answer his pocket phone, stiffen angrily, look quickly to where Shepherd's car was swinging out of the car park and respond abruptly.

'For Christ's sake, when did this happen? I'll be back right away!'

It was the first time Neil had witnessed the man energized. He ran to his car and away. Neil waited a beat, then followed, rewinding and playing the tape at the word that jarred his brain: 'running up the beach shouting "Sare-sha! Sare-sha!" Then boom! Up he went.'

'Sare-sha,' Neil repeated. 'Where have I heard that before?'

Keeping Roper in his sights Neil glanced in his mirror and was surprised to see a car he'd noted earlier still behind him; someone else it seemed was following Roper. Neil whipped across a red light; to a shriek of brakes and angry horns, the tail did the same. Then as if deliberately inciting him, the car drew alongside, the man stared hard at Neil, roared past, and cut in sharply across his front, forcing him to slam on the brakes, then accelerated away.

The man driving was not unlike Petrov in age and build. What intrigued Neil was the hair, close-cut in Russian military style. Neil took the bait. He guessed from the route that Roper was on his way home. He reached for his cellnet to contact Control but the emergency braking had thrown it across the car, out of reach. The high-speed chase hurtled them into narrower and narrower country lanes until Neil's quarry swung up a dead-end forest track. The man was trapped. Neil followed, but the car had vanished. Bewildered, he jumped out and looked around. Behind him the quarry's car roared into life, reversed at speed from its leafy hiding place and stopped. The escape was blocked and the man had a gun.

Neil dived for his gun, hidden in his car, but the aggressor was too sharp. Bullets spat at Neil's feet, keeping him at bay, while the gunman took out tyres, aerial and glass. Neil rolled for cover. The gunman advanced, then stopped – something had caught his eye. Two bird-watchers, petrified, stared back. The marksman aimed the gun, the men fled, but it was enough. Flattened to the ground, Neil crawled away into the undergrowth, only to hear the screaming engine of his adversary's car as he abandoned the hunt and raced away.

Roper was being carried out in a body bag when Neil reached the house. The men waited while he pulled down the zip. He blanched at the contorted face, the wide unseeing staring eyes. Roper's neck had been snapped.

Black met him, her face pinched and grim. 'What the hell happened to you? Why did you go out of contact?'

He tried to explain; the old trick, the hunter turned hunted, his RT out of reach, but the result was the same, he'd been sidetracked and Roper was dead.

'One decoys you while the other waits for Roper,' Black concluded.

'What about Annië Shepherd? Does she know?'

'No. I don't want to frighten her, make her run. She's at home. We've put surveillance in place.'

Neil was astounded. 'Surveillance! She should be

brought in. Her and everyone else in the cell. She's next, for God's sake!'

'Exactly! That's why we need her out there,' Black said coldly. 'How do you know it's a cell?' she added.

'Roper mentioned "the others" when they were talking in the restaurant. We've got to bring her in, she's our only means of finding out what this is about.'

'She's also our only known target for this hit team to go after and I want them as well.'

Neil was rigid with anger but the stubborn cut of Black's set mouth warned him against further argument. He watched the police outside combing the garden for scraps of evidence. Inside it was the same. He looked round again; a couple of chairs were turned over, the inevitable signs of a struggle, but other than that . . .

He took Black's elbow and guided her out of earshot. 'This place hasn't been turned over. It was in the same mess when I was here last night. They weren't looking for anything. The only thing they came for was Roper. And when he wouldn't play ball, they . . . And there aren't just two of them, there's three. The one I followed was not one of those in the blow-ups.'

Black glanced at him with a quick frown. 'There's something else,' she informed him. 'As you know we've been tracking the Iran–IRA relationship for some time. Yesterday we struck lucky, arrested two Iranians with a huge quantity of heroin on its way to the Rah. We picked them up in Athens.'

'Major Turner's last port of call! As far as we know,' Neil pondered. 'And possibly the reason for Hogan's call on the Iranians in The Hague. No doubt he was there to finalize the deal or the transit. Let's walk outside.' He stepped around the forensic team crawling around them. Black followed.

'There's no way, I suppose, that Turner could be

234

involved in the IRA?' Neil began. 'Perhaps he acted as their liaison with Iran?'

'Never! I'm certain. I knew Turner, he was exceptional, a man of the highest integrity. I'd stake my life on him.'

Neil glanced across, surprised at the betrayal of emotion by this normally very detached, dispassionate woman.

'We worked together once,' she said quietly. 'He saved my life.'

Neil, fellow trooper, understood the loyalty. 'Nevertheless,' he went on, 'his murder was not a casual killing. You don't shoot someone through the head for just sitting in a car. And at close quarters too. Seems to me, he was parked by that airfield waiting for someone. There were several cigarettes lying around, he must have been there for some time. Yet according to the Military Intelligence report no one at the airfield knows anything or heard a sound.'

'Unlikely anyone from there was involved. Surely to allay suspicion, common sense would have made them move the car elsewhere?'

'They could have been disturbed, of course . . .'

Neil offered Black a cigarette, noticing for the first time, the greying hair at her temples, the tired lines around the eyes. She drew in deeply, exhaling the smoke from delicate nostrils and pursed lips, watching it billow white in the cold air.

'Seems to me,' she said finally, 'Turner witnessed something he shouldn't. It would be too against character for anything else. He stumbled on something inadvertently and was killed for it, and I want to know who by. There are just too many coincidences creeping in for his murder not to be part of this investigation.'

'Or for him not to have been involved,' Neil couldn't help adding. 'One thing we have not considered – what if he was one of "the others"? Another member of the cell? Maybe the hit team, whoever they are, knew of his involvement and got to him first, and when he wouldn't cooperate, they were forced to go to Petrov?'

Jane Black did not like what she heard, hostility sparked from her eyes, but there was a dawning feeling that events were moving out of control and if they lost the woman, the only contact they had from Petrov's list . . .

'I suppose it's feasible,' she replied frostily. 'We'd better bring Annie Shepherd in.'

CHAPTER EIGHTEEN

Down in Archives Andy was working late. Except with Andy there was no early or late. Archives was his life, he was always there, always available. He was a creature of the vaults, his hair a crown of awry spikes, his face pale from lack of daylight and open spaces, his eyes weak behind pebble glasses. Nevertheless he exuded boundless enthusiasm and energy for the job and like Gault, his mentor and friend, his memory was formidable.

'Lebanon,' he muttered, studying the blow-ups. 'I keep thinking Lebanon. It will come.'

Neil's description of his car-chase adversary produced no recollection whatsoever. It was Gault who spotted him. Archives was his second home. He wandered in while Andy and Neil were poring over files and boxes of prints and picked up the blow-ups, looking through them while Neil described again the Russian-looking man.

'Could be anyone,' he said. 'Are these all the prints from the video?'

'All the relevant ones,' Andy said. 'We've got film lasting all night, ending with Neil's visit in the morning. We've isolated all the prints around the two men, plus any other likely figures and some, like those of Neil leaving the building, all in separate piles. I've gone through them, there's no one fitting the description that I can see.'

Gault ambled over. 'Do you mind?' he asked, and

picked up a stack, sat down with a magnifying glass and began scrutinizing each one carefully.

'Sare-sha . . .' Neil began.

'*Saorse*. Hogan still using it?' Gault answered automatically, without looking up.

'That's it!' Neil exclaimed. 'That's where I've heard it. He used it as a nickname.'

'Pseudonym,' Gault corrected, eye glued to the glass. 'It's Gaelic, means freedom, remember? There was a revolutionary socialist group, Saor Eire, back in the thirties. Hogan joined a left-wing splinter group, same name, Saor Eire, in the sixties. Oh, this is interesting! Petrov's apartment, third floor, someone's at the window as you are leaving. See, the curtain's pulled back. Anyone else in there with you?'

'Definitely not.' Intrigued, Neil peered at the magnified blurred image. It was either someone bald or with a close-shaved head. There seemed little doubt it was the man who'd shot at him.

'We'll blow it up, see if we can get a clearer picture, but someone was there in the room after you left, and got a clear look at you,' Gault warned. 'I don't think he was anything to do with the other two hit men at all. This was taken a good twelve hours or more after they'd left.'

Neil did not need Gault to add more, it was becoming all too clear. 'In other words,' he said, 'whoever it was – thought I had murdered Petrov. Which also means the car chase was no decoy. It wasn't Roper he was after, it was me.'

John Neil needed some air. He left the two boffins closeted together trying to identify the three men and left the building. There was something missing in the puzzle. Events were in motion, accelerating even, but towards what? He decided to walk home. His car anyway was in for repairs. Besides, he needed time to think, to

238

work things out. He couldn't rid himself of the feeling that things had taken on a new sense of urgency, and orchestrating it all were the ruthlessly ambitious jet-setting Hogans.

This wasn't just a new IRA offensive, retaliation for the one he'd aborted, this was something far more sinister, and high-powered City men like Brendan Rylans and Patrick Heaney were all involved – or being used?

From that meeting in Dundalk it was obvious Rylans and Heaney both were in the business of laundering dirty money, financing arms for the IRA. But did they also know what Neil now suspected: that they were being used to fund terrorism and bloody revolution in Europe on behalf of Iran?

Somehow, Neil had to get into Sinead's office. The report had come back negative on both Rylans' and Sinead's client list and business dealings. Everything appeared to be bona fide. Neil had expected no more.

He crossed Bayswater Road, still thronging with people even at this late hour, and plunged into the deserted streets and squares beyond. Deep in thought he turned into the road leading to his own apartment. Suddenly two figures leapt out from behind and threw him hard against one of the parked cars that lined the pavements. Instinctively he whirled round; his back-handed fist cracked the temple of one, his forearm rammed against the throat of the other, forcing him back at a run, until his head crunched against a wall. Jason Sturden, managing a grin, lifted his arms in surrender. Neil stepped back, the high-octane energy ebbed. Sturden rubbed his neck and leered in appreciation of the aikido attack.

'Takes one to know one. Falklands, yeh? Bit special, eh? Now nobody cares,' he said.

Neil stood loose on balanced feet, saying nothing, his

glance flicking from Sturden to the stirring figure of his other assailant.

'Relax. That was pretty fancy! Miss it all, do you? The excitement? The camaraderie? Tough living alone on civvy street, eh?' He winked knowingly. 'No lady friend? No boyfriend?'

'No!' From the shifty look in the rodent's eyes, Neil guessed he'd searched his flat, been round asking questions.

'Oh, we've been there, Tarleton and me. Army uses you, then ... There's a few of us, old soldiers – none in your class – meet for a drink. Join us, tomorrow night.'

'I choose who I drink with.' Neil's hands were poised, ready.

Sturden noticed and laughed. 'I told you, relax! Nobody'll touch you. Could be worth your while, wheelman.'

Neil's expression did not soften but he nodded slowly. 'Tomorrow night then.' He backed away and watched Sturden pull his mate Tarleton to his feet. Only when their car roared away did he relax.

Holding his coffee and hot dog up high, John Neil, City messenger, eased his way through the lunch-time crowd, jostling around the hot-dog stall.

'I'm living on these bloody things, no time for anything else,' he grumbled to the slim back of his controller. Black moved aside to let someone pass, then fell in beside him.

'The coffee's foul.' She poured it away and lit a cigarette.

'The tea's worse.'

'I'll buy you a slap-up dinner when this is all over.'

'If I haven't died of salmonella first.'

She looked at him gravely. 'That bad, eh? Me too.

Annie Shepherd's in a safe house, stonewalling like crazy. I didn't tell her Petrov and Roper were dead. Thought that would make her clam up even more. Just told her Petrov had talked, named the two of them. Looked at me as if I were Alice in Wonderland on magic mushrooms. Swore she'd never heard of Petrov or Roper, of course. We'll keep trying but with nothing specific to pin on her...'

'Just hold her as long as you can. And don't let her go without telling me. And Major Turner's girlfriend, Liz Baker?'

'The same, still insists Turner never confided anything. Still continuing with her training at the military school – still under surveillance. And I have to admit, I still think she's telling the truth. Stalemate!'

'Not quite. My new pal, Jason Sturden, has taken me to his heart and is introducing me to a few friends tonight. He promises it will be worth my while. We'll see. What I do need is to bug Rylans' office plus I need surveillance in a room opposite Cottrells, telling me what's going on in there.'

'Done.' She looked at her watch. 'I'm late. A conference about a conference. Keep in touch.'

That evening as the last of the staff left, John Neil sat on the edge of Rose Herbert's desk, detaining her gossiping while through the open door he monitored the late-night office routine: the cleaners' arrival, the partners' departure, the executive suites left open or locked. Only Sinead Hogan's office seemed sacrosanct.

'What's Hogan up to? Back soon?' he asked casually.

'No idea, luvvie. She often disappears. Sets up deals all over the place, Eastern bloc a lot of the time. Like Rylans, she's there now, Budapest. Back tomorrow.'

'Doesn't anyone else look after her clients or use her office?'

'She'd go mad if they did.'

He slid off the desk, checking his watch. 'Sorry Rose, kept you talking long enough and I've got a date. See ya.'

He sat beside Sturden with Tarleton in the back and felt the adrenalin surge through him. Not only had they just passed the very spot where Turner had died with no reaction from either, he'd noted, but they were now pulling into the car park of the same run-down airfield. A weathered sign carried the legend, 'Flaxfield Flying School'.

Had it not been for the sight of two executive jets, a 'Jet' helicopter, and a Cessna, parked nearby, Neil would have assumed the place was derelict. He took in the 'temporary' war-time huts, the smattering of workshops and hangars and entered the equally dilapidated building that housed the reception, office and bar. Neil was struck by *déjà vu*: he'd waited for hours in places like this, with his stomach in knots, waited for the call, for the op to begin.

Neglect and smoke hung heavy in the dingy air, nicotine stained the walls, second-hand sofas bulged and sprouted springs or horsehair and chipped Formica tables bore the marks of years. Here men still waited, drinking, smoking, playing cards – except the call never came. The last op was long over and they were no longer needed.

He joined Sturden, Tarleton and Francis, the owner, in a game of poker, but he had the feeling he was there for more than just a game of cards.

'Jason tells me you were in the Falklands?' Francis spoke with an aristocratic accent despite his dishevelled

242

appearance. 'What op?' He shuffled the cards with nicotine-stained fingers and dealt.

'We were in before anything started. Argentina – mainland, clocking airfields.'

'One of the élite. How very impressive!'

'They didn't think so or I wouldn't be here. Now I no longer exist.'

There was the sound of an aircraft landing. They looked up expectantly.

'Bit early,' Francis said.

'You fly?' Neil asked.

'No longer. Gets in the way of my drinking.'

Jason pushed back his chair. 'When you can't do it, teach it. That right?' and he walked off without explanation.

Francis gathered their glasses. 'Same again?'

Left with Tarleton, Neil fidgeted. 'Karsi?' he asked.

He located the lavatory and pushed on, following the path already taken by Sturden, through a storeroom and office until he reached a large hangar, where a small plane was in a state of repair. He ducked behind it as he caught sight of a man in his forties peeling off his helmet and flying suit. There was a rattle of plastic. Sturden pushed aside some sheeting and appeared carrying two holdalls to add to the one already there. The pilot seemed agitated. He had something urgent to impart to Brendan Rylans, he said, Sturden had to get him to Cottrells fast. As if on cue, Francis appeared. The pilot, learning that Rylans was in Budapest, became even more unnerved. 'The bastards,' Neil heard him shout. They were making even heavier demands, insisting he brought in double the amount and before the end of the month! Francis looked equally disturbed. Sturden was suddenly walking towards Neil, carrying two more holdalls. Neil crouched low and moved away.

Neil walked back into the bar as Tarleton entered. It

was obvious from the relief on his face he'd been looking for him.

'Bit of a bug, I think,' Neil said with a grimace. 'Too many hot dogs!'

Jason Sturden was at reception, waiting to leave. The pilot was with him, filling in his flight book. He looked up suspiciously at Neil.

Sturden introduced them. 'Alec Dwyer, pilot – Pat Beale, the new messenger at Cottrells and ex-SAS. Give us a hand,' he said to Neil, indicating the five holdalls standing by. Following the others, Neil picked up the last bag.

They drove back in silence. Dwyer, in the passenger seat, was rigid with tension; from the pallor of his skin and the beads of perspiration which he constantly mopped with his handkerchief, Neil decided the pilot was in a state of high anxiety.

They dropped Neil off at Marble Arch. He wanted to walk, grab something to eat, he told them. He also wanted to make his report. He took out his cellnet and contacted Control. Black listened intently.

'The pilot's name was Dwyer. Alec Dwyer. Not the same one I saw doing the Dundalk run. Although I'd guess from the weight of the holdalls it was cash again – but a lot more of it. There's something very heavy going on there. The pilot seemed desperate – scared. And the owner too, Francis, was pretty wound up. Some-one's definitely leaning on them, putting the pressure on Rylans. What's the connection in Budapest? Did you find out?'

'We did. Rylans brokered a deal there three years ago, took over a failing construction company, Nagy. Turned it around – now it's very successful. He deals through a major bank over there – all very legit. If he's doing anything illegal, it must be either coded vocals or voice patterns GCHQ can't pick up or it's all genuine. And the same goes for Sinead Hogan.'

'Time for humint to take over, eh Boss?' Neil teased.

'Fuck off and out,' she responded in a delicate tone.

The lighting was low, the office doors open, the army of cleaners spread throughout the floor were at their various jobs. Working alone at a computer, studying the keyboard and the manual, was John Neil.

He felt a rap on his arm. 'Move over a minute, love. I just wanna get under your desk,' the cleaner said, staring nosily at the screen. Neil slid back his chair and lifted his feet while the woman vacuumed round him.

'That all you can do?' she snorted. 'My kid can do better than that, wizard he is and he's only eight. Makes them little hedgehog things run around!' She chortled and moved away, heading next for Rylans' suite.

It took Neil seconds to pick the lock and he was into Sinead's office. Systematically he began his search. The desk diary revealed little, the usual appointments, the usual reminders. The current dates were left blank; in fact, Neil noted, apart from the last day of the month, heavily circled in red, there was nothing else entered for the rest of the year.

Knowing his time was limited, he'd already planned his search. He accessed her computer and checked the files; nothing stood out as unusual. He keyed in to various ones at random; everything appeared normal. Her diary file matched what he'd already read, except against the circled date the screen now printed *Saorse*!

Neil was suddenly aware of voices. The vacuuming had stopped. Quickly he closed down the computer, checked the room and slipped back to his desk. The cleaners were preparing to leave. He could see them gathering their things together, ready to move on to the next floor. He knew he had but a few minutes before security arrived to lock up. As the last woman squeezed into the lift and the doors closed, he nipped into Rylans' office and made straight for the curtain rod, fixed the tiny microphone to the end and adjusted the angle. The lift was rising again. In no time he was back at his desk assiduously tapping the keys. The lift stopped, he didn't even glance up. He'd expected the security man; the voice he heard was Rylans', irascibly demanding what the hell he was doing there. Behind him, looking on with interest, were Sturden and Alec Dwyer, the pilot.

Neil had already decided on the face he would present to Rylans – spirited, firm, respectful but not ingratiating. It was an approach intended to impress and as he rounded on the man and explained that he had only three months in which to prove himself and had been granted permission to practise on the computer, he saw his ploy had succeeded.

Rylans, impressed, leaned in to look at his screen.

'*Twinkle, twinkle little star* . . .' he read out. 'Very good. May I suggest that's enough schooling for tonight? Mr . . .?'

'Pat Beale, sir. I'm the new messenger.'

Rylans smiled briefly, nodded and walked into his office calling to Alec Dwyer to follow him.

Jason Sturden pulled up a chair. 'There are easier ways of getting in than this.' He rapped on the computer.

'I had enough taking orders in the army,' Neil grumbled, concentrating on exiting the machine. 'Still, I don't want to lose this job.'

'Listen to me and you won't.' Nervously his fingers drummed on the desk. They stopped, he spoke. 'Sometimes things here come up a bit quickish – interested, wheelman?'

Neil's eyes narrowed. 'Like what?'

Sturden assumed innocence. 'Nothing dangerous, just

delivery – collection – the usual. Bit more money in this, though.'

Neil stood and picked up his coat from the back of his chair. Sturden followed, stretching nonchalantly. 'Think on it, wheelman,' he said and winked.

John Neil closed his eyes and listened again to the taped conversation from Rylans' office. It explained the pilot's agitation the previous night.

The 'double amount' he was being pressurized into transporting referred to cocaine. The man behind it all was a Mr Osuna, who was also coercing Rylans into finding a tame banker as a future conduit for money into Hungary. All was to be in place before the end of the month. Neil smiled grimly on hearing Sturden so readily offer Pat Beale's services as an extra mule and driver to cope with the rush order. He cocked his ear to the machine and listened intently. It was Dwyer speaking.

'With all this extra, there's no way I can carry that other lot. It's too much.'

'We have to.' Rylans was quiet but emphatic. 'She has us over a barrel. We have no choice.'

'Listen, you can stash a few bags of dope, but her stuff's in fucking crates! This next one's a big bugger. And with double the other. Surely I could do it next time?'

'It will be too late. I've fought against it, believe me. If we don't deliver and in time . . . She means what she says, make no mistake. There won't be a next time! Somehow you have to do both.'

'Bloody Irish bitch! It's my neck on the line . . .'

'It's all our necks on the line . . .' Rylans' voice trailed off but his desperation was clear.

The tape finished. Neil stretched back his shoulders

and picked up his mug of coffee, drank and wrinkled his nose.

'It's cold now. Make me another cup please, Suze.' He smiled his crooked smile. The young tape operator dimpled and jumped up.

Jane Black raised an eyebrow. Neil looked questioningly and resumed analysing the tape.

'So Rylans is in it up to his neck. And Dwyer . . .'

'Squadron Leader Dwyer, ex-Tornadoes, now of RAF Manningdene . . .' she interrupted.

'Is using his new position in Transports and government property to do a little moonlighting.' Neil, sitting at the desk opposite Black, leaned forward, his elbows on the table, his fists clenched together tight against his mouth, his eyes narrowed in deep concentration.

'Sounds to me like a Hogan pincer movement has Rylans nicely trapped. Declan Hogan sets up the deal, let's say a drug cartel posing as a legit business, Sinead introduces it to her lover and senior partner as an exciting new project. Rylans using his clout in the new marketplace brokers the deal in Hungary. The big bucks are rolling in before he realizes he's not only dealing in dirty money but the drug barons have him by the balls. And so does Sinead! Hence he's blackmailed into helping the IRA as well as being open season on the drug market.'

'And what better way of laundering money than the stock market? We've suspected it's been going on. It's catching them at it. With the new technology dirty money can be wired into legitimacy in no time.'

Neil pushed his fingers through his hair. 'We should be able to follow that down the line. What's worrying me is what's in those crates and what this deadline means. Everything seems to be pointing to the end of the month. What is happening then that's so important?'

'I've got this damn conference, but apart from that . . .'

'Crates has to mean arms of some description. Could it be a special little something coming in from Iran? But then how the hell would Dwyer get that and from where? Unless . . . that was where Major Turner came in?' He glanced significantly at Black. 'Let's get all Dwyer's official movements over the last few months and where his Transport command are destined at the end of this one. Meanwhile I think it's time I met Liz Baker.'

'There's a job tonight. You on, wheelman?' The lift doors had been closing when Sturden jammed them with his foot and jumped in with Neil.

'No, not for me, thanks all the same.'

Sturden pressed the button and the lift ground to a halt between floors. 'Oh, I'd say it was just the job for you. What d'you think?' And he held up a photograph of Neil carrying the holdalls.

Neil glared at him.

Sturden grinned. 'We all need a little encouragement now and again,' he said as the lift started up. 'See you tonight, late. I'll call you on this.' He pushed a portable phone into Neil's pocket. 'Be ready, wheelman.'

Captain Liz Baker, selected from the cream of the army for training in Military Intelligence, knew she had seen John Neil before and she knew where and when. She watched him, walking restlessly about the room, she answered his questions, presented a pleasant face – he was after all a figure of authority – but she regarded him with suspicion. This was the man she'd seen slip by her on the stairs. This was the man who had searched the flat that day, not long after Bob was buried. She'd rushed in and from the window she'd seen him look at another man getting into a car further down the street and the two of them, in separate cars, had roared off together. One of the cars she was convinced was the one that had tried to mow her down.

She'd been ordered to answer whatever he asked but she did not trust him. Somehow he was involved in her fiancé's death, she was sure.

'You have to be honest with me, Captain,' he was saying. 'I am here to find out who killed Major Turner and the only way I can do that is if you tell me everything.'

She wanted to scream out, You did! Bob was wonderful, a man of integrity, whose work was his life. Why were they all trying to make her condemn him? Somehow, someone was trying to frame her fiancé – to make him the fall guy, the scapegoat. But for what?

'Major Turner and I were deeply in love. We both are – were – totally pledged to our work. Anything that was open to discussion, we discussed. Anything that was confidential never passed our lips,' she said quietly for the millionth time. 'Therefore I know nothing of his undercover work in the Middle East or anywhere else, come to that. You have copies of all the interviews. I have nothing more to add. Besides which it is late and I'm tired.'

John Neil could see the stress in the young woman's face. He changed tactics. 'I'm sorry, I understand how distressing this is. We valued Major Turner very highly . . .'

'Then why do you want to prove him guilty?'

'We don't. But there has to be a reason for him to be killed in cold blood like that. And you have to know something, whether you admit it or even realize it. Why else would someone try to kill you?' Neil paused. 'Those three weeks in Athens – have you any idea where he could have been or what he was doing?'

'I've answered this so many times. No, I have not!'

The shrill ring of the portable phone startled them both. She watched closely Neil's dark expression, his curt response.

'I have to go. We'll talk again.'

She opened the front door to let him out. Her police guard was missing.

'I sent him off for a coffee.' Neil smiled apologetically. 'I'll have him back right away, don't worry. Just make sure you lock your door.'

'Tell him not to disturb me. I'm off to bed. Goodnight.' She slammed the door and made a performance of rattling chains and shooting bolts, listening for his footsteps to fade as he ran down the stairs. Swiftly she grabbed a coat and followed.

Keeping his car in her sights, she kept her distance, trailing him across the river, to the seedier areas of South London: Brixton, Peckham, New Cross. He turned off the main road and began weaving through the darker side streets. She was almost upon them before she knew it. He'd pulled onto a piece of wasteground that acted as a car park to a pub across the road. She drove past and saw him greet another man already there, waiting. By the time she'd parked and sidled back, Neil was walking towards the pub carrying a bag, a grip of some sort. She pulled back into the shadows of a doorway but not before she'd recognized the other man, who was putting a full plastic bag into Neil's car, as the accomplice she'd witnessed in the street below her flat. She looked back, surprised to see Neil entering not the pub but a late-night corner store next to it.

His accomplice was now seated in his car, his eyes glued to a lit window above the store. Neil emerged with a West Indian in tow. They crossed over to his car and opened the boot. Neil held up the bag. At the same time another man, carrying an identical bag, walked out from the shop to meet with Neil. They both checked the contents of each other's bags, exchanged them and, satisfied, parted. Even to Liz Baker it was obvious Neil and his accomplice were handing over drugs in return for cash. Was this why Bob Turner was killed? Were they trying to implicate him in some way? Or maybe, like her, he'd discovered John Neil was playing a double game.

She edged out of the doorway and, still keeping to the shadows, drew nearer. She saw Neil hand the full bag of money to his partner and heard the triumphant chortle as his partner crowed that their success deserved a big drink.

Incensed, she stepped out. 'I'll join you in that,' she said loudly, her voice ringing with contempt.

As soon as she'd done it, she knew she was wrong. Neil spun round, his face in despair. His accomplice blanched, looked from her to Neil, realized they knew each other and cursed.

'You bastard!' he yelled viciously at Neil, who now stood between him and his car. 'Oh clever! Oh, very clever. Tricked us all, didn't you? Who the fuck are you?' He began stumbling backwards, turned and broke into a run, the bag swinging in his hand. Neil started after him, pounding across the uneven ground to the wasteland beyond. Liz Baker followed. Desperately, impeded by the bag, Sturden clambered over rubbish. Fear gave him a lead. He leapt at a fence, scrambled over, and fell into a scrap yard. Neil was catching up. Sturden swerved round a car wreck, Neil went over the top, there was only a yard in it. Neil threw himself at Sturden's legs, caught him in a rugby tackle and sent him flying. There was a scream, a deafening crack, a sickening crunch – then silence.

Liz panted to a halt. 'Oh my God!'

John Neil pulled himself slowly to his feet. From the girl's face, he knew Sturden was dead. He saw the concrete block where Sturden had cracked his head but, worse, he saw the ugly spear of rusty iron that bayoneted Sturden's throat.

Neil looked round. There were no witnesses. He eased the bag of money from the dead man's fingers and shoved it in his coat. The girl was speechless.

'I am investigating the death of your boyfriend,' he said in cold fury. 'And you have just blown my cover. What the hell were you doing following me?'

'I thought you were involved.' She shivered. 'Did he kill . . .?'

'I don't know,' Neil said abruptly. He gave her a gentle push. 'Get home fast. Act natural. This is your first job, soldier. Don't blow it. Next time I ask about Turner, I want to know everything. Now go!' Separately, they made their way to their cars.

'Sturden's dead,' he reported to his controller. 'Cover me with the police.'

Next morning Neil whistled into work as if nothing had happened, amazed to see the place crawling with police. It was later that morning that Rylans called him into his office. The man was jittery with nerves. Neil repeated his story. He and Jason Sturden had completed the deal, then they'd split, Sturden with the money. He'd told the police he didn't know Jason.

Rylans was staring white-faced through the window. 'Jason liked you. Said you were to be trusted.'

Neil looked at the man's back – and decided a straight answer was called for. 'Well, I didn't like him. I was blackmailed into that drug delivery. I shoot from the hip, Mr Rylans, and I don't like being threatened. He said if I didn't help, I'd be blown away.'

Rylans swayed gently on his feet. Then he started and it was as if the floodgates had opened and he didn't want to stop. It was more or less as Neil had surmised. A firm posing as oil traders with huge sums to invest had been introduced to him. He'd recommended Hungary, a construction company in need of an enormous cash injection. They'd undercut everyone and now were the success story of Budapest. When he'd discovered the money came from drugs, the country was into recession and he couldn't afford to stop. Now he was at the mercy of every drug cartel in Colombia.

'Just like you, they had me over a barrel and now just like them, I have you.' He turned round and faced Neil. His eyes were dark and haunted. 'I want you to replace Jason.'

Dressed in a formal suit Neil reported for duty that afternoon. Rylans was on the phone, finishing a call.

'Will you please find Mr Paric and tell him it is of the utmost urgency he contacts me.' He slammed down the phone and plunged his head in his hands. For a moment Neil thought he was crying.

'You all right, sir?' he said.

The man looked up, his face grey. There was raw fear in his eyes. He slumped back in his desk, then with a huge effort pushed himself to his feet. It was as if he hadn't heard the question. 'Drive me home, Beale.'

On the drive home, Rylans retreated into himself, but as they pulled into his drive and he saw the other car there waiting he sat up in shock, glaring wildly about him as if seeking escape.

'Oh Christ, she's here. She's let herself in. Christ! What does she want now?'

Neil knew it had to be Sinead Hogan, the very last person he wanted to see.

'Wait here, Beale. I want an excuse to get away. Give me fifteen minutes, then come and get me. Make some excuse . . . I'll leave the door on the latch.'

The man seemed to have aged ten years. He dragged himself reluctantly to the house and went in.

Neil waited, then slipped out of the car, keeping his

head down as if checking the bodywork or tyres. He heard voices raised in anger and with head low walked purposefully to the entrance. If anyone had been watching they certainly were not there to bar the way. He pushed, the door opened slowly, revealing a sweeping staircase which wound up to lofty heights, lit by an enormous stained-glass window. He edged in, thick carpeting muffled his footsteps. There was no need to go far, Sinead's Irish brogue, scornful, derisive, resounded in the spacious hall.

'Greed got you into this, Rylans, not me. Your own selfish greed! I don't give a damn what their demands are, all I care about is my delivery. Because if I don't get my delivery and on the date promised, there won't be a corner left on this earth but I'll come looking. I promise you that!'

'This is the last time, you bitch. I've had enough. No more! I'll rot in jail before I do anything else for you.'

'Then rot,' she spat out. 'Once this is over you'll do exactly as I want and you know it! You're too much the coward and you love money too much to say no.' She snorted disdainfully. 'The crate will be at the airfield on the twenty-eighth. Please don't think of playing games, Rylans. Nothing is going to stop us. This is the big league now. You cross us and not only will your life not be worth living, your death will be hell!'

'What are you and your fanatics up to this time, Sinead? What're you blowing up now? The Baltic Exchange not big enough for you? You're mad, you know that, don't you? You and your brother are fucking certifiable!'

There was a loud slap as she hit him across the face. 'You're hysterical, Rylans,' she said in a soft, sinister tone. 'And you're in it up to your neck. Never forget that.'

Neil nipped into the cloakroom and locked the door,

just as she swept out of the house. He heard her rev hard on the engine and the spit of gravel as she accelerated away.

He left the house and rang the bell before re-entering. He found Rylans collapsed in a chair, a broken man. There was a raised red welt across his face. He stumbled to his feet when Neil walked in, and crossed to an antique drinks cabinet. With shaking hands he poured himself a very large Scotch, threw it back and poured again. In between his head jerked convulsively as if he was suddenly afflicted with a nervous twitch. The spirit seemed to soothe him. He seemed to shake himself back to some form of control.

He picked up the phone and dialled, his back to Neil. 'Thomas Paric, please ... Mr Rylans. Have you given him my message? ... Then when will he be back? He must call me. Please stress, it's urgent, a matter of life or death!'

He'd drunk almost three-quarters of a bottle before they left.

'Where're we going, sir?' Neil asked.

'I'll direct you,' he said, staring through the window.

It was dark, they were heading down a narrow country lane, when Rylans instructed him to stop. Their headlights reflected on a car parked in a layby. Tarleton was in the driving seat. Neil pulled up, facing him. Before he dimmed his lights, he saw Dwyer escorting a man in his fifties towards them. Rylans swung open the door, the man got in beside him.

'Good evening, Mr Osuna,' Rylans said.

Dwyer slid in the front, next to Neil. He reeked of fear.

Osuna was angry, very, very angry. In measured tones, with the voice of reason, he pointed out that he had worked hard to fulfil the arrangements. Everything was in place, the merchandise ready for collection on the appointed date, but where was Paric? Rylans had promised the banker would respond in seven days, but already ten days had passed and still no word. His voice rose to a scream. Dwyer he could trust but Rylans was reneging on his word. Nothing would appease him now but the presence of Rylans with his tame banker, Paric, in Cyprus. Not hiding somewhere in Budapest, but Cyprus, where they could meet face to face as a gesture of trust. Otherwise his life would be forfeit.

He stormed out of the car but not before Dwyer whispered frantically to Rylans, 'For Christ's sake, get him! Get Paric. I'll get the money in place.'

It was late when Neil dropped Rylans off. The man was exhausted, he hadn't uttered a word on the journey.

'I won't be in the office tomorrow. There's a Harley Jason used.' He flapped a listless hand towards the garage. 'I'll call if I need you.' He practically fell out of the car.

'I'll be on my mobile, sir.'

Rylans held up a hand in acknowledgement.

Neil found the Harley Davidson and rode into town. It was the best bit of his day.

Jane Black took his report. 'Cyprus! That figures. There's a Tornado bombing practice at Akrotiri Air Base scheduled for the end of the month. Dwyer picks up the drugs, flies them to RAF Manningdene, then on to Flaxfield. Easy! We just have to catch them at it.'

'Still doesn't explain Petrov's list. Or what Sinead Hogan is up to. Because whatever it is, whether she gets her crate or not, she's going through with it.'

Black was silent. 'I'm going to have to let Annie Shepherd go. We've nothing on her,' she said wearily.

'No! Let me talk to her. My car's ready, I'll pick it up and drive to the safe house first thing, early. It's time she knew Petrov and Roper are dead – time she was scared witless.'

'She could run, then we'd have nothing.'

'We have nothing now. We have no idea who the hit men are. They could be Russians guarding the secret. Someone saving their own hide. Or something to do with the Hogans. Roper mentioned an Irish boy, remember? We need some answers.' Neil stopped. Something flicked across his subconscious and surfaced as a photograph. 'What time is it? I want to check something. I'll be with Liz Baker. Let her know I'm on my way.'

She answered the door in her dressing gown, led him into the sitting room and sank down in a chair.

'I won't stay long but I do need some answers,' Neil said. 'The truth this time. This photograph.' He picked up the one he'd seen Sturden studying, of Liz and Turner on holiday. 'It is Cyprus, isn't it?'

'Taken two years ago. My mother has a holiday house.'

'Could that be where Turner went after Athens? Cyprus?'

'I don't know.' She looked away defensively.

'Captain! I cannot conduct this inquiry if you don't cooperate,' Neil growled.

The girl paled, obviously shaken. Then hesitantly she began to talk. 'He called from Athens, wanted me to join him in Cyprus. I couldn't because of the course.'

'So he stayed at the house anyway?'

She shook her head. 'The house was already rented.'

'Who by? Someone he knew?'

'No. I don't know. We just rented it out, when we didn't need it.'

'So where did he stay in Cyprus?'

'I don't know. He just wanted to rest before he came home. Nothing else, I swear!' The girl was sobbing bitterly. Neil was satisfied she had nothing more to add but at least he now knew Major Bob Turner was in the same place, at the same time, as the Tornadoes' last bombing exercise and Dwyer's last courier run.

Neil picked up his car early next morning. The Harley attracted too much attention. The safe house was in the country, west of London. At that time the roads heading out of town were easy. He was feeling pretty bleary-eyed as he followed the country lanes. He wound down the window and took a deep breath. He didn't even see the van. It careered out of a side road right in front of him. He swung the wheel, the car reared up over the verge, plunged into a thick thorn hedge and stopped abruptly, smacking him forward. Dazed, bruised, he was hauled from the car, his legs folded under him. He came to, sitting on the grass propped against his car, and focused on the man peering down at him. It was the close-shaved head he registered first, then the gun pointing at him. Before he could move, he was jerked to his feet. He swayed. A hand back-swiped his mouth, a fist rammed his stomach, he doubled over and fell. Neil peered up at the white blob swimming in and out of his vision. It spoke in a heavy guttural accent.

'Now you tell me why you kill my friend Petrov?'

John Neil struggled to concentrate, to play for time, but a vicious kick close to his kidneys warned him this was not a man to toy with, this was a professional killer.

'I did not kill him. He was dead already. A heart attack!' The blood streamed from Neil's split lip.

'You beat him up, you make the heart attack!'

'No! We were doing business together. I didn't want him dead. He had information to sell, I had the money to pay him, money he needed for a heart operation. Someone else got there first. Moscow maybe . . .'

'Liar! Why would Moscow care about old secrets?'

But the man was listening. Neil pressed on. 'Someone

cared enough to kill off his sleepers. Roper, for instance. You can check it out. Petrov gave me two names: Roper and another, two members of his cell. I'm on my way now to see the other one, before whoever got to Roper gets to her. It's the truth, for Christ's sake. Listen, we have visuals from the traffic camera opposite Petrov's building. Stills of you holding back the curtain watching me. Stills of the two men who were there before us . . . who killed Petrov.' Neil started to get up.

The man kneed him in the chest, holding him down, while his silencer dug under Neil's chin, forcing his head back, making him look at him eye to eye. 'What are their names, these killers? Who are they?'

'We don't know.'

The man's finger was on the trigger, the muzzle bit deep into Neil's flesh. 'Their names?' he screamed.

'You kill me you'll never know.' Neil was choking. He felt the pressure relax. 'I'm the best bet you have. Let me go and I'll find them. I want them as much as you.'

The man stood up. 'You find them or I will find you. There is a number. I leave it in your car, an international service. When you know, call. Use your own name – leave a message for John Neil.' Like a boxer the man stepped lightly away.

'Give us a hand,' Neil groaned, surveying his car, but the only response was the van accelerating away.

Jane Black met Neil as he limped into the gloomy hall of the Gothic mansion that served amongst other uses as a safe house.

'He did make a mess of you,' she said unsympathetically. 'You can clean up in here.' She pushed open the door to the cloakroom where Dettol, cotton wool, plasters were neatly lined up, next to the wash bowl.

'See, you do care!' Neil grinned, then grimaced. 'Ouch! My mouth!'

Black leaned in the open doorway and consulted her notes. 'You're sure he was German?'

'East German, probably Stasi. Trained security, definitely. He knew exactly where to hurt.'

'And he convinced you Moscow had nothing to do with it?'

Neil nodded, holding a towel to his sore face, gingerly patting it dry.

'Then let's see what Shepherd has to say. She's waiting in interrogation. Everything you asked for is in here.' She handed Neil a large envelope.

Annie Shepherd was sitting at the table opposite an empty chair. A flicker of recognition crossed her dark features but the where, the why, and the when of their meeting seemed momentarily to evade her. She frowned, her arms crossed defensively. Without a word John Neil sat down opposite her, took a cassette from the envelope and slotted it into the tape machine already set up on the table. He sat back and waited. It was the taped conversation at the restaurant, the meeting between her and Roper.

It took a moment for the voices to register but when they did, Shepherd sat up, her mouth open in shock. Furious, she snatched at the machine. Neil caught her hand. Her eyes burned into his but slowly her resistance waned. She sat back, grim, mute with anger. Still Neil did not speak. As the tape ended, he drew out the autopsy pictures of Petrov and slid them under her downcast gaze. He saw her eyes widen in horror. She squirmed in her seat, her mouth down-turned, her face pale.

'Someone did that to force Petrov to give your names. And when he did, they went after Roper.' Gently he slipped her the shots of Roper, brutalized, defiled, ugly in death. She gasped hoarsely and clutched at her mouth,

261

gagging in horrified disbelief, unable to tear her eyes away from the clinical definition of Roper's distorted features.

Neil grabbed her wrists. 'Annie! Listen to me, Annie. You have to believe me, whoever did this to Roper will have no compunction in doing the same to you. The only way you will survive is if we catch these men first. You have to tell us what they want from you. Why were you on Petrov's list? What were you recruited to do?'

He could see she was in shock. He shook her, called her name and watched her dazed eyes begin to focus.

'You have to tell me, Annie. You have to trust me. They have your name, Annie! Do you understand?'

She shivered, tears welled in her eyes, she was clearly terrified, not thinking. Again he forced her to look at the shots, again he played the tape.

'Others, Roper said. Who are the others, Annie? Who was the Irish boy? Where was he killed?'

'What will happen to me?' There was a hint of defiance.

'We'll keep you safe until the men are caught.'

'And then?'

'That's not up to me but you're in no position to bargain. Let's save your life first.'

She began frantically, 'It was over for us long before they called it off. We decided, Bill and I, after North Africa, the Irish boy, we'd get out. We wouldn't answer the call. When it came we wouldn't . . .'

Neil took her hands, held them, spoke calmly, quietly until her panic ebbed and died.

'From the beginning,' he said.

It was the time of Vietnam, Nicaragua, Chile, the CIA. They were in their twenties, they wanted to make a difference, to right the wrongs. They'd been recruited from university, at a Young Socialists' conference in Berlin. Their mission – sabotage – to precede and facilitate a Soviet invasion of Western Europe. Each cell was to concentrate on specific targets. Their target was the power and communications industries. She recited like an automaton, her face devoid of expression. They'd been trained in Czechoslovakia, '75–'77, Libya in '83. A package tour to Tunisia then a flight across the border . . .

'How many in your cell?' Neil prompted.

'Four in each cell. Grant, Harris, Roper, Shepherd. I was the coordinator. I was the only one who knew the identities of the other three and how to contact them.'

'Do you have the addresses now? Of Grant and Harris?'

'George Grant . . .' As she began, Neil looked up at the camera recording the interview and gave a curt nod for Control to send the order, to bring them in.

'Does the name Bob Turner mean anything to you? Maybe not in your cell but in another? At one of your training sessions?'

She shrugged helplessly. 'We never knew each other's names.'

'And the Irish boy?'

'Just another student. I could tell you what we called him. It wouldn't mean a thing.'

She was emotionally exhausted, he let her go.

Jane Black was on the phone when he walked into the control room. She waved at him to wait and continued with her conversation. 'Are Trade and Industry happy with the way things are being organized? And the minister's making a personal appearance? Fine, as long as we know.'

She pulled a face as she replaced the receiver. 'All this for a trade conference. I don't know why . . .' She stopped herself in mid-grumble.

Neil smiled sympathetically. 'So,' he summed up, 'we bring in Grant and Harris but unless Andy comes up with anything, we're no nearer our two hit men. Unless our East German friend can recognize them.'

'How did he find you by the way?'

'Tracking device fitted to my car. Drove it today – first time since he shot it to pieces. I nearly wrecked it again.'

The phone rang. Black listened. From the way she tapped her pencil and pursed her mouth, Neil could tell the news was not good. She replaced the receiver with a deep sigh.

'George Grant was reported missing three months ago. His wife went to the police, hasn't heard from him since. Could be he was the first victim. They're faxing the report now.'

They sat around listlessly, preoccupied with their own thoughts, waiting for the fax to arrive. When it did it added little. His wife stated he'd been depressed. She didn't think it was another woman. He hardly went out. No friends or relatives. Recently he'd made two over-night business trips to London, stayed at a hotel in Kilburn, The Cushendall. She thinks it could be loss of memory.

'Mmm . . . forgot he's got a wife's more like it,' Black muttered cynically.

'Tut, tut, Miss Sharp,' Neil mocked. 'Kilburn,' he mused. 'IRA country. What was he doing there?'

The shrill ring of Neil's cellnet startled them both. 'Yes, sir,' he answered, holding up his hand to silence the controller. 'Oh, good, sir. Tonight? And my passport? Fine. Yes. Flaxfield. See you there.

'Rylans,' he explained. 'He's got hold of Paric, his tame banker. He's obviously agreed to play ball. We have to get his payoff in place tonight, which also means he's agreed to meet Osuna in Cyprus.'

'It's all falling into place. With Hungary not yet in the EC, it doesn't have to report any unusual movement of money – dirty money can pour in regardless. Osuna, a typical Colombian drug baron, launders money through Spain to the Baltics. Rylans brokers the deal and Paric, a willing banker in Budapest, gains brownie points – rebuilding his nation.'

'Rough justice?'

'Don't even think it,' she said.

Neil was on his way back into town when he received an excited call from Andy.

'I told you, Lebanon!' he said.

They met at the hot-dog stand in the City, not far from Cottrells.

'Food doesn't get any better,' Neil grumbled through his hamburger. 'OK, let's see what you've got.'

It was a shot of a group of youngish men and women laughing together before a tented awning in a desert setting.

'These came in four or five years ago. Cyprus station bribed the cook to get them,' Andy said proudly, his mouth full. 'Hot dogs are good, you should try them. Think I'll have another.'

'Those are definitely our two hit men, bit younger. So what was this, a training camp? "Jumfradi",' he read out, from a scribble on the back of the photograph.

'More a sort of safe haven for terrorists. Every known group, Red Army, IRA, ETA Basques, et cetera, joined up to exchange experiences, plan revolution, the usual PLO holiday camp activities.'

'And these two? Names? Nationality?'

Andy shook his head. 'No go there, I'm afraid. Obviously terrorists . . .'

'Great, Andy, just great!'

Neil headed towards Flaxfield. Frustrated at his lack of progress he'd risked leaving a message on the East

German's service number. Hopefully, by now he'd have checked out Roper's death and wouldn't take another shot at him, Neil thought uneasily as he approached the layby he'd designated as a meeting place. On the other hand, he may not have got the message at all. There was no sign of the German's van. Neil pulled in. Time was not on his side, he had only thirty minutes to reach the airport and already it was getting dark. He looked round anxiously, listening for an approaching vehicle. Finally he gave up, turned out of the layby only to find the German barring his way, his gun at the ready.

It was a quick exchange. It had to be.

Neil showed him the stills from the video film, and the two men in Lebanon. The man studied the photographs and shook his head. 'I will look into it,' he said.

'There's another man from Petrov's list gone missing, Grant,' Neil told him. 'The fourth, Harris, we're still trying to trace.'

'And the girl?'

Neil looked at him in surprise. 'Safe.'

'Look after her,' the German said.

As John Neil drew near to Flaxfield he made one last contact with Control and learned that Harris had moved on from his last known address to a hill farm somewhere. They were tracing him. So, too, were others. Two men had been asking after Harris's whereabouts. The local police were investigating. A description of the men was following.

Dwyer was waiting for him at the entrance to the flying school. He led him directly to the workshop round the back.

'Where's Rylans?' Neil asked. 'I thought I was meeting him here?'

'You're helping me tonight, Beale. Put this on.' Dwyer

pulled two heavy-duty flying suits out of a locker and handed one to Neil.

'Here, what's going on? Rylans said it was a delivery job.'

'It is – a delivery to Latvia! We've got some money to put in a bank in Riga. You're going to open an account. Here, take these.' He pulled out two cases, both combination locked.

Equipped with helmet and parachute, Neil followed Dwyer to the Cessna out on the runway. The pilot slid back a panel section under the fuselage and stashed the cases.

'Half a mill in cash in each of those babies,' Dwyer said with a grin.

In the cockpit Neil sat alongside the pilot, watching him complete his pre-flight checks, his navigational map, marked with arrows and ringed with red, strapped to his knee. In this, his world, Dwyer's actions were precise and automatic and for the first time since Neil had met him, he seemed relaxed.

'We'll be dropping in for fill-ups on the way.' Dwyer pointed to the map. 'Flying low level, below the major radar traces. OK?' The engine sputtered into life.

Once in the air, the pilot pointed to a large packet behind them. 'That's for you. Your instructions for opening the account. Take your time. It's going to be a long flight.'

Dawn was streaking the sky when Neil felt Dwyer nudge him awake. He stretched and looked out, feeling the aircraft slowly begin its descent.

'It's a training area, para jumps, night drops. Peasants are used to people dropping in,' Dwyer explained.

It was a flat, featureless area, bare of anything except a few larches and silver birch, trailing early-morning mist. There didn't even appear to be a runway; even so Dwyer touched down with expert delicacy, bumped

267

lightly along the uneven ground, brought the light craft to a halt with effortless ease and taxied into the shelter of the only copse in the area.

John Neil was full of admiration.

Pleased, Dwyer laughed. 'After Tornadoes, this is a doddle. You can land these anywhere,' he said. 'OK, let's move fast. Keep eyes and ears open. The sooner we're out of here the better.'

While Neil stripped off his flying suit and smoothed down his hair and civvies, Dwyer pulled the cases out of the hidden compartment. Neil's stomach was in knots. Dwyer had not been too forthcoming on procedure. Neil had the feeling that other than getting him there, he didn't want to know.

'Now it's your turn to perform,' Dwyer said, handing him the cases. 'Good luck! I'll be waiting.' Neil followed his eyeline and saw a car lurch out from the other side of the copse.

A tall, bony young man, shabbily dressed in an over-size suit, jumped out almost before the car had stopped, his hand held out in greeting. He grasped Neil's hand. 'Kot,' he said, and still on the run, took one of the cases, put his hand in the middle of Neil's back and ushered him back to the car.

The dreary landscape was soon replaced by the equally depressing outskirts of the Baltic port. Drooping tele-graph wires guided them in along a road long in need of repair. Utilitarian concrete blocks of flats reared up through the drizzle, followed by sturdy, square buildings, colourless and grey, built to withstand the harsh winters; long neglected by the years of Russian rule.

The bank was housed in one such building. Kot led the way. A long queue of set-faced people shuffled slowly forward in grim acceptance. Kot swept past them to a cashier, ignored the person being served, and whispered confidentially. The cashier delivered the message immediately. Neil was struck by the lack of curiosity. No one turned to look at the stranger in their midst, no one complained at the interruption. Perhaps, he thought, no one dared.

A door opened and they were discreetly beckoned in. Faces of the new regime adorned the faded, painted walls of the manager's office, a small room, carved from a bigger one divided by cheap partitions. The desk was wooden, simple, old. Everything was basic, poor quality, from the chairs to the carpet. Only the computer was new.

The bank manager, a man in his late thirties, greeted him brightly and demanded Neil's passport. A telephone call had prepared them for his arrival, he said. The formalities were a contrivance, a nod to legality, Neil realized; nevertheless he played it according to his instructions.

He wished to open an account to facilitate oil trading between his own company and Latvia, Neil told the manager. Kot translated.

'We count it now,' the manager said. The cases were lifted on to his desk. 'Number?' he demanded, indicating the locks.

'Three, three, one one. Here's the inventory.' Neil held out a sealed envelope.

The manager ignored it and opened the cases revealing the tightly-packed wads of bank notes.

Two tellers were called in, followed by two armed guards. Neil looked around uncomfortably. 'Sit,' Kot instructed him. He was there for over an hour while the used notes, in a variety of denominations and currencies, were counted into neat piles and the information fed into the computer.

'Now,' Kot translated for the manager, who had two large forms open before him, 'specimen signatures and name of company.'

Neil handed him the sealed envelope. The manager, not to be deviated from his routine, now accepted it with a business-like nod and a question.

Kot translated. 'What arrangements do you want made for regular information concerning the account?'

'No statements. No correspondence. We'll make contact as and when we need to. Any one of those three signatures can operate the account, opened in the name of the Swiss Company, SA,' Neil recited.

The manager perused the document before him, entered names on the two forms, the amount deposited, handed a copy to Neil and kept the duplicate himself.

'Is that it? Is this all I get?' Neil asked as the manager stood ready to dismiss him.

The manager frowned at Kot's translation and the guards looked questioningly at him. 'That is all anyone gets. Is something wrong?' Suspicion was heavy in the air. Neil shook his head, smiled and couldn't wait to get out.

They arrived back at the plane to find Dwyer pacing nervously and smoking. On the wing of the Cessna was a soldier, his Kalashnikov casually pointing at Dwyer, while another armed soldier covered their arrival.

Neil, carrying the empty cases, emerged slowly from the car. 'What's going on?' he whispered to a very nervous Kot.

'They want to know where you are going now,' Kot translated.

'England,' Dwyer retorted hoarsely.

'They want payment,' Kot said. Disguising his relief with a show of reluctance, Dwyer agreed fifty dollars each.

'They want double,' Kot called out, 'for not seeing the plane!'

With his hands up, Dwyer jumped up onto the wing, indicating he was getting his wallet. The soldiers watched him carefully, their weapons cocked. Dwyer held up his wallet. Immediately, the soldier next to him snatched it from him and backed away towards their car, covering them with his gun. The second one jumped into the driving seat and the two of them drove off laughing.

'Thank God for that! I thought we were in real trouble there,' Dwyer grunted, reaching into a money-belt under his jacket. He peeled off a bundle of notes and handed them to Kot with thanks.

'You go home now,' the Latvian said earnestly. 'I think is best.'

CHAPTER NINETEEN

Rylans was waiting for them at the flying school. He walked out to greet them as they jumped down from the Cessna, listening anxiously to the details of their report.

'So why is Paric playing me around? I was worried something might have gone wrong,' he muttered, half to himself, half to Dwyer. His face was gaunt, his eyes dark from lack of sleep and the nervous tic in his cheek warned of a man on the edge. Exhausted though they both were, Dwyer and Neil changed out of their flying suits and followed him into the bar for a drink.

'The money's all in place,' Rylans called out to Francis. 'So why is Paric playing silly buggers and why can't I raise Osuna?'

'Not my side of things.' Dwyer held up his hands. 'Listen, I have to get back. I'm on duty in three hours.'

'Yes, yes, you go.' Rylans threw back a Scotch. Not the first either, Neil noted, watching the man's agitated movements as he roamed the room.

'Grateful, Beale, grateful, for what you've just done.' He pulled out a chair beside Neil and sat down. 'There's something else,' he began – nervously he chewed at the skin around his thumb nail.

'A girl, there's a girl, we have to get rid of her. She knows something. We must eliminate all risks.' His thumb was raw. 'I've thought about it a lot. There's no other way. Tarleton will help.'

Neil was stunned. 'I think you'd better explain a bit more, sir,' he said, playing for time. 'You've got a major operation coming up and you want to jeopardize it by murdering a girl because you think she knows something?'

'Think, who said think?' Rylans shouted. 'I know! Why else would she have police and army protection?'

There was the soft chirrup of a phone. Rylans leapt to his feet, his gaze fixed on Francis who had picked up the receiver. Francis listened, nodded and held out the receiver to Rylans.

Rylans strode over and snatched at it. 'Tomas!' he said in a forced jovial tone. 'Yes, yes, here there are no microphones.' He listened intently, but his mouth gaped slackly. 'When did Osuna agree this?' he rasped, then coughed and tried again, pulling his shoulders back, firming his tone. 'Yes, of course. I look forward to it. Your ticket will be sent to you.'

He replaced the receiver, his back to the room. 'You have no choice in this matter, Beale. Survival is the eliminating of risk – eliminate all risk, all worry . . .' He turned, shouting savagely, 'The girl is a risk. I want no more risk. I want her eliminated!' He slammed his fist on the bar.

Francis was immediately by his side, calming him, his hand on his shoulder. When he spoke again Rylans was icy and cold, but underneath Neil knew he was shattered.

'You have seven days, Beale. The venue has been changed. We will not be going to Cyprus.'

Neil was blitzed. He drove back to London in a daze, his brain too tired to function.

Black, relieved to hear his voice, listened to his report.

'I want out of this! I will not harm that girl,' he said adamantly.

'You have to stay. This is a major, major smuggling ring you've uncovered. The operation has to continue. We have to know the new venue.'

'But not by killing the girl. You think your way round that one, Boss. 'Cause I ain't hurting anyone else.'

'You don't have a choice. You're under orders, soldier. Now get some sleep and report to me tomorrow.'

They met in a coffee bar. Black ordered him a double espresso and threw down a photo, the Lebanon shot of the camp at Jumfradi.

'I've seen it,' Neil said wearily.

'Not this one. Look again. Andy found it last night.'

Neil peered at it, then held it up the better to catch the light.

'My God!' he said.

'And the description of the two men enquiring after Harris? Varied of course, according to the eyesight of the witnesses, but on one thing they all agreed – they both spoke with an Irish accent.'

'And here,' said Neil, pointing at the photo, 'standing next to them is my friend Hogan, to prove it. So what the hell are they up to? I hope you got to Harris.' He saw by her face they had not.

'We sent in an armed response team, but the hill farm was deserted and of Harris there was no sign. There was also no sign of a struggle. He'd been there, we have witnesses, but . . .'

'And Grant went missing in Kilburn?' Neil said

thoughtfully, adding, 'I think I'll have another chat with Annie Shepherd, maybe she can throw some light on it.'

Annie Shepherd was looking through her bedroom window as he pulled up before the safe house. She came down the stairs, anxiously examining his expression, hoping for good news.

'Have you got them?' was her first question.

He shook his head. 'And we haven't traced Harris or Grant either.'

'Do you think they've got them too?' she asked.

'Let's hope not. We need to talk.' He led her into the interrogation room where their conversation could be recorded.

'Were either Grant or Harris Irish or connected in any way?' he asked.

'Definitely not. They would have said. We had to declare things like that.'

'Tell me about the Irish boy.' Neil noticed her flinch before she looked away.

'He was with us, training in North Africa. They sprang a surprise on us on a night exercise running up a beach, simulated explosions, gunfire, that sort of thing. Except one of them wasn't simulated, I mean . . . he, the Irish boy, trod on a mine. It was real. The bastards had planted a live mine! Blew him to pieces. Almost . . .' She was distressed at the memory. She buried her face in her hands.

'What do you mean?'

'He wasn't quite dead when we got to him. Grant put him out of his misery. Harris watched. You could see it gave a kick. I loathed him, he was a sadist, made my skin creep. They were both furious when Gorbachev called off our operation – said it was the only thing made their lives worthwhile.'

'What does *Saorse* mean to you?' Neil asked.

' "Sare-sha", the Irish boy always shouted it. I thought it was the name of his girlfriend. He said it was some group he belonged to, back in Ireland. He talked to Grant and Harris more than me.'

Neil was directed by Jane Black to meet her at a large country house where preparations were under way for the impending trade conference. He pulled up before heavy iron gates and was surprised at the appearance of armed policemen who carefully examined his ID, then checked with Control on their radio transmitters before allowing him to pass.

'Bit heavy for a trade conference,' he commented when he caught up with Black. He pulled her to one side and began expounding his theory.

She looked at him sceptically. 'I suppose it is feasible. If Grant was frustrated by the mission being cancelled, I suppose he might have tried to sell his talents to the IRA . . .'

'No,' Neil said carefully, 'not the IRA. I believe they turned him down. Instead he remembered the group the Irish boy had told him about, *Saorse*, the radical Saor Eire, and set out to find those instead. I think that's what Grant was up to in Kilburn. Remember the report. First time his wife said he returned depressed, second time he returned elated, happy. That's when the Hogans got in touch. Grant told them about the cell, their expertise in sabotage. The Hogans must have thought they'd hit gold. They'd found the ideal nucleus for a new radical army. Only trouble was, Shepherd was the only one who could coordinate their reunion. They had to go after Petrov. Probably they gave him the idea he had something to sell. And when he didn't talk but wanted to bargain they sent in the boys.'

'What about Roper and Harris?'

'Roper I assume didn't want to know. Harris, I would imagine, is now part of the team.'

'All supposition, Neil. We need facts. And I don't want you doing anything that will jeopardize this smuggling operation. Crack that and we defuse whatever little plan Sinead Hogan has in store. The others we can get later.'

'And what if we don't? What about Annie Shepherd? We can't hold her for ever.'

'No, you're right. She may be the price we have to pay.'

'Well at least we value something,' he commented bitterly, acknowledging the armed security checking everywhere. 'The ministers of Trade and Industry will be comforted to know that.'

Neil could see Jane Black standing on the steps below the grand portico, watching him drive away. There had been a reticence about her today, a lack of interest. Normally she encouraged his conjecture, then tempered it. Today she'd dismissed it out of hand. Maybe she was under orders . . .

He suddenly felt very alone. It was like a game, a game of chess. He needed old Petrov, the chess player. Neil smiled grimly to himself. He'd been so near checkmate, only to be outmanoeuvred. Now to get back in the game, he had to take a risk. He knew what he had to do. He also knew he possibly would not come out alive, but it was a risk he had to take. But first he had to find out the location for the meeting between Paric, Osuna and Rylans and to do that he had to kill the girl.

Chapter Twenty

Tarleton's eyes bulged, hypnotized by Neil's proficient handling of the automatic as he checked and loaded it and fitted the silencer to the dull grey steel muzzle. He jumped as a car roared past them on the main road and revved the idling engine of his car, parked at the exit to the layby, where they waited.

Neil, taut, upright, glanced at his watch. His eyes narrowed.

'Any time now,' he growled. 'OK, this one.'

Liz Baker, driven by her military escort, shot past in her car, her window down, tapping her fingers to strains of Coleman Hawkins. Tarleton pulled out as her car disappeared round the next bend.

'Gun it,' Neil instructed him. 'The next bend's a tight one, we'll take him there.'

Tarleton accelerated, came fast at the bend, overtook their quarry and slammed on the hand-brake, spinning the car, violently cutting across that of their victim, forcing it off the road to a screeching halt. In a flash Neil was there. He fired four shots through the open window.

Tarleton was transfixed. 'Now! Come and look! Come on!' Neil screamed at him. White-faced, he stumbled across. Neil grabbed his shoulders, forcing his head to the window, making him look. Tarleton reeled away, retching.

*

Rylans sat alone at the bar in the flying school. It seemed to be the only place where he felt safe. He hadn't shaved, his breath stank of cigarettes and booze. He poured a shot of whisky for himself and a vodka for Neil and raised his glass. Neil noted his hand was shaking.

'Thank you, Beale. Jason said I could trust you. He was a rogue but I miss him. He understood this dark world. I don't.' He looked at Neil. 'You all right?'

Neil glanced sideways at him, his lip curled in disgust. 'Whenever you do it, whatever for – king and country or like this girl – the bile in your gut sets like a rock and it never lets go.' He downed his drink and smacked the glass down. 'So, what did I do it for, Mr Rylans?'

'I'm caught in a trap. I found a quick way out of the recession and now the people who run the black side of my business won't let me go. Our Mr Osuna, for example.

'So this weekend I am ordered to buy, collect and sell two million dollars' worth of cocaine. Jason arranged the market end.'

'Christ, how do you collect a stash like that?' Neil gaped in disbelief, leading him on, pouring him another drink. The floodgates opened. Rylans confessed it all: the pick-up in Cyprus, Dwyer's transportation to RAF Manningdene, and on to Flaxfield and Francis. Half the money they'd placed in Riga was the sweetener for Paric's cooperation in Budapest. Now he said Osuna was demanding more, insisting Paric should meet with them personally, with proof of account numbers and documents. That way Paric's face would be known and he would realize that when Osuna said play the game or be killed, he meant it. Paric, poor fool, Rylans concluded, still thought he called the shots and wisely or foolishly had stated he would meet Osuna only at Flaxfield.

'I must be there too, Paric insists. He says he feels safer among friends.' Rylans laughed cynically.

'Why are you telling me all this, Mr Rylans?' Neil said uneasily.

'I told you. Jason said I could trust you,' he answered plaintively. 'And I have no one else. You impress me, Beale. You understand this black world, like Jason. I need you with me, to protect me. There are others . . .'

'What others?' Neil asked.

'Just others . . . dangerous people.' Rylans looked around nervously, then plunged his head in his hands. 'Why won't these people leave me alone?' he moaned, rocking to and fro in agitation.

'It doesn't explain why I had to kill the girl,' Neil said. He stopped rocking, his blood-shot eyes narrowed cunningly. 'I've told you, Beale. She knew something of all this. She hadn't talked as yet, obviously, but I'm vulnerable enough. She was a risk I couldn't afford.'

It was clear the man's nerve was cracking. One moment he was lucid, rational, the next paranoid. Neil left him drinking steadily, his life on hold, until the meeting was over.

'Did you get all that?' he asked Control.

'Every word,' Jane Black answered. 'The Tornadoes and transport left RAF Manningdene first light this morning. Squadron Leader Dwyer is on his way to Cyprus. We won't touch him there. We don't want to do anything to alert the others but when he returns to Flaxfield, we'll be waiting. We'll round them all up together.'

Annie Shepherd had identified the East German. Schroeder, she called him; the man who had recruited them at the student conference in Berlin.

Neil met him outside the old East German Embassy.

'*Wilkommen*, Herr Schroeder,' he said. 'I thought you might like to see the old place again.'

'Annie Shepherd remembered me,' the man laughed, then added seriously, 'you have them? The men who killed Petrov?'

'Not yet. How come he meant so much to you?'

'He found me, trained me, was more a father to me than my own father. Only when he was dead did I realize he was the only friend I had. You have someone like that?'

Neil shook his head. 'Unfortunately I do not – which is why I have to ask you for a favour.'

After Belfast, John Neil knew the last place in the world he should go to was Kilburn. He pushed through the crowded bar of the Cushendall. Irish accents were thick around him, suspicious glances slid over him and he felt the adrenalin surge in his veins. He paid for his drink, leaned over the bar and whispered in the barman's ear. A while later, when Neil emerged from the gents, someone was waiting for him. A sharply dressed man in his thirties leaned indolently against the wall, blocking his way.

'You said you had something for the right pair of ears,' he said.

'That's right,' Neil said.

'So what's the agenda?'

'This man I happen to know is not who he says he is.' Neil handed him a photo of Grant. 'I think certain friends might be interested to learn that, friends of *Saorse*.'

The man glanced at him slyly. 'Stay around,' he said.

It was late, the bar was closing and Neil had heard nothing. He was considering asking for a room for the night when the message came; he was wanted in the back.

Neil pushed through the lingering crowd to the door leading to the gents. That was the last he saw. A hood was thrown over his head, his mouth was taped and his hands were tied behind his back. He made a pretence of struggling, then gave in and was hustled down the corridor and out into a waiting car.

He guessed there were three of them. They drove for about fifteen minutes, stopped and bundled him out. Heavy wooden doors banged shut behind him, the floor beneath was hard like concrete and there was the smell of oil. They thrust him down on an upright wooden chair and lashed his bound wrists to the back, his feet to the legs. Abruptly the hood was ripped from his head and a flash bulb flared, blinding him. He realized they'd taken a Polaroid of him. The hood was back on before his sight had had time to adjust. He could identify none of them.

Neil tried to calculate the time he was there by the hands of poker being played by the two men left guarding him. It was cold, the chair was hard and his muscles ached from the limited position.

There was a sudden rapping on the door. He heard the young men murmur, hesitate and call out. Obviously satisfied, they opened the door. Neil heard it creak and scrape on the rough concrete floor, then bang shut. He strained, listening, trying to guess who it was, what they were doing, if his gamble had paid off.

Footsteps crossed the floor. The hood was snatched from his head. He screwed up his eyes against the sudden harsh light. When he opened them, Sinead Hogan stood before him, smiling indolently, her hip cocked, her hands in her pockets, her long eyes half closed, mockingly. A young man with a gun stood by, holding the hood. Another was near the door.

'Well, well, if it isn't Christmas and aren't you just a wicked present?' Her voice was husky, low and sensual.

There was another loud rap at the door. Without taking her eyes from Neil, she waved for them to open it. 'That'll be him,' she said.

The door opened, there was a muffled crack. The young man hurtled back, a bullet through his head. In the same instant, Schroeder dived through the door, still firing. The second man flew back, killed by a bullet to the heart. Sinead spun round, blood spurting from a wound to her shoulder. Schroeder, back on his feet, kicked shut the door as Sinead darted for a fallen gun. Schroeder was too fast. He kicked it away from her grasp, lashed out with the back of his hand across her face and sent her reeling against the wall.

Still covering her with his gun, he pulled out a knife and cut free Neil's hands and feet. With a grimace, Neil ripped away the gag covering his mouth.

'She's expecting someone else,' Neil warned.

'He's already dead, outside,' Schroeder answered.

He handed Neil a gun and hauled the dazed woman to her feet, pushed her down on the chair and bound her hands and feet tightly. Sinead glared defiantly at Neil.

He stood in front of her and held up the photos of the two hit men taken from the video. 'We know these men killed Petrov and Roper. Tell us who they are and what they are up to.'

Sinead didn't even look, just glared murderously at Neil. Behind her Schroeder yanked at her head, forcing her to look at the stills.

'We haven't time to play games,' Neil said roughly. 'We'll do what we have to.'

Sinead sneered. 'Come on then,' she said. 'Let's see what you can do.'

'I think you need some air,' Schroeder announced. 'You take a little walk. The young lady can tell me. I would like to know why she ordered the killing of my friend Petrov.'

When Neil returned he blanched at Sinead's bruised face. She was trembling, tear-stained and bleeding but she was talking. Their names were Tony Lynch and Mark Grady, she told them. There was a price on their head for disobeying orders.

'Your cousins?' Neil said with disbelief.

She nodded. It was as Neil had surmised. Grant had approached them with the idea of finding his old cell, the nucleus for a revolutionary army, expert in sabotage. They'd gone to Petrov for the names. He'd wanted money; they killed him. Roper too, when he'd refused to join them. Harris and Grant were back together.

'For what? What are they all up to?'

'You'll have to kill me first,' she said defiantly.

'First you, and then your cousins. Believe me I will find them,' Schroeder promised. Neil knew it was true. Schroeder nodded for Neil to leave.

He heard the shot as he closed the door.

John Neil slammed Francis against the wall. 'Tell me who killed Major Turner,' he snarled, his arm pressed against Francis's throat. 'Rylans won't and Sturden's dead. It's up to you.'

Francis was choking.

'Tell me.' Neil exerted more pressure.

'Dwyer!' Francis croaked. 'It was Alec Dwyer.'

Neil let go, the man fell forward. 'Why? And tell me the truth. There's someone here who's interested.'

The door to the hangar opened and Liz Baker walked in. Francis started back, shaking. 'I thought . . . you . . .' he stuttered.

'The truth,' Neil said sternly.

Staring at Liz, Francis began. 'Dwyer saw Turner in

Cyprus, hanging around the base. Only Intelligence are allowed to do that. Dwyer was bringing in cocaine. He thought Turner had seen him. Then when he saw him hanging around here . . .'

'Was Turner involved in any way?'

'No. Otherwise Dwyer wouldn't have killed him.'

'I expect he was simply plane spotting,' Liz Baker murmured brokenly. 'They fascinated him. It was his hobby.'

There was the sound of a car approaching. Neil pushed Francis in front of him, dug the muzzle of his automatic in his back and frog-marched him to the bar.

'In position. Osuna is here,' Neil announced into his radio control. With Francis in front of him, a glass in his hand, they went out to greet Osuna. He walked towards them, his two minders behind him. Francis and Neil stepped aside and ushered them in. The Armed Response team, Military Intelligence, Police were all waiting.

By the time Tarleton drew up before the flying school with Rylans and Paric, only Osuna's car was visible. The three got out. Rylans took Paric's arm and led him to the door where Neil was waiting to meet them. Liz Baker stepped out.

Rylans fell back, his face ashen. 'What the hell's going on . . .?'

'You bastard, Beale!' Tarleton yelled, lunging towards Neil, then stopped. Armed police were suddenly everywhere. Paric and Rylans didn't even try to run. For Rylans, Neil thought, it was almost a relief it was over.

The Cessna was coming in on course. Francis, his voice firm, normal, at his radio control, was calling final instructions for the craft to land, closely watched by Neil and Military Intelligence. The runway was clear, the

Cessna barely a few metres off the ground. Without warning Francis suddenly shouted out, 'Get away, Alec. Get away!'

Dwyer tried to lift the aircraft, but cars were suddenly everywhere, chasing him from behind, heading him off from the front. From flight control, Neil watched the light craft jump and hop frantically like a wounded bird desperate to escape, panicked by the circling cars. Then it stopped and in the silence, over the air, they heard the shot and saw the blood splattering the glass of the cockpit.

Jane Black was at the country house. It was the eve of the conference and the participants were arriving for the first-night reception.

Neil took the call on his RT as he was driving back.

'Well done, Neil. The operation was a big success,' Black said.

'A big success,' he said dryly.

'On both fronts.' She paused. 'It was a ground-to-air missile in that crate, I understand. So with that defused and Sinead Hogan out of the way, we've decided to let Annie Shepherd go. You can give her the good news.'

'How's your conference going?'

'Nightmare. The Americans may talk tough but they want more security than anyone. Now they're demanding to see all the clearances on all the caterers. They'll be wanting food tasters next to check for poison.'

'For trade talks?'

'Everything and anything that involves Northern Ireland is a headache, even trade.'

A red light flashed in Neil's head. 'Tell me again,' he insisted urgently. 'What's going on? Who's there? This is important.'

'The Americans are here to discuss a big investment in the Province.'

'And they want guarantees . . . from Sinn Fein?' Neil demanded. Black was silent. 'Come on, tell me. Sinn Fein? Who – who's there, for God's sake?'

'All the important ones,' she said quietly.

Annie Shepherd was waiting for him. She jumped in the car. 'I hope I recognize their faces,' she said. 'It's years since I last saw them.'

'It's vital you do, Annie. Otherwise, Sinead Hogan or not, your friends Grant and Harris are going to blow the whole lot sky high. You were coordinator. What were their particular roles?'

'Harris was quartermaster – weapons, that sort of thing. He kept stuff at his farm . . .'

'You mean like detonators, explosives?' Neil persisted. Annie nodded. Neil looked grim and put his foot down on the accelerator. 'No wonder Sinead kept her secret. She knew they could fight on without her or her missile.'

They roared up to the country house.   ·

Jane Black was waiting. 'I don't see how they could have got a bomb in here, we've had this place and the grounds bottled up for days.' She hurried them inside.

'Not a bomb. If they were planning on a missile, they've probably resorted to a mortar, or something similar. Start looking, Annie. Either Grant or Harris could be here. We'll need RTs.'

The grand entrance hall was set for the reception, a buffet table to one side, tables and chairs arranged around the sweep of the central staircase where waiters rushed up and down with trays of drinks.

'Where's everyone now? Sinn Fein, ministers?' Neil demanded.

'Most are still in their rooms, others are gathering in

the library upstairs, before coming down for the reception,' Black explained, anxiously. 'We still don't have anything to support this theory of yours, Neil, so keep it low key, for goodness' sake. We don't want a hint that anything's wrong.'

'Delay the reception as long as you can,' Neil instructed. 'If there's going to be an attack that's when it will happen. When everyone's gathered together. Keep them upstairs as long as possible. Give us a chance to look around.'

Upstairs Neil and Annie Shepherd fanned out among the guests, checking everyone, everywhere: caterers, waiters, even security.

They joined up at the head of the stairs just as the Sinn Fein party and their minders were walking up. Neil abruptly wheeled away and crossed to stare out of a window. Annie joined him.

'I never thought I'd end up worrying about their security,' he said bitterly. 'Let's try the roof, see if we get any joy up there.'

They found their way up, through endless corridors and stairs. The roof was vast.

Control came through on Neil's RT. 'I can't hold them back much longer. They're beginning to go down to the reception. Have you found anything?'

'Nothing yet. Could you send someone at least to keep a lookout up here?'

'Fine. But with no stronger evidence, I have to let the reception begin.'

Neil led the way back down. It was Annie who let out a sudden gasp.

'That tray!' She pointed to a tray of drinks on a chair in the corridor. 'It wasn't there when we came up.'

As if on cue, a waiter walked out of a room next to them, greeted them politely and moved forward to pick up the tray.

'George!' Annie cried out. 'George Grant?' The waiter spun round, his eyes wide in disbelief, a gun suddenly in his hand. Neil threw himself forward, blocking Annie, just as the gun fired, catching his shoulder. He stumbled, unbalanced by the impact but only for a second. As Grant raised the gun again, Neil hurled himself at the man's legs. Grant staggered, his weapon still aimed at Neil, his finger found the trigger. Gunshots exploded, reverberating down the narrow corridor.

George Grant toppled forward. He was dead before he hit the ground.

The two armed policemen at the end of the hallway slowly lowered their weapons.

In the silence that followed, they heard a distant voice. 'George! You OK? Can you hear me? What's going on?'

Neil rolled the dead man over. The transmitter fell from his hand.

'George! Come in! Answer me . . .'

'That's Harris,' Annie whispered, transfixed, her face white.

There was a rolled-up paper jutting from the dead man's inside pocket. Neil snatched at it. It was a map. Frantically he turned it around, at the same talking into his RT.

'They're using a mortar. Wait, wait, the mortar site's marked. The other side of a wood.' He fired off directions, a grid reference, urging them to hurry.

Neil wandered over to the window in the upstairs room, waiting for the call from Control. His shoulder, though bandaged, was throbbing.

Downstairs the reception was going smoothly. He'd heard the speeches echoing up the stairs and he thought of those initial talks at the big house in Dundalk and he remembered Eilish.

289

One voice in particular caught his attention. He peered over the balcony. Paul Heaney, top financier, Irish-American, covert IRA, was speaking, radiating pride and self-satisfaction. He'd orchestrated the meeting, achieved his coup. He'd make a fortune! They all would in their way. Money, power and egos worked the room . . .

The old chess master must be looking down and laughing at the absurdity of the game: Sinn Fein leaders here being courted, auditioning democracy, while back in Belfast Provo justice continued to require the cruel maiming of young people for crimes the Provos themselves had instigated and encouraged in the first place.

But the light of peace was glimmering.

Neil hoped Kevin, after his kneecappings, was safe. He hoped young Michael wouldn't hate him. And that Fergal would forgive him. That all the sacrifices on every side, down the years, would not be in vain.

Jane Black walked in. 'They've got him. Harris was parked in a van. The mortar would have devastated the whole front of the building, and everyone in it,' she said. 'No sign of the two Irish boys.'

'We don't have to worry. Schroeder will deal with them,' Neil told her.

She turned to Annie Shepherd, who was sitting, shocked and white-faced. 'You're safe to go now. Someone will drive you home.'

They watched her leave.

'And me?' Neil asked. 'Can I go home?'

His controller nodded. 'The back way, I think. There are people down there . . .'

'Who wouldn't appreciate what I've been up to.' Neil gave a short laugh.

'We'll call you,' Black said, watching his receding back.

'I'm sure you will.' Without turning John Neil raised his hand in acknowledgement. Scotland – his mountains were waiting.